Thirst Trap

GRÁINNE O'HARE

Thirst Trap

PICADOR

First published 2025 by Picador
an imprint of Pan Macmillan
The Smithson, 6 Briset Street, London EC1M 5NR
EU representative: Macmillan Publishers Ireland Ltd, 1st Floor,
The Liffey Trust Centre, 117–126 Sheriff Street Upper,
Dublin 1 D01 YC43
Associated companies throughout the world

ISBN 978-1-0350-4619-5 HB
ISBN 978-1-0350-4620-1 TPB

1 3 5 7 9 8 6 4 2

A CIP catalogue record for this book is available from the British Library.

Typeset in Bembo by Jouve (UK), Milton Keynes
Printed and bound by CPI Group (UK) Ltd, Croydon CR0 4YY

Visit **www.picador.com** to read more about
all our books and to buy them.

For my friends, with love

My own brain is to me the most unaccountable of
machinery – always buzzing, humming, soaring
roaring diving, and then buried in mud. And why?
What's this passion for?

Virginia Woolf

They were not perfect, but they were my friends.

Girl, Interrupted

ONE

one

any old moment

It is almost midnight, and the three of them are trying to persuade a member of door staff to let them bring a houseplant into the nightclub. Maggie, Harley and Róise take turns to explain that the plant was a birthday present given earlier this evening by a friend who went home around nine, apparently blind to the practical challenges of accommodating a cactus on the dancefloor. Róise turns thirty next week and was informed by the gift-giver that this particular breed is known as an old lady cactus, on account of its white cobweb of spines. Maggie resents overhearing this information. The sea-urchin crown of the plant has, in her mind, taken on the earnest personality of an elderly woman for whom Maggie now feels responsible, despite Róise having been assured that it doesn't need much watering and should in fact thrive on neglect. They are allowed eventually to check the plant into the cloakroom with their jackets, and Harley pays the attendant with a five-pound note she has folded into eighths to stop it springing back scroll-wise.

In the club, Maggie notes with disappointment that the spinning pole has been removed from its plinth on the dancefloor.

Maggie has been coming here with Harley and Róise since they were eighteen. She once engaged the pole too aggressively in a dance tribute to Wham! and needed medical attention for a bruised perineum. She claimed to the doctor that it was a cycling injury and had to sit on a ring-shaped cushion for a week afterwards, feeling like a humbled pet in a cone collar. That night has gone down as one of the greats in their group lore. They had gone into town on a Friday afternoon, chasing a rumour that Jimmy Nesbitt was drinking at the Sunflower; the rumour turned out to be unfounded, and the night ended at four a.m. with Maggie injured and Harley getting off with two cast members from a touring production of *Cats*. Only Róise had been uninvolved in the drama of it all, spending that night on the edge of the dancefloor with her face lit by the midnight fridge glare of her smartphone screen, messaging her new boyfriend. She does not use a smartphone anymore; her new phone is an old phone without any apps or features. Her then-new boyfriend is her now ex-boyfriend. The two things are not unrelated.

Harley offers Maggie and Róise a hit of her MDMA in the club toilets in the same casual way you might ask *shall we get a flatbread to share?* As a rule, Maggie declines when people offer her recreational drugs, citing a previous 'bad experience' which she hopes makes it sound like she did something fiercely rock and roll like smoking a load of crystal meth and waking up on an ostrich farm in Lurgan four days later. (Her friends have pointed out that Lurgan is not remotely rock or roll, nor does it, to their knowledge, have an ostrich farm. 'No, but you get the gist,' Maggie says.) When Maggie claims she had a 'bad experience',

4

she means that her sole previous experimentation with illicit substances was at a house party in the Holylands many years ago when she accepted a bump of coke that turned out to be heavily cut with washing powder. She sneezed and it stung with flowery freshness; it is not an experience she has been keen to repeat.

This time, Maggie accepts a line from Harley and it feels like someone has pushed a cocktail umbrella up one nostril and opened it inside her head. Harley is cursing, her face performing a montage of elastic contortions like an actor preparing to go onstage: lion-face, lemon-face, lion-face, lemon-face. Róise is ostensibly unaffected by her own line until a single traitorous tear crawls out of the corner of her eye.

'Fuck me,' Harley rasps, 'that *burns*. Should've crushed it more.' She swipes her bank card clean of residue on her tongue as if she's clocking in (or out), then pinches between her eyes with a pained expression. 'Sorry. It'll pass,' she says. 'Give it time.'

Back on the dancefloor, a cool, white buzz begins to creep outwards as the glass shards dissolve in the bridge of Maggie's nose. She plucks absent-mindedly at her top where the under-carriage sweat has fused it to her skin. She is wearing a light grey Blondie T-shirt with no bra, and is regretting it now that two dark, drooling crescents are imprinted on its fabric. She makes accidental eye contact with a woman as she does so, and the woman smiles at her in a way that implies underboob under-standing. The woman fans her face with her hands in sweaty solidarity and shouts over the pounding dance track, 'IT'S BOILING, ISN'T IT?'

'I'M MELTING!' Maggie hollers in agreement, her reply helpfully coinciding with a drop in the music to sound like the frenzied screech of the Wicked Witch of the West.

'WHO'RE YOU OUT WITH?' the woman asks.

'JUST WITH FRIENDS!' Maggie snatches at the air vaguely behind her.

'HAVE YOU PULLED?' Harley blares in her ear, closer than Maggie realized.

'WHO ARE YOU HERE WITH?' Maggie asks the woman, ignoring Harley.

'WORK NIGHT OUT!' she says, indicating the group dancing near her. One of her colleagues jabs a thumb towards the smoking area, and she asks Maggie, 'DO YOU WANT TO COME OUT FOR SOME FRESH AIR?'

'OH I'M GRAND, I DON'T SMOKE!' Maggie deliberately misinterprets. The woman smiles but does not persist, vanishing in the dense crush of the crowd around them. Maggie unlocks her phone, snaps a blurry panorama of the club, a swaying wheat field of arms against a neon sky.

'You're lit,' someone assesses (accurately) from behind her. Maggie turns and sees Cate there, smirking at her. Her pale face and witch-black hair are bleached with blue light, her eyes are smoky and wicked. Maggie starts and, spooked, her breath briefly deserts her. She is suddenly very conscious of the perspiration gathering in the hollow of her back. Cate is wearing a black vest and denim shorts and there seems to be not a lick of sweat on her, as though her body has its own microclimate unaffected by the claggy humidity of the nightclub. She seems somehow able to make herself heard without screeching over the music as Maggie has been doing since they arrived.

'WHAT BUSINESS IS IT OF YOURS?' Maggie shouts back. The euphoria from the drugs has begun to blissfully saturate her body, and the impulse to pull Cate into her arms is suddenly so strong she almost forgets she is dripping with sweat like a basted chicken. In her first year of university Maggie had gone out a few times with a classics student who told her jokingly about the *lesbian rule*, which Maggie initially thought must be some unofficial commandment of the community, but turned out to be a historical tool of masonry made from lead on the island of Lesbos, an instrument that could be bent and fitted to any curve. She feels in this moment as though she could pliantly and happily mould her entire body around Cate's like a second skin, flattening and shrinking and concaving to fit.

'MAGGIE.' Harley's hand is on Maggie's elbow as she cocks her head brusquely, summoning her back to dance with them.

'YOU REMEMBER MY FRIEND CATE!' Maggie says by way of introduction. Early on in their acquaintance, Cate set a precedent for introducing her as *my friend Maggie*, prompting Maggie to refer to her with the same platonic prefix. In the six months they have known each other, Maggie has never broached the subject of whether Cate might have any interest in becoming her *friend* in the Victorian sense of two female companions who live together for decades in sapphic harmony only for historians to footnote them as pals in spinsterdom. They have never been on anything as formal as an actual date; their encounters have been a chaotic tide of late nights and last minutes. Maggie has tried to buy into the idea that it is a very chic, adult thing to be friends who casually sleep together; however, when she is presented by Cate as *my friend Maggie* she feels like a toddler trailing around after an assigned buddy at a new school.

'WHERE WERE YOU BEFORE THIS?' Maggie asks Cate nonchalantly – or would, if it were possible to be nonchalant screaming over the top of B*Witched while everyone on the dancefloor is violently céilí-ing around them. Harley keeps bumping into Maggie as she bounces, which Maggie suspects may be on purpose.

'House party,' Cate replies, rolling her eyes. 'Dead.' Cate attends house parties with the air of a touring foreign dignitary whom the organizers have been privileged to host. Maggie cannot imagine her wedged in a beanbag and churning craic in a desperate bid to keep hold of people's attention. She has an old-world It-girl sort of energy, Maggie thinks, like Zelda Fitzgerald or one of the Mitfords. You would never see Cate idling awkwardly in a corner at parties, pretending to check her phone until her friend returned from the bathroom.

That is how they met – at a house party, when Maggie was in the kitchen trying to negotiate the cork out of a wine bottle with a large hairclip. 'Need a hand?' Cate asked, looking curiously at her.

Maggie relaxed her face from its tug-of-war grimace and attempted a careless laugh. 'This might be a lost cause.'

'Apparently,' Cate told her, 'if you take off your shoe, put the wine bottle in it, and smack it against a wall, it's supposed to make the cork come out.'

'Sounds like witchcraft to me,' Maggie said, stepping back and examining the hairclip wedged half in the cork like a knife in a corpse.

'Try it, you never know.'

'You want to try?'

'I'd much rather spectate and laugh, if I'm honest.'

'Your shoes look more appropriate.' Maggie was wearing canvas trainers that were peeling at the sole; Cate had on a pair of snakeskin Doc Martens.

'There isn't a corkscrew in here?' Cate asked, checking the cutlery drawer.

'Oh no, there is,' Maggie replied. 'I just thought I'd introduce an element of unnecessary challenge.' Cate laughed, and triumph leapt in Maggie's stomach at having clawed back some dignity. She added, 'I assumed it was a screw-top. It was four pound fifty in Lidl.'

'*Lidl*,' Cate said, almost wistfully, as if Maggie had mentioned an exotic country she'd visited during her gap year. '*Best wine.*'

Half a dozen wallops of Cate's boot-heel against the wall, and the cork had crept out of the bottle far enough for Maggie to pull it free. 'I think I owe you some of this,' she said to Cate.

'Go on, then.' Cate smiled.

'WATER,' Harley commands Maggie now, cocking her head towards the bar. Harley's jaw is clenched, and Maggie is not sure it's the drugs. She has never much liked Cate, viewing it as a personal affront whenever she turns up to derail a perfectly good night out. Harley is the self-appointed director on most of their party sprees, her orders often having an undertone of subtle reprimanding, although it is impossible for Maggie to take her too seriously as a tyrant when her long face, small dark eyes and white-blonde hair give Harley the perpetual look of a suspicious possum.

'BAR?' Maggie says to Cate.

'Yes, come on,' Cate replies, as though it were her idea. She brackets Maggie's hips lightly between her hands and walks her through the crowd. Maggie wonders briefly whether this is a move to annoy Harley, since Cate has never much liked Harley either. She decides she doesn't mind if it is.

Harley throws an arm around Róise's shoulders to steer her away from a woman on a hen night bending the ear off her, and they lead the way to the bar. Róise mouths the word *shots?* or perhaps it's *shots* without the question mark, since she doesn't seem to wait for an answer. When the shots are placed in front of them, Róise's eyes are already lowered to the salt-sprinkle on her wrist so when she murmurs '*Sláinte*', she looks almost reverent, as if giving a solemn toast at a wake.

Maggie forces the shot down roiling, the lime wedge slammed straight between her teeth, where it seems to dry and shrivel instantly to potpourri. She sips from the pint glass of water Harley hands her. An acidic burp flares in her throat, and she is forced to excuse herself just as the ABBA megamix begins, which is wholly out of character for her.

She is confused and horrified by the strange black caterpillars in the toilet bowl, until she realizes her cheap false lashes, loosened by vomiting, have given up and dropped off. You fought bravely, friends, she thinks through the gauze curtains lowering over her brain. Rest easy.

Harley's body stiffens with morning-after rigor mortis when the man in her bed rolls over to nestle against her. She hates waking up next to people. Her bedroom does not seem her own with a stranger present; it feels like a crime scene she has been barred from fully entering until the police have given clearance. She feels as though she is standing behind fluorescent tape, peering at carefully numbered articles of evidence strewn across the floor. A foil wrapper from a brand of condom she does not buy, and the condom itself lying unfilled nearby like the abandoned hide of a shedding reptile. Boxers patterned with the face of a cartoon character she vaguely recognizes. Her wastepaper basket moved to the side of the bed in case he needed to vomit again.

Harley remembers having very brief, very poor sex with this man. 'I don't think this is happening, is it?' he slurred after trying to push inside her with what felt like a deflated party balloon. She resented him throwing the question out to her as if the not-happening was something for which she should be held jointly culpable, and not the fault of the nineteen or so pints he'd had that evening. He rolled out of bed and she had thought he was going to get dressed and order a taxi, but he instead stumbled with coltish uncertainty to the bathroom, and she had to listen to copious boking through the wall for the next half-hour. He reappeared at her bedroom door like a toddler who'd had a night-mare and mumbled, 'I know you said you didn't want me to stay over . . .' and she said, 'It's fine, just crash for a bit until you're feeling better.' They went to sleep lying parallel in bed with as much intimacy as two neighbouring bodies in a morgue. Now it is the morning and she lies with her back to him as something fully alive and solid nudges against her tailbone. Before she can begin to contemplate what to do about this, she remembers what day it is.

She curses under her breath, stumbling around in the chalky half-light of the early morning, reclaiming her scattered clothes and wits. 'I didn't think my morning breath was *that* bad,' the man jokes, watching her get dressed without making any effort to do the same.

'I'm sorry, but you need to leave. *I* need to leave. I have somewhere to be.'

'Is this your way of telling me you've got a boyfriend?'

'It's my way of telling you to put your fucking pants on and scoot.'

He swings himself humbly out of bed and starts fussing with his underwear and socks. Harley takes a brush to her tumbleweed-textured hair and adds, with a little less aggression, 'Are you feeling better?'

'Loads better, yeah. I'm really sorry about last night. I don't normally get sick.'

'It could happen to anyone, honestly, don't worry about it.'

Apparently encouraged by this, he says, 'Have you got time for breakfast? Do you want to go somewhere?'

'I can't; I'm already late,' she tells him. He seems to accept defeat, dressing quickly and leaving with an uncomfortable

'Thanks . . . all the best . . .' as though departing a job interview he senses has not gone well.

Harley waits to hear the front door close before heading down to the kitchen. Her temples throb with each step and the dread has already begun to set in. Róise is downstairs already, apparently not in much better shape, inhaling the fumes from a cup of coffee without quite being able to bring herself to drink it. She stares unseeing at the cactus on the kitchen counter, which they almost forgot to rescue from the cloakroom, after all the effort they had made to get it in there in the first place. Róise is dressed in a baggy black sweater over grey plaid trousers. Harley throws her Afghan-lined coat over the kitchen chair and wonders if she ought to wear something more sober. Róise's style is that of a cool yet formal English teacher (autumn tones, lots of tartan, corduroy blazers and seven different weights of turtleneck) whereas Harley likes furs and leathers (all fake) and the occasional bit of vintage Halston (or real, when she can afford it, which is rarely). Róise's look is arguably more suited to this morning's church setting, but Harley cannot be bothered to change.

'Where's Maggie?' Harley asks. The last exchange she remembers between them is Maggie pulling her into a fierce hug after they located her in the bathrooms, her mouth clacking with dryness next to Harley's ear as she said, 'I'm having the best night, I love you.'

'She went home with your one from the club. The usual suspect.'

Harley rolls her eyes. Not only does Cate mess Maggie around without shame, she also checks the most contemptible box on Harley's list of red flags: scabbiness. She knows that Cate is well off on account of her parents owning a handful of hotels in the city centre, and yet she never seems to pay for drinks and always bums cigarettes off other people. She also didn't contribute anything for the bumps of MDMA she accepted last night, which Harley only offered to seem polite.

'Have you heard from her? Is she up?' Harley realizes she has left her phone in her bedroom and almost weeps at the thought of having to tackle the stairs again.

'She's up. She's dying. Says she'll meet us at the church.'

Róise phones to book a taxi as Harley throws together a cocktail of Dioralyte and cystitis remedy in a pint glass of tap water, downing the lot with two paracetamol. She hasn't passed water yet and feels the sting of an oncoming UTI like a tight coil of barbed wire.

'Did you have fun?' asks Róise, in reference to the man who left two minutes ago.

'That's for me to work out with my future therapist.' Harley frowns. 'Did we all get a taxi back here together? You, me and . . . him?'

'Yes. He talked a lot to the driver about Newry City's performance in the league.'

'Mm. Are they doing well?'

'Better than expected but still below average. According to him. Do you care?'

'Of course not.'

*　　*　　*

14

When they turn up the street in the taxi twenty minutes later, Róise tells the driver, 'Anywhere here is fine.' They pay him in coins sticky with liquor and lever themselves out of the car. Harley consults her reflection in the wing mirror of a parked Honda Civic. She has rubbed the ashy mascara from under her eyes and applied a fresh layer of foundation. 'I look like a dead clown,' she confirms as she catches up with Róise. They pass the scene of last night's crimes. The kerb, painted colourfully like a rainbow-brick toy town, looks grubby in the early morning; Union Street is littered with takeaway cartons and fag ends and charred embers of rapture. The club doors are barred like a sacred cloister.

They meet Maggie at the door to the church. Select strands of her long fox-coloured hair look slightly damp, and Harley suspects she may have had to rinse dried vomit out of them. Maggie has touched up her own face with Cate's concealer, which is slightly too pale even for Maggie's fair complexion; she looks like a child sick with chickenpox, patchy with calamine lotion. 'Maggie, come here a second,' Harley mutters, blending Maggie's makeup with the pad of her thumb. Someone passes them on their way into Mass and looks sympathetic. Harley realizes it must appear as though she's tenderly wiping Maggie's tears.

The three of them slide into a pew halfway down the church, next to Maggie's brother Liam. 'Are there toilets in here?' Harley whispers to Liam, as solemnly as she can manage. He stifles a laugh and mouths, 'I don't think so.' A middle-aged woman sitting in front of them reacts with palpable disapproval, as though Harley has asked for the WiFi password.

★   ★   ★

It is one year since Harley, Maggie, Róise and Liam were in this church for Lydia's funeral. Maggie and Harley had been friends with Lydia since they were five. The three of them met Róise when they were all in the same class at secondary school, although she had her own group of friends back then. When they went to Queen's at eighteen, Lydia did her undergraduate degree in Business Management, while Maggie, Harley and Róise all studied English. The four of them spent their evenings in the Parlour bar bonding over whiskey and Romantic literature (and, as they became drunker and less pretentious, Jägerbombs and *Gossip Girl*).

Lydia began dating Maggie's brother not long after uni, a development of which Harley heartily approved (partly because Lydia's previous boyfriend had been a dairy farmer who wanted her to move to his homeland in the Fermanagh countryside and get to work on the five to eight children he intended to sire). Maggie took a little more persuading; she reacted at first with the air of a put-upon diplomat who would one day have to broker a peace treaty between two warring nations, should the relationship end badly.

'It won't end badly, I promise,' Lydia had said.

'You can't know that!' argued Maggie.

They told her that if it was causing her genuine upset, they would agree to just be friends. Maggie considered that although she would feel extremely uncomfortable if they had an acrimonious break-up, this was very much a what-if, whereas the discomfort she felt at dictating who her friend and brother should or should not ride was very real and present. Eventually, she relented.

Lydia was the first of them to get a proper job for a corporate surnamed firm after university. By the time they were twenty-four, Maggie was working as a legal secretary, Harley was employed as a hotel receptionist and Róise had found a position in a recruitment agency that was at least secure and well paid, even if it was a corporate hellscape. They heaved their duvets and books and board games to the four-bedroomed house they had found to rent in south Belfast. Lydia took endless trips to charity shops and St George's Market and brought back prints and ornaments she thought were interesting, comedic sexual health posters from the 1920s to hang in the bathroom and a brass umbrella stand in the shape of a wombat that sat in the hall. Six months after they all moved in, Lydia was found installing a ter-rarium in the front room to house a small domestic turtle, whose name (she advised) was Barnaby. They lived there together – the four girls and Barnaby – for almost five years.

Not long after Lydia died, Maggie, Harley and Róise were informed that she had left Barnaby to them in her will. None of them knew quite what to say. Harley, for one, took some time to process the notion that anyone their age had a will, and won-dered whether that was something she ought to have, until she considered that she had nothing to bequeath beyond a tattered stack of novels that ranged from *Bleak House* to *Breaking Dawn*, and several Spandau Ballet vinyls.

They have kept the turtle, though none of them feel par-ticularly maternal towards him. 'Lydia wanted us to have him,' Maggie pointed out sadly at the time. Harley looked at Róise and knew what she was thinking – that they weren't in any position to say what Lydia wanted at the time of her death, since she had perished very suddenly in a road accident with none of them present, and they hadn't actually been on speaking terms with her at the time it happened. Barnaby sits in the corner of the front room like a witch's familiar still loyal to Lydia, and sometimes when Harley has stumbled in particularly intoxicated, she has convinced herself that he is glaring at her with knowing disdain.

The matter of the house was more difficult to negotiate in the aftermath of Lydia's death. Róise said she thought they should move out immediately, that the place was teeming with *bad energy*. Maggie seemed on the fence, nostalgic and saying that it was a home of many formative memories, but admitting that the house was starting to look shabby and that the landlord's stopgap repairs were beginning to show. Harley didn't want to leave at all, concerned that they would struggle to find somewhere for the three of them to live and that it would mark the bifurcation of their shared life into separate streams. She found herself pointlessly resenting Lydia for kick-starting this process, by making stupid mistakes that had fractured the friendship group, and then by dying before any of it could be resolved. Harley knew deep down that it would have happened anyway, that one or more of them would eventually move in with a partner or want to upgrade from their damp and battered dwelling; and yet there was another part of her that had thought they might continue on as they were, grouped together with the peaceful simplicity of a well-loved sitcom.

They agreed they would give it six months and review again in the summer. They had a rolling tenancy; the landlord asked that they give two months' notice should they want to move out. When the summer came, Harley had no desire to bring up the subject unprompted, and Maggie half hoped that a decision either way would be made for and without her, so did not mention it. Róise was miserable after a break-up, as well as grieving Lydia's death, and she sank into a listlessness that barely allowed for deciding on a coffee order, much less whether to pack up her life and move it elsewhere.

Now, a year after Lydia's passing, they are still there together, and they have not discussed what to do about their living situation. Lydia's parents came to reclaim some of her possessions, but apart from this, no one has been into her room. As the anniversary approached, Harley felt as though a reckoning of some sort was surely looming. Róise would suddenly snap into action and decide to move out, or the landlord would tell them the house was going to be sold, or a phantom would burst forth from Lydia's abandoned room and send the whole place crashing down around them.

Harley suspects that Róise scheduled her birthday night out for the eve of Lydia's anniversary in the hope that she would pass out drunk in the small hours of the morning and sleep through Sunday; and then Lydia's mother contacted them last week to say that a Sunday morning Mass at St Patrick's was being dedicated to Lydia's memory, if they felt they'd like to come along. There was a reluctant agreement between the three of them that not going would seem cold, and so they told Lydia's mother they would see her there. Róise had already paid a deposit for her birthday dinner, two friends with children had arranged babysitters, and one was getting the train up from Dublin, so rescheduling would be tricky. There were, of course, adjustments that could have been made – going home earlier, drinking less tequila, not getting a bag of MDMA for the night – but they instead treated these matters like regional employees with mandatory tasks imposed on them by a distant CEO. They had no choice but to shrug and say, 'Well, it's not ideal, but it's out of our hands.' Back when Lydia was still living with her parents and grudgingly going to church with them on feast days, she had spent many a year hungover and sweating during the Passion of Christ at the Good Friday service. Harley did not envisage her being offended by their bedraggled presentation at the memorial Mass.

Lydia's mother and father are sitting two rows in front of them in the church. Her dad is wearing a zipped-up anorak over his Sunday suit, his knee jerking up and down as he flips through the pages of the order of service, as though checking to make sure Mass hasn't undergone any radical changes since he was last in church a week ago. Lydia's ma is wearing a navy dress. Apart from at the funeral, Harley has never seen her in anything that isn't brightly coloured and patterned with flowers. She always used to wear earrings the size of wind chimes, but today she wears small silver studs. Harley wonders whether her entire wardrobe is in mourning now, imagines her stirring the florals in a vat of black dye like a teenager entering their goth phase.

Harley does her level best to swallow the mushroom cloud of heartburn that has erupted in her chest. It is painful, the kind of angry acid reflux that makes her fear she is decaying and collapsing from within. Maggie had her thirtieth birthday a couple of months ago, Róise's is this week, Harley's will come next, and Lydia's never. Things seem to have barrelled in Catherine-wheel fashion towards the end of this decade, their roaring twenties, and this year more than ever Harley has swung between cautious thoughts of *you only live once* that tell her she should be taking better care of herself, and caterwauling thoughts of *you only live once!* that argue she shouldn't be wasting precious time taking better care of herself. Her heartburn fades almost as quickly as it came, and Harley knows she will make a jokey comment later about being in a church and bursting into flame.

The pint of water has passed and is pressing insistently on Harley's bladder by the time they stand for the gospel. Her pelvic floor, while robust, is struggling. 'Just need some air,' she whispers as everyone choruses, 'Thanks be to God,' and she hobbles out of the chapel.

There are no toilets in the church, but there is a small car park round the back. Harley is desperate, and not (she assures Jesus, should he be listening) trying to be deliberately perverse. She goes back in for communion.

omagh sapiens

Róise turns thirty on a Friday, almost a week after the birthday celebrations with her friends. She arrives at work with no fanfare or ceremony; she never lets anyone know when it's her birthday. She gets out of the lift on the thirteenth floor of the building and crosses the office, an open-plan space made almost entirely of windows. The people who populate the recruitment firm sit in glass rooms against the sky-high backdrop of outside, as though they are perched in the clouds and doing the work of angels.

Róise sits down at her desk and checks her email and is relieved to see that her calendar is empty for the day. Barely a week seems to go by without a department-wide invitation to someone's birthday celebrations, always with titles like *Sandra's birthday lunch – BYOB (Bring Your Own Buns!)* or an itinerary for post-work drinks at the most over-hyped cocktail bar in town. On this morning's commute, Róise convinced herself that she was about to be ambushed with a birthday lunch arranged by her colleagues. She cringed at the thought of the clandestine collection of loose change in a brown paper envelope, a card smuggled ineptly between desks for people to sign. She imagined being presented with a gift card for H&M, a gesture that would make her feel obliged to contribute to all her co-workers' future birthday gifts, regardless of how little she knows or likes them. Juliet from the marketing department would bring in a spread of snacks and traybakes to arrange across a table in the middle of the office, and it would turn lunch into an uncomfortably communal affair where they would all be forced to talk to each other. Róise would be asked if she's doing anything to celebrate her birthday, and she might disclose that she went out with friends at the weekend, and Sandra from HR would remark, 'I've never seen the attraction of clubs, myself. You can't hear yourself think – I just don't understand the appeal!' and Juliet would warn Róise that her hangovers are about to get cataclysmically worse now she's in her thirties. Juliet is only thirty-three but speaks to Róise with the air of a sage old crone dispensing wisdom to a fresh-faced whippersnapper.

Awkward workplace birthday rituals are something Róise has never particularly warmed to. Even so, there is a small part of her that, when Adam passes her desk mid-morning, wishes there was colourful bunting or a plastic tray of cupcakes or someone loudly wishing her *happy birthday!* that would catch his attention, to let him know that today she is not simply his admin assistant; she is the Birthday Girl. The term would ring sour and infantile in anyone else's mouth, but the thought of Adam using it in reference to her makes Róise's breath catch slightly.

Róise worked with Adam for over a year without thinking of him as much more than a name in an email signature. A couple of months ago, she was ahead of him in the canteen queue when the server asked her how she took her coffee, and she said, 'Black,' and Adam commented, 'Girl after my own heart,' and Róise found herself blushing. The blush was not covered by her makeup because she wasn't wearing any. She realized that she had not worn makeup all year; she had been rolling out of bed to go to work and then leaving work to go home and get back into bed again, and had not thought there was much point in wasting cosmetics on this bleak itinerary.

Blushing in front of Adam seemed to indicate that the cryogenic numbness of her heartbreak was at last beginning to thaw. Róise had been single since the break-up last year and did not remember the last time she'd had a notion for someone. She felt a sudden rush of embarrassment, as if she had just realized she'd been walking around the office for months with her skirt trapped in her knickers. She wondered if he had said that – *girl after my own heart* – because he saw her as his dull, sexless assistant who barely spoke and had started coming into work with unclean hair, and he wanted to bestow some attention on her out of pity. Maybe he thought her pathetic for blushing at such meagre flattery. Maybe, she thought, you're overthinking it.

Róise wore makeup to work the next day. She spent half an hour in front of the mirror giving herself a 'natural' look – pale foundation and subtle pink lips and a soft outline of kohl around her eyes that looked like the dainty remains of last night's mascara, as if to say, 'This is what I'd look like if you woke up next to me.' The minimalism of the effect was ruined by Juliet stopping at her desk and cooing, 'Ooh, you going somewhere nice,

Róise?' when Adam was in earshot. While he likely had not registered the difference in her appearance, Juliet's remark drew attention to the fact that Effort had been made on her part, and her cheeks coloured again (though less visibly this time).

Against her better judgement, Róise opens a social media tab on her work computer when she sits down after lunch. Maggie has tagged her in a birthday post, a photo from their school formal in 2006 in which Róise is sitting looking unimpressed, with a bottle of tequila in one hand and a whole turnip in the other. None of them can remember why. Róise had been closer with a different group of girls back then, although they drifted apart after going to university. Those girls went to teacher-training college together and gradually migrated back to their old secondary school on placement and supply and eventually full-time employment. Róise has met up with them occasionally since, but it generally turns into an hours-long faculty meeting, the conversations punctuated with insincere apologies of 'God, Róise, this must be so boring for you to listen to.' The gossip about their own former teachers was a huge novelty the first couple of times, but after the third update on staff conflict over an art teacher's maternity leave, Róise realized she did not care. Several of these women are still with the boys they brought as their formal dates, married with mortgages and gardens and babies. Any time Róise broke up with a boyfriend in her twenties, they leapt into action, asking their husbands and brothers whether they knew any eligible single men who might want to take her out – although the way they said it sounded more like they wanted someone to take her *in* as one might a rescue dog. *Róise is looking for her forever home.* She hasn't seen most of them since her last break-up, reluctant to face their pity and their questions. Some of these women have tagged her in posts similar to Maggie's, photos taken on the dancefloors of Stiff Kitten and Limelight ten years ago, when they were all still wearing skull-print scarves and plastic chokers that looked like neck tattoos. Facebook volunteers a photo memory from Róise's twenty-fifth birthday – *Share to your timeline?* it suggests. Harley stands cartoonishly tall in heels with the chest and hips of a sixteenth-century wet nurse (her own words), and Maggie is tucked under her armpit wearing an oversized *Jurassic Park* T-shirt that she insisted would work as a dress, although it looks somewhat like she tumbled out of bed and forgot to finish putting clothes on. Róise cannot exactly judge her for this, given that in the photo she herself is wearing a woollen wrap dress tied around the waist, which she likely chose for the close resemblance it bore to a housecoat. Róise's hair in the picture has been straightened with the meticulous aggression of flowers dried and pressed in a vice; it has taken years of oils and butters and scolding from hair stylists to resurrect its natural curls.

Lydia stands next to her in the line-up, cackling hysterically at a joke Róise cannot remember. Lydia always complained about this photo, saying she looked like a maniac. Róise has always disagreed with this assessment. She resents that Lydia's image could be captured in such a moment of abandon and still make her look like a beautiful dead wife in a Hollywood movie, laughing and windswept in a montage of the hero's memories. Lydia was long-limbed and dishwater blonde, with a shaggy fringe that forced you to look for her eyes, which smiled at you as soon as you found them. She wore cat-flicks of black eyeliner, and red lipstick that left blood-orange prints all over cups and glasses and cheeks, but never seemed to bleed out from her lips.

Róise ignores the birthday messages, closes the tab and takes her mug to the office kitchen.

Adam comes into the kitchen a minute later with his coffee cup. Róise almost wishes he would point at hers and say, 'Black, yes?' although she cringes at the idea of him storing this small, silly memory and pulling it out months later, almost as much as she cringes at the fact of her storing this small, silly memory for herself.

'Róise, before I forget,' he says, spooning coffee into his cup, 'could you do me a favour and rearrange my meeting next Monday with Jenny Whelan? I think I'm still going to be in recovery that afternoon.'

'Ah,' Róise deadpans, 'weekend coke bender planned?'

It might be the first joke she has ever made to him. It lands successfully, and he laughs. 'A lot less rock and roll, I'm afraid: root canal on Monday morning.'

'Sure, I'll reschedule it.'

'What've you planned for the weekend, then – wild one yourself?'

'Going home for my birthday,' she murmurs, taking advantage of the cue.

'Oh? What day's your birthday?'

'It's technically today.'

'You kept that quiet!'

'State secret,' she says in a stage whisper.

'Am I allowed to ask what age you are, or is that classified information too?'

'It's the big one.'

Adam raises his eyebrows. 'You're looking well for sixty.'

Róise tightens as she tries not to laugh out loud. 'Thank the Botox.'

'Well, I hope you're having a drink tonight to celebrate.' She isn't about to tell him about Saturday night's festivities, so she lifts one shoulder in a way she hopes is coy and enigmatic. Adam laughs. 'Enjoy yourself, birthday girl,' he says, and shoots her a wink.

At home in Omagh on Saturday, Róise's mum is scandalized that she went into work on her birthday. 'Could they not have given you the one day off at that place?'

'I wasn't fussed about it.'

'Surely they could have spared you for the day . . .'

'If I'd *asked* for it, Adam would have let me. Holidays are never an issue, he's really good about that kind of thing.' Róise would never tell her mother about her notion for Adam, but she lauds him in other ways, feeling as though her professional praises are sly euphemisms for other, darker things. *He's such an attentive team leader. So dedicated. Incredible work ethic.* The formality of saying this to her mum gives Róise a strange kind of thrill, as if Adam is tracing his tongue up the inside of her thigh under the table where no one can see.

Róise, her mum, and her older sister Ciara are having breakfast at the coffee shop near the courthouse, strawberry compote bleeding into pillowy pancakes, and tiny potholes of butter pooling on golden toast. Róise remembers that her ex-boyfriend Brendan simply did not believe her when she told him the town centre had artisanal cafes nestled among the chemists and charity shops. Like a lot of people who'd grown up in Belfast and had never gone far outside it, Brendan assumed that once you started driving out from the city, it was countryside until you hit Dublin. He once went on a stag do to Derry and asked if he'd get a phone signal there. For the first year of their relationship, he thought Róise was from some kind of Brian Friel backwater, with fields and a post office and very little else.

Róise's mother has bought her a new phone for her birthday, a smart, slimline model with multiple camera lenses, and she has also included a thick detachable cover. Róise lied to her mum when she started using a drug-dealer Nokia several months ago, saying that she had dropped her iPhone in a toilet and was saving for a new one. 'It's meant to be good, that one,' her mum says enthusiastically, tapping a finger on the box. 'And I've got you insurance if it breaks, although the protective cover looks like it's made out of recycled tractor tyres, so you should be grand.'

'Aww. Mummy. Thanks, that's . . . You really didn't have to.'

'Don't be daft, it's your birthday.'

When their mum excuses herself to visit the bathroom, Ciara asks, 'Have you heard from Daddy?'

'I got a card from him. He sent me book tokens.'

'Are book tokens still a thing? I swear I've not seen one in the wild since primary school.'

'Apparently they are. I did check the expiration date to check he wasn't re-gifting me ones from 2002, but no. Valid till next winter.'

For Ciara's thirtieth birthday, their dad had presented her with re-gifted Nathan Carter tickets that his mother had given him as a misguided Christmas present. Their paternal grandmother had a habit of buying their dad concert tickets in threes, because she wanted to encourage him and his new partner to mend things with Róise's mum; this time, her granny had seemingly put an awful lot of faith in the healing power of Irish country music. When Róise was ten, her dad left her mum the day Tyrone got a particularly brutal thrashing in the GAA finals. The two things weren't related, although for the first three days Róise's mother did not query her husband's absence, thinking three days was an understandable respite to need after such a painful sporting defeat. It turned out he had run off with a woman called Diane, who worked in the bingo hall near the Derry Road roundabout, and who looked like an ice-cream-van drawing of Róise's mum: similar in essentials but strangely distorted, a budget imitation of the original. Róise moved to Belfast with her mother and sister just in time to start secondary school.

(Róise and Ciara went to the Nathan Carter gig for a sort of masochistic laugh. They sold the third ticket and spent the money on a bottle of the most expensive tequila they could find in the big Asda. They drank the whole lot before the concert and

Ciara did the splits during 'Wagon Wheel', ripping her trousers along the full length of her crotch.)

'Has he said anything to you about Christmas?' asks Ciara.

'No. Why?'

'He's invited me and Domhnall and Finn to have Christmas dinner with him and Diane. I said no, obviously.' Domhnall is Ciara's husband and Finn is their eight-month-old baby. Róise thinks her father views Ciara's healthy, functional family unit as proof that his failings as a partner and parent have not impacted his daughters too badly as adults, and therefore aren't something he ever needs to address or apologize for. He regularly offers to babysit Finn, and he invites Ciara and Domhnall for lunch every couple of months. He texts Róise occasionally to ask when she's next in Omagh, although he never offers to visit her in Belfast. At the end of last year, he began to communicate with her almost exclusively via screenshots of motivational quotes, lines about finding light in dark forests or learning to swim in choppy seas. Róise decides not to tell him she has a new phone, lest he resume this disturbing practice.

Her ex-boyfriend Brendan once jokingly diagnosed her with 'daddy issues' when she told him she thought Charles Dance was a bit of a ride in *Game of Thrones*. She argued that it was frankly insulting to Charles Dance to suggest she was only attracted to him as a result of trauma inflicted by a negligent parent. 'The man is a theatrical powerhouse,' she said, 'and a stone-cold fox.' Róise wonders what Brendan would think if he knew she was lusting after someone senior at work. She wonders if he thinks about her at all anymore.

counsel culture

For as long as Maggie has been seeing Astrid, she's been dying to ask her where she gets her nails done. She wonders what Astrid's code of practice says about that kind of thing, since for all Astrid knows, Maggie could be looking to stake out a nail bar with a view to following her home and kidnapping her family.

'How was Therapy?' Astrid asks her, amused.

Therapy (capital T) is a club that Maggie and Harley went to at the weekend while Róise was at her mum's. It is the kind of tragically pretentious establishment they do not generally frequent, one with exotic dancers pouting on podiums raised above the dancefloor, perma-tanned bodies rippling as they swing fiery batons around their heads – although Maggie seriously questioned the wisdom of having naked flames in a room where the atmosphere is so heavily saturated with Lynx Africa. The club's social media promotion promised complimentary flutes of champagne for everyone who arrived before ten thirty, except they weren't real flutes because the club seemed only to trust its clientele with plastic, and they weren't really complimentary when entry cost twelve pounds, and the drinks were so lukewarm and rancid Maggie could not be sure whether it was champagne or fresh piss put through a soda-maker.

Therapy (small t) is also an only slightly less harrowing appointment Maggie attends for fifty minutes every Monday. She has been having panic attacks since university and they have been getting slowly worse since Lydia died. Her last major one was several months ago at a family wedding, when she bolted during her Grand-Uncle Tiernan's lewd toast and caused a small landslide of salmon and knock-off Bollinger in the process. Maggie's Aunt Aoibhlinn sent her a link to an online directory of counsellors and told her to choose one in the mid-price range. Maggie insisted it was unnecessary, but Aoibhlinn wouldn't take no for an answer. Maggie's mother had taken her own life at the age of twenty-one, when Maggie was a year old, and she had been raised by her aunt and uncle alongside their son, Liam.

Liam is two years older than Maggie and when she came to live with them, he boasted to everyone at nursery that he had a new baby sister. Nursery staff and parents were congratulating Aoibhlinn for weeks when she came to pick him up, many remarking on how well she'd looked both during and after pregnancy. She spoke gently to Liam at home, saying, 'I hope you and Maggie will love each other very much, pet – but you know your mam and dad aren't her mam and dad, don't you?'

'I *know*,' Liam said, rolling his eyes as though she was insulting his three-year-old intelligence.

'So she's not your sister.'

'She *is*.'

Aoibhlinn decided to leave it at that.

By the time she was a teenager, Maggie could have papered her bedroom with all the mental health leaflets and laminated prayer cards her aunt and uncle had given her over the years. When Maggie herself turned twenty-one, she came out as gay to her aunt (accidentally, in the homeware section of TK Maxx), and Aoibhlinn, though clearly blindsided, quietly accepted this information without comment or judgement. Maggie doubts her aunt will ever turn out for a Pride parade, but every so often she receives a text from Aoibhlinn telling her something like 'Just caught Saint Vincent (not de Paul!) on TV doing Glastonbury . . . is she on your music radar? Very talented' or 'I watched *Carol* last night . . . assume you've seen it. Lives up to the hype!' which Maggie finds in its own way pleasantly validating.

Maggie and her friends used to laughingly refer to the panic attacks of her early twenties as 'getting the D', because of the specific things that sent her into crisis: deadlines, debt, drinking, dentist (she ground her teeth so violently that she had to have two of her molars crowned by the time she was twenty-five). As she got older, these anxieties mutated into larger fears that were less easily catalogued, so when Harley would ask with quiet sympathy, 'Are you getting the D?' it referred to a more nebulous sense of dread and despair, the source of which Maggie was often unable to pinpoint.

The proverbial 'D' that Maggie has been getting over the past year is (rather unoriginally, she thinks) death. She remembers seeing an advertising campaign years ago, featuring a whimsical song entitled 'Dumb Ways to Die', that was designed to promote safety on the railways. Maggie finds nowadays that she has to flatten herself against the wall of any station platform as a train comes in, imagining herself slipping and shredding under its wheels like one of the cartoon bean-people in the advert. When a bus comes down the road in her direction she veers as far away from the kerb as she can get without being fully in someone's hedge, suddenly terrified that she might keel over into the middle of the road and be walloped by the number 61. She finds herself short of breath walking over bridges, the railings seeming frighteningly low and easy to topple over into the Lagan beneath. She can no longer go near open windows more than one storey off the ground, gets panicked in glass lifts and on Perspex bar balconies, as though the panes might break like the skin of a bubble.

Maggie has considered telling her aunt about these anxieties. If she ever does trip in front of oncoming traffic, or pitch into the river because a teenager zooming past on a bike made her lose her balance, she would like to spare her family the horrid speculation about whether she, like her mother, did it on purpose. Aoibhlinn had always referred to her sister's death as 'the accident', even when Maggie was an adult and knew that her mother had gone to very deliberate lengths to ensure the end of her own life. (When Maggie talks about Lydia's accident, she finds herself calling it 'the crash' to differentiate between the two.) She has decided that telling her aunt she has waking nightmares about falling off the edge of a building would cause more concern than reassurance.

Maggie's counsellor is an Australian woman not much older

than her. Astrid is short and round-faced and wears a lot of scarves, around her hair and neck and wrists, as though she is being held together entirely by strips of colourful knotted fabric. She maintains a strict poker face at what Maggie thinks are her most juicy disclosures, but often reacts with animated sympathy or horror to more trivial things, like Maggie telling her Cate's star sign.

'Therapy was fun,' Maggie tells Astrid. 'I mean, it's expensive as balls and the music is shite and the people are worse. But I had fun. I didn't text Cate. A good night.'

'A good night,' Astrid repeats, nodding slowly.

'Yes.'

'How are you feeling about Cate?'

Maggie shrugs. 'I haven't heard from her.'

'That's not what I asked.'

Maggie and Cate did not have sex the first night they met, despite the heady fuel of the supermarket wine they had so triumphantly uncorked together. They crossed paths again several weeks later, at a hen party for one of Maggie's school friends. Maggie had begun drinking heavily after committing an early-evening faux pas, in which she'd lauded the bride for hosting a normal, one-night hen in her home city, instead of a week-long carnival of tiaras and cocktail-making workshops that cost six hundred pounds a head. Maggie had not seen the social media posts of the bridal party's five-day trip to Barcelona, where they were photographed in silken party sashes outside the Sagrada Família and made their own wine in a Spanish barn.

She stood next to Cate at the bar without realizing who she was at first. 'Maggie?'

She turned her head and recognized Cate but forgot her name. 'Hi! You're . . .'

'Cate. We met at Dervla's house party.'

'I used your shoe to open my wine.'

'You're welcome.'

'What are you doing here, how do you know the bride?'

'Work. You?'

'School.'

The woman behind the bar came back with Cate's drink, blood-red and crowned with a half-moon slice of orange.

'Negroni?' Maggie guessed.

'Negroni sbagliato,' Cate said, taking a small sip. 'Prosecco instead of gin.'

'Why not both?'

'Why not, indeed?' Cate smiled. 'Are you going to the wedding, then?'

'Aye.'

'Plus one?'

'No. My girlfriend and I broke up a couple of months ago.'

'Oh? Sorry.'

'Don't be. We fell out over Repeal.' Maggie's last relationship had been a three-month affair with a girl from Galway who had voted against repealing the eighth amendment because she thought that if abortion services became accessible then 'people would just take the piss'. Maggie learned this information while they were both in a queue for the Centra deli counter, and she had ended the relationship by the time they reached the till.

Cate listened to Maggie sharing this backstory, and then said, 'Are you seeing anyone now?'

Maggie paused, suspicious. 'Why?'

'I'm nosy. Do you not like being asked?'

'Usually when people ask me it's because they want to set me up with their one lesbian friend.'

'Is that a problem?'

'Yes, because everyone's one lesbian friend turns out to be either some weird lass with gills and a passion for taxidermy, or someone I've already gone out with. Or both – the two aren't mutually exclusive.'

'So are you gay or bi or . . . ?' Cate had the same mildly perplexed look that Maggie sometimes got from straight men, men who asked her this question in a tone that suggested they were entitled to an answer and would ask to speak to a manager if they deemed the answer implausible.

'Filthy homosexual.'

'I'd never have known; your nails are too nice.' She nodded at Maggie's art deco manicure.

'Everyone says that. "*Oh, I'd never have guessed!*" '

'So *are* you seeing anyone now?'

'Jesus, stop flirting with me,' Maggie said flippantly.

'Why?'

Maggie's eyebrow shot up. 'Are *you* . . . ?'

Later, in the pub's empty smoking area, the negroni sbagliato taste was bitter and sweet when Cate kissed her – something

Maggie now jokingly reflects upon as an omen. A week later she looked up what *sbagliato* meant and found it translated to 'mistake'.

For a while now, Maggie has had a recurring fantasy about Cate in which the two of them are together and Maggie receives a piece of bad news – anything from unsuccessful job applications to family deaths to friends falling down stairs and being hospitalized with non-fatal injuries (Harley and Róise taking turns to play this role in her mind). She dreams of Cate softening and shushing in the face of Maggie's distress, the two of them bonded by tears.

Maggie cried a little in the taxi to Lydia's memorial Mass last Sunday; partly from grief, partly from the hangover, and partly because Cate had not offered to go with her. They had woken up early that morning, and Cate had pressed her hands into her eyes and groaned, 'I'm fucking dying. I would honestly prefer not to be perceived.'

'I've got to get out of here soon, don't worry about that.'

'Somewhere better to be?'

'It's Sunday; I've got Mass.' Cate snorted, and Maggie said, 'I wish I was joking.'

'Light a candle for me, then.'

Maggie, who had expected Cate to ask her why she was going to Mass, decided to reply as if she had. 'I don't know if I ever mentioned this,' she said, looking at the cobweb threads on the ceiling, 'but one of my best friends died a year ago. It's her anniversary Mass today.'

'Oh, I'd no idea. That's rough.'

Cate fell back into a doze and Maggie wondered which stung her more: the fact that, despite her feigned vagueness, she distinctly remembered having told Cate about Lydia before now, or the fact that Cate had been unable to summon a response more tender or sympathetic than *that's rough*.

Maggie reasoned afterwards that it was foolish expecting Cate to offer to accompany her. Cate had not known Lydia and did not even know Maggie all that well. By the end of the day, Maggie had convinced herself that perhaps Cate had even wanted to come to support her, but had not wanted to encroach on Maggie's company during a difficult time. Maggie notes now that Cate has not contacted her since to ask how the service went, or how she is feeling, and allows herself a little light denial, speculating that Cate may be trying to be sensitive and give her some space.

Astrid asks Maggie how she's feeling about Lydia's anniversary. 'Guilty,' says Maggie.

'Can you talk a bit more about that?'

Maggie shrugs, shifting with discomfort in her chair. 'I'm alive and she's not. And I was really hard on her before she died, because of everything that went on. I was probably even harsher than Róise, and Róise was the one who had the most reason to be angry, to be fair.'

'Mm?' says Astrid, looking as though she expects Maggie to elaborate. Maggie wonders if this is some kind of established talking therapy technique, getting her to go back over the particulars again, or whether Astrid simply does not remember.

Astrid sits with a pen and a stylish leather-covered notebook closed in her lap during all their sessions; Maggie hasn't seen her open it once. She decides to shift the subject slightly. 'I feel like our house is in much worse shape than it was when she died. Lydia always kept on top of everything. I'm pretty sure Barnaby's off his food, there's black mould in the upstairs bathroom and I think there might be dry rot under the stairs. I'm thinking of messaging our landlord. Not about the turtle, obviously. Just about the damp.'

'How are you feeling about still living there?'

Maggie thinks sometimes about how it would be to leave, for somewhere different but the same, a halfway-similar house-share for the three of them without the ghost of Lydia whispering out of every plug socket. She imagines she could live quite content-edly by herself, but there would need to be some inciting incident to set this in motion; Harley and Róise deciding they wanted to live alone, or move away. She can be adaptable to change, but she does not want to be the person to effect it.

At the end of the session, Maggie ventures, 'I love your nails, by the way.'

Astrid flexes her hand out flat in front of her as though she'd forgotten her nails were decorated at all. She thanks Maggie, and volunteers no further information.

After leaving Astrid's office and stopping quickly to buy an over-due lunch, Maggie half jogs towards the courthouse entrance, choking down the last of a sausage roll and brushing herself down before she gets pastry flakes on the marble floor.

Maggie's footsteps echo along the corridor as she makes a quick bathroom stop before heading to the office upstairs. The courthouse is a grand building with Corinthian columns and a lot of dark wood panelling, and the first time Maggie came here for work she expected the toilets to have ancient cisterns suspended above her head and rusty bolted doors, but they are disappointingly modern.

She had thought about training for the bar when she was applying for university, imagining it would be fun to swan around an ornate courthouse in a wig and robes, coming home to a glass of expensive sauvignon blanc from her wine fridge after a long day of serving justice. She shared this notion with Harley, who pointed out that Maggie had left the school debating society after one meeting because it felt too much like arguing and made her cry.

Secretarial work suits her much better, although it does also make her cry sometimes. She works in the Family Division, in the department that deals with adoption cases. A few months into the job, one of the barristers, Ann, was chatting to her about her Christmas plans, asking if she spent the holidays with her parents, and Maggie gave a summary explanation of her family circumstances.

'Oh, I see,' Ann said, pausing to take off her glasses. She often does this while speaking, as if marking out a small pothole of silence for others to stumble over. 'Is that why this job appealed to you?'

Maggie did not want to say that the job had not necessarily appealed to her, that she had been sent there by a temp agency and she needed to pay bills; nor did she want to say that she thought about her mother when she was processing adoption paperwork, that she wondered what would have happened if she'd had no family to take her in, whether she would have had a social services file and an earnest childless couple trying to prove to a panel that they were the best people to look after her. She reads court reports written by social workers detailing how the single mothers involved are unable to parent safely because they are mentally ill, suicidal, have self-harmed in front of their children, and she wonders if such a report would have been written about her own ma, had she lived longer.

In the bathrooms, Ann comes out of a cubicle at the same time as Maggie. 'Nice weekend, Margaret?' she asks. She is the only person who ever calls Maggie that. 'I had a grandmother called Margaret,' she once said by way of small talk. 'She went by Peggy, though.'

'I'd like to have been called Peggy,' Maggie replied.

'Were you named after a Margaret?'

Maggie said only, 'Yes,' and did not elaborate, not wishing to disclose that she had been named (only semi-ironically) after Margaret Thatcher. Maggie had been born on the day in September 1988 that the then prime minister made an unannounced visit to Lisburn, and her grandparents had missed her birth because they were at the pub engaging in bottomless anti-establishment discourse and similarly bottomless pints.

('Your ma was very relieved,' her Uncle Sean told her. 'If your granny had got to the hospital in time, she'd have banished the nurses and delivered you herself.'

'I didn't know Granny was a midwife,' remarked Maggie.

'She wasn't,' said Sean.)

'Yes, it was lovely, thanks,' Maggie replies. She can almost still feel the sticky imprint of cheap sparkling wine between her fingers as she starts to wash her hands. 'Good weekend yourself?' she asks, looking round to see Ann lifting her trouser leg and straightening a compression sock.

'Excuse my immodesty,' she says. 'First half-marathon in ages. I've not been properly training. Who has the time?'

'I didn't know you ran,' Maggie comments lamely into the bathroom mirror, pretending not to have caught sight of Ann's anklet of blue veins.

'Good for the soul. Do you? Run?'

'I don't even run for the bus.'

Ann laughs curtly, rinsing her own hands and snatching up a paper towel on the way out. 'You should try sometime. Excellent antidote.' To what, she does not specify.

The house is empty when Maggie arrives back. She kicks off her boots and nudges them into the shoe rack near the door, next to lethal heels she hasn't worn in months and running shoes she hasn't worn at all. She ordered the latter online last year when she and Lydia kept making aspirational drunk plans to go jogging together, plans that were ultimately never followed through. Maggie has never had cause to run in her adult life, unless you count the time she chased down someone who tried to steal her jacket at Belsonic. She did not bother trying the runners on when they arrived, and they are stuffed with lungs of cardboard, stickers still taped to the soles. Maggie puts them on now, sitting on the bottom stair in the hallway. They feel garish and clunky like a toddler's bootees on her feet, and the insides are cushioned with a keen, happy-to-help insole. She stands up. On a whim, she sprints up the stairs, down again, up again, down again. She stops just as suddenly when she remembers there's rot below, imagining the steps collapsing and swallowing her like some hideous beast with jagged, splintered teeth.

the STIs have it

Harley is given a number in the hospital clinic and told to wait. When her number is called, she is given a yellow card and told to wait some more. She watches the antiques programme on the waiting-room television, trying to guess whether each grotesque item will make a profit or a loss. The programme ends and rolls on to a property show, a couple in matching gilets touring empty houses and squinting at mildew. Harley stops paying attention and picks up a magazine from the table. It is an end-of-year issue with a month-by-month summary of the highs and lows of the year. She wonders whether she should do something similar when she's in with the doctor and they ask her to recount the last few months in sexual intercourse. *Culchies had a real moment this season and we were SO here for it. Eating ass made a surprise (but not unwelcome) comeback!*

At Therapy on Saturday night, Harley picked up a twenty-year-old boy who had misplaced his friends on a uni bar crawl; he was wandering around the club looking up at people like a lost child in a supermarket, sweat collecting in the ditch of his clavicle and around the neck of his superhero T-shirt. He began to make small talk with Harley at the bar in a way that was in equal parts endearing and neurotic; he seemed to feel the need to find an ally as a matter of urgency, as though anyone left alone when the lights came on would be escorted down the stairs and shovelled into an incinerator. He was surprised to learn that Harley was twenty-nine. 'You don't look it!' he said, apparently impressed, seeming to think she had outrun the ravages of age that should by now have wizened her. In bed she found him inexpert but very open to direction. He held his arms obediently above his head when she told him to, graceful as a ballerina. He did not ask for her phone number the next morning but instead vowed to look her up on Instagram.

She realized the day after that they had neglected to use protection, and that she was in the risky penumbra of her fertile window. She also thought the twenty-year-old seemed the earnest, pliant sort who was routinely dragged into bed by his more confident friends and peers, and as a result was likely riddled with chlamydia.

Harley had been on the pill for years but had stopped taking it two months ago, convinced it was giving her mood swings. The side-effects of the pill had never been referenced in the sex-ed classes their all-girls' Catholic secondary school had cryptically named 'Personal Development'; the pill had, in fact, never been mentioned at all. There was an uncomfortable silence, punctuated with sniggering, when their teacher asked how they could protect themselves from pregnancy. Harley had eventually volunteered, 'Contraception,' by which she meant 'condoms'. She could not bring herself to say the latter; pronouncing the word aloud in class seemed as inappropriate as physically flicking one in the teacher's face. At the time, Harley did not even really know what condoms were, imagining them to be made from some kind of waterproof material similar to a cagoule. It did not matter; the teacher informed her that while Harley was technically correct, there were some methods of contraception that she could not officially sanction, and changed the PowerPoint slide to a large WordArt display that said simply, ABSTINENCE.

Harley had received no hand-me-down advice from either of her older sisters. By the time she was a teenager, Liz had gone to university, and Marianne had run away to London with her boyfriend at the time. Her mother might not have raised the subject of sex at all had she not found and confiscated a small stack of teen magazines from Harley's bedroom, all of which featured articles about safe sex, which her mother assumed she had read. Harley had not actually paid these very much attention; she mainly smuggled these illicit publications into the house because she was in love with Sarah Michelle Gellar and used to cut out photos of her and paste them into a scrapbook like an adolescent serial killer. She did not understand what 'safe' meant in relation to sex, thinking that it perhaps referred to internet safety and online dating – that safe sex was sex that didn't end with you being murdered by a stranger you met on OkCupid. When she tried searching it online, a large red X came up on both the school computer and the family desktop, with an accompanying paragraph telling her that the search results had been blocked.

Despite her curiosity as a teenager, Harley did not end up having sex until her early twenties. No one particularly appealed to her; the boys in her classes at uni talked at length but said little of interest, and lads in the clubs she went out to carried themselves with transparent desperation. At twenty-two she had a short affair with an academic in his mid-thirties who seemed to enjoy her inexperience. This made her self-conscious and keen to catch up with her peers, to expand her meagre bank of anecdotes. She set about doing so, and she has not stopped since.

The doctor who services Harley is, she observes, annoyingly handsome. She uses her weekly planner as a memory prompt for rattling through her most recent sexual partners, and at one point feels the need to clarify: 'I'm just checking dates, I haven't – you know, taken notes.'

He laughs. 'Hey, I'm not judging. Whatever works for you.' She wonders if he means that, about not judging.

She is swabbed and scraped and sent away to piss in a cup. She lies on the table and tries to relax as the speculum is cranked wider. She gets an absurd mental image of the doctor opening her cervix with a circular wave of his hand like the space wizard from the superhero films conjuring a portal from the air. She considers asking the doctor if he can see into another dimension down there, but decides against it. The IUD being inserted feels like a bad period cramp, pain blossoming in her abdomen; and then it's done. Harley is given a party bag containing a pregnancy test to do in three weeks' time (just to make sure), a home testing kit for chlamydia (should she need it in future), and a generous batch of condoms. She would have loved some pink-frosted birthday cake wrapped in tinfoil, but has to make do with the chocolate biscuit the doctor gives her to take with ibuprofen. 'You did great,' he tells her, nodding. She feels a shimmer of pride like a child being given gold stars for a spelling test, although she supposes he would hardly have yelled, 'What the fuck was that display, soldier?' if she'd cried her way through the entire procedure.

When Lydia died, Harley still owed her money for the abortion she'd had in 2013. At the time, Lydia was coming to the end of her first month after a work promotion, while Harley was on a zero-hour contract at a city-centre bar whose cheapest pint was more than her hourly wage.

Harley told Lydia about the pregnancy first, for practical rather than sentimental reasons. Maggie had just been charged three hundred pounds for a dental crown and had advised she'd be dining on toast for the rest of the month. Róise had all but fallen out with a friend from school after footing the cost of both their trains and hotel rooms for a wedding they were attending, with the promise that she would be paid back (she wasn't). Harley did not want to ask either of them for money. Lydia made a good salary and sensible savings, and she was a planner, a fixer. Harley told her first in the guilty hope that she would take over all the arrangements like a travel agent.

Before the request was even in Harley's mouth, Lydia insisted she would help. Harley protested unconvincingly: 'This is your first decent pay cheque – you're meant to spend it on a ridiculous handbag.'

'You're my ridiculous handbag.'

'I'll pay you back. I promise.'

'We'll sort it out. Don't worry about it.'

Harley had a consultation with the pregnancy advice service, who told her the earliest available appointment would be at a London clinic. Harley felt her face drain of colour as she looked at Lydia; she'd expected to be getting the ferry to Liverpool. She mouthed, 'London?' at Lydia, who flashed her a silent thumbs-up.

The cheapest flights were at seven in the morning, and Lydia fell into a doze on the plane. Harley was desperate to sleep but forced herself not to, as though Lydia had treated her to an exclusive getaway and to nap would seem somehow lazy and ungrateful.

The appointment was at ten o'clock. The consultant who saw them was a woman in her forties with a thick Lancashire accent and a choppy ice-blonde bob. (When Harley had her own hair bleached and cut the following year, she wished she'd had a photo of the doctor for reference.) 'Once you're under, the procedure should only take around five to ten minutes,' she explained, 'and you'll need to rest in the recovery area for maybe half an hour, an hour afterwards.'

'And that's it done?' said Harley.

'It's not a lengthy procedure,' the doctor reassured her.

'Neither was the conception,' said Harley.

'And you'll need someone to stay with you for the next twenty-four hours. That's just standard for anyone going under general anaesthetic.' The doctor looked at Lydia and smiled. 'Have you both come over from Ireland or do you live here?'

'We came over from Belfast,' said Lydia.

'Oh, I've been to Belfast! The *Titanic* museum's fantastic, isn't it?'

'Never actually been,' Harley and Lydia both admitted.

'Good night out, Belfast, isn't it? I'd love to go back. Shall we get started, Charlotte?'

The sudden veer away from small talk, and the use of Harley's given name, threw her briefly. Mum had named Harley and her sisters in the style of a Regency mother: Elizabeth, Marianne and Charlotte. (Dad had wanted at least one good strong taig name in there somewhere; they would have been Eimear, Méadhbh and Cliodhna if he had had his way, but it was the mid-80s and Mum was worried about what those names might mean to others if they heard them in the wild.) When Harley was very young her dad had called her Charlie, which Mum disliked because she did not want anyone to mistake it for Charlene, a name she thought sounded common. Harley did not especially like Charlie either, and during the summer between primary and secondary school, announced she was changing it to Harley after Harley Quinn in the Batman cartoons. Her sister Marianne had recently started skipping school and smoking, and Mum did not have the energy for any additional battles; she assumed this rechristening would be a short-lived phase, and did not argue with her. She didn't seem to notice it had stuck until Liz and Marianne started calling their younger sister 'Harlotte' as a joke, and by then it was too late.

'Oh – aye, fire away,' Harley said to the doctor.

In the pharmacy that afternoon, Harley inspected the shelf of sanitary pads, and asked, 'Do you think I should get bigger ones than usual?' The ones marketed as barely-there gossamer napkins would clearly not suffice, and she examined a pack that looked as though they had been designed to bandage battle wounds in World War II. 'I mean, how much blood do you reckon there'll be?' she asked, picturing a biblical plague-style cascade of crimson.

'The doctor said it would be just like a normal period,' Lydia said firmly. 'Get the big 'uns and you'll be grand.'

They walked to the tube station on Baker Street and tried to meet the surging pace of the lunchtime rush. Harley broke into a light sweat. The cotton pad they had given her at the clinic felt thick and unwieldy between her legs. As daft a notion as it was, she could not help worrying that the people around her would clock her walking awkwardly and somehow know why. She quickened her pace.

Lydia admired the long ribcage of arches lining the station platform. 'People over here don't know how good they have it,' she remarked. 'All you hear the Brits complaining about is train delays. I'm so sorry you have to wait five extra minutes for a tube inside a literal work of art. Try missing a Sunday train to Derry and having an hour to kill at fucking Yorkgate.' Lydia had a lot of opinions about train stations. She could often be found chatting to people at parties about what a shame it was that Aldergrove station had sat disused since the 60s, when it would be such a convenient transport link for the airport. She found it absurd that Belfast Central station was so named given how un-central it was. Not long after Lydia died, Belfast Central was renamed

Lanyon Place, which Harley thought would have given Lydia a lot of new material, since the station wasn't even located on Lanyon Place but on East Bridge Street.

Lydia had got a good last-minute deal on a hotel in Elephant and Castle. Late in the evening they ordered Chinese food and sat on the double bed and saw that *Trainspotting* was on TV. 'Which one would you be?' Lydia asked, even though she already knew the answer. The four of them had been through every beloved book and film and series and assigned each other characters in the style of a teen magazine personality quiz. Sometimes they took themselves out of it and spent time pairing the main cast of one text with another: Merry and Pippin were Lydia and Kitty Bennet, Amy March was Blair Waldorf, Mark Renton was Carrie Bradshaw, and so on.

'Apparently they're making a sequel,' said Harley, stabbing her fork towards the TV screen.

'Bound to be shit, isn't it. Nostalgia porn for the fans.'

'Cast are all still rides, at least.' Harley felt a sudden rush of warmth in her crotch, and got up to go to the bathroom. The pad was drenched in scarlet, and she rolled it up and packaged it neatly in the wrapper of a fresh one.

'My pants are a crime scene,' she told Lydia when she returned. 'What happens if I get blood on the sheets – will they care?'

Lydia took a folded black towel out of her holdall on the floor. 'They won't care, but here, this should help. Brought it just in case.'

A crashing wave of shame washed over Harley, more potent than any she had felt all day. She had asked for Lydia's help for cold, practical reasons – she had money and was good at planning things – and had not considered the main reason Lydia was a good person to have around at a time like this: she was kind.

Harley sat on the towel, and they watched Renton read a letter from Diane – *I'm not pregnant, but thanks for asking* – and by the time Begbie turned up in London on the run from armed robbery charges, she had begun to cry. Lydia shuffled up beside her on the towel and guided Harley's head towards her shoulder. Harley still remembers the smell of Lydia's Britney Spears perfume mixed with egg-fried rice from the takeaway.

Harley comes home to an empty house after her doctor's appointment. By three in the afternoon, she is on the sofa with a hot-water bottle and a glass of wine. She groans aloud when someone knocks at the front door; Maggie or Róise must have ordered something online. Harley considers letting the postman leave it next door, but their neighbour is a close-up magician having a mid-life crisis and the last time she tried to collect a parcel from him she had to endure an elaborate roleplay with an oversized handkerchief and a live ferret. She answers the door reluctantly with her hot-water bottle clamped to her womb and sees it is not the postman but their landlord, Frankie.

'Bad time?' he queries.

'Yes,' she replies. 'I only receive gentlemen suitors between midday and one. This is most improper.'

Frankie doesn't laugh, and his response suggests he has either not paid attention to her riffing or is choosing not to engage with it. 'Maggie messaged about the damp in the bathroom. I was going to take a look.'

Harley looks suddenly scornful. 'There's no damp in the bathroom,' she says, her tone defensive.

He raises an eyebrow, apparently unconvinced. 'I can come back another time,' he says. 'But it'll only take a minute, I just need to see what the damage is.'

'Come on in,' she concedes, stepping back into the hall. She follows Frankie up the stairs and idles by the bathroom door as he inspects the walls.

He mimics her incredulously: ' "There's no damp in the bathroom"?' The corner above the shower is black with caviar-clusters of mould.

'Obviously there's *damp* in the *bathroom*,' she sighs. 'But that's no different to anywhere else. It's not like it's a massive problem — it's not hurting anyone.'

Frankie looks at her with obvious bafflement as to why she is speaking about the damp as though it is an ugly yet beloved family pet. She is annoyed with Maggie for whingeing to him about the mould before consulting her. Their living situation, to Harley, seems impossibly fragile; one structural instability too far (she is convinced) could see the landlord giving them notice, or jump-start Róise into talking about moving out again.

Then again, she supposes, Frankie does not seem overly keen to boot them out. He inherited the house from his father and does not seem interested in being a career landlord. He seemed appropriately uncomfortable when he came round to update their rental agreement after Lydia died, telling them that he had removed her name from the contract and that he had adjusted the rent so they wouldn't have to pay her share.

Frankie rarely visits the house, although Harley sees him every couple of weeks as he also sells her drugs at a very competitive rate. He is a tall, taciturn man in his late thirties and he wears a navy peacoat, and his general willingness to buy and fix things in the house over the years has meant they have very little to complain about. Harley engages in gentle flirtation with him, which he reciprocates infrequently enough to make him seem interesting.

'I'll maybe get someone in,' Frankie is saying vaguely about the mould.

Harley shrugs. 'Grand. Just let us know.' She nods at the clothes drying on the radiator. 'If I'd known you were coming round I'd have put away my pants.'

'Lies,' he scoffs sportingly, taking a photo of the damp with his phone. A small thrill flares between Harley's ribs and dies just as quickly as he answers an incoming call and excuses himself from the bathroom.

Harley follows him downstairs, the weathered wood of the steps bowing and creaking beneath their feet. She hovers around the kitchen, making tea she won't drink. When Frankie gets off the phone and comes to find her, she says, 'Sorry, do you want a tea or anything? Irish coffee? Saying that, we don't have any cream. And the coffee's run out. So it would just be whiskey.'

'No, thank you. I'll just head off. I'll give you a shout about the bathroom.'

'Sound. I might drop you a message about picking up next week?'

He nods vaguely, already back on the phone. 'Cheers, Harley,' he says, and leaves.

The teabag bobs around the hot water's surface, lace-skinned and flexing like a jellyfish. A barbed ache twists in her abdomen and almost brings tears to her eyes. She hugs her hot-water bottle close and returns to the sofa, leaving the cup of tea behind.

m'lady doth protest

Róise is, she decides, not suited to dating apps, because she finds most men extremely visually unpleasant. She resents the apparent lack of effort made by men on dating apps to conceal this. It is also never clear which person in any given sweaty Magaluf group photo is the proprietor of the profile, and rarely do any of them look particularly promising.

She downloaded the app to her new phone after finding a carrier bag of Brendan's T-shirts when she was cleaning out the wardrobe. One of the photos on her profile is a picture he took when they were out for dinner in Dublin. Another is a photo with Maggie and Lydia after they went to see Florence and the Machine in concert. Róise wonders if this is too morbid, imagines a man texting *You look gorgeous in this photo!* and her responding *Thanks! The woman on my left is dead now!*

She looks at the photo and tries to imagine what Lydia would have been like on dating apps. Róise and Lydia had both met their exes in the wild, so to speak, and she remembers them discussing how relieved they were not to have to use technology as a means of meeting people, as though they were old women reminiscing in hushed tones about a local tragedy that they had narrowly avoided decades earlier. Perhaps Lydia would have gone on the apps too, after things ended with Liam. It feels strange to think of Liam as Lydia's ex, since they broke up only a short time before Lydia died, and no one else apart from Róise, Maggie and Harley knew that it had happened, or why. Liam told them he couldn't face the thought of explaining the break-up to anyone, least of all Lydia's parents. Róise understood; for her own part, it was easier to lean into the role of the grieving friend than it was to tell people they'd fallen out, to tell them she'd spoken to Lydia every single day for years and then not at all for weeks, and now she could never speak to her again.

In different circumstances, Róise thinks as she flicks dully through men's bios, she and Lydia might have entered the trenches together, auditing each other's profiles and swapping screenshots of embarrassing messages. Róise wonders whether the brusque efficiency Lydia applied to other areas of her life would have made for a successful virtual courtship. Her most oft-used solution to any problem – personal or professional – was *why don't you just ring them and ask?* and Róise can picture her immediately requesting the contact details of a potential score on a dating app and phoning them up to arrange a meeting. Some people would likely find this refreshing, endearing, while others would block the number and wait patiently to be murdered in their beds.

But it is impossible to know now that Lydia is gone; and given the scale of their final fallout, it would be just as unlikely were she still here. Perhaps Harley would have taken Lydia out on the pull instead. Róise had stopped speaking to Lydia almost instantly, after what she did; Maggie, similarly fuming, had been more than happy to follow. Harley joined them dutifully although she seemed less comfortable about it, keen for the conflict to pass and for things to go back to the way they'd been, as if that were possible.

After dismissing about forty men in a row out of revulsion, indifference or confusion, Róise reluctantly swipes right on a man called Will who is wearing a Tyrone jersey in one of his pictures. They match, and he sends a message around thirty seconds later. It feels instantly unnerving, as though he has been waiting in a hedge for someone to walk past, leaping out at the earliest opportunity. His chat, Róise soon discovers, is excruciating. As soon as she tells him she studied literature at university, he begins to speak almost exclusively in jokey Shakespearean dialogue. Very early on in the exchange, he unsubtly floats the notion of her coming round to his place tonight. *I will summon thee an Uber!* he insists. *Wherefore art thou, Juliet?* She tells him condescendingly that 'wherefore' does not mean 'where'. She then points out that Juliet was fourteen and she does not think it an appropriate literary allusion given what Will is implying he'd like to do to her in his bed (which he has informed her is situated in a house in the Holylands that he shares with five other lads, all undergraduates ten years younger than him. He tells Róise he is doing an MA in journalism, as though this justifies his living situation). She takes a deep breath and suggests they meet for a drink later in the week instead.

This sort of transaction had been unnecessary when she

started seeing Brendan. They had managed to circumvent the uncomfortable formality of first dates by meeting across a bar and regularly going home together when his shift had ended, and over several months staying longer together in bed the next day, which transitioned to getting out of bed to eat and drink and watch films together, and by the time they began to actually pre-arrange times and dates to eat and drink and watch films together, the awkwardness had dissipated.

The first time they had had sex was after a lock-in, during which Róise had broken the pub fruit machine by feeding forty-seven beer caps into the coin slot. Brendan told her that he had taken responsibility for it, which she thought was very nice of him, until she confessed this to some of his co-workers years later, and one of them sniggered, 'Yeah, he told everyone it was you.' It transpired that she had been known colloquially as 'the Bandit' for years behind her back. ('Joke's on Brendan,' Lydia had said at the time. 'What a boss nickname.')

Róise used to like watching him pull pints behind the bar, looking at the perfect right angle of his bare arm as he eased the tap handle down and imagining resting her head in the crook of his elbow. She used to fancy his arm had the same bend, his face the same expression of calm focus, when she was going down on him. 'You can put your hand on my head, you know,' she told him once when they were in bed.

'I thought you said you didn't like that.'

'I don't mean *push* my head down. I mean, just . . .' She demonstrated.

'Ahh, grand. Like you would a dog.' Brendan pursed his lips. 'That came out wrong.'

'That's what she said,' Róise murmured, and they laughed in the way you always did at things that were hack jokes in normal conversation but seemed the height of witty repartee when you were naked and alone with someone you had a notion for.

Róise is not a regular smoker but on a nervous whim buys a pack of menthols from Centra and lights up on the roof terrace of Lavery's when she arrives; it gives the entire encounter more of a sense of chatting to a stranger she has met by chance in a smoking area rather than someone with whom she has arranged an official rendezvous.

Will bounds towards her, seemingly overjoyed, when he arrives. He looms expectantly over her rather than taking the seat opposite, and she half rises to give him a flimsy hug by way of greeting, her cigarette end dropping ash down the back of his coat.

'Well!' he exhales as he sits, looking her up and down. 'Well. Wow.'

Róise pretends not to have heard, peering at the cardboard sleeve on the table advertising drinks offers. 'Do you like rum? They've got a deal on, six fifty for a double and mixer.'

'I'm sticking with pints, I reckon,' he replies. He looks at Róise's full gin and tonic and seems crestfallen, as though he was determined to offer to buy the first round and she has robbed him of the opportunity. Even so, he says, 'Can I get you anything? Another . . . ?'

'No, thank you, I'm all good!' she says, sipping from the top of her drink.

Will returns to the table five minutes later with not one drink but three: two beers for himself and another G&T for Róise. She deflates at the notion of having to stay for a minimum of two rounds. '*So*,' he says, with a head-tilt and tone straight from a *Carry on* film. 'What's a girl like you doing on an app like this?'

Despite Róise feeling at every stage of the date that things are going badly, he seems, by contrast, to think they are going extremely well. She bites down on her derision when he tells her he is a *movie nerd*. He does not seem to know much about actual filmmaking, but likes to simply reference things in the film canon that he has seen, namedrop their directors, and say, 'I can't believe you haven't seen it!' He, by contrast, has never seen *You've Got Mail*. She tells him coldly that it is essential viewing and he responds with a jolly salute and a 'Yes ma'am!' She tells him not to call her 'ma'am' and he calls her a spoilsport. He also uses the word *groovy* apparently unironically, which she finds very difficult to allow.

When, after an hour and a half, Róise says, 'I'm really sorry, but I'm going to have to shoot on after this!' and makes up an excuse ('It's my friend's leaving do, sorry!'), Will looks surprised.

'O-kaaay . . . well, where are you meeting?'

She wonders if he is asking out of simple curiosity, or if he intends to walk her there, or if he might even be angling to be invited. 'I'm just heading *that* way and they're going to text me

66

where they are.' Róise gestures towards town (although she is
going in the opposite direction) and quickly plunges her hands
deep in her coat pockets to hint that she does not intend to
hug him.

'Well, can I walk you—?'

Róise cuts him off more sharply than she intended. 'No! No,
you stay here, finish your drink – I'm grand. Get home safe!'

At home in bed, Róise starts browsing films and ignores the
WhatsApp message that Will has already sent her. Before she has
settled on what to watch, another notification from him pops
up; he has messaged her on the dating app this time, perhaps
concerned she has not seen his previous text. *Hey there, pleasure
to meet you, good lady! Tell your friend I said bon voyage! Just putting it
out there . . . when you're done for the night with the gals, I'm only a short
taxi ride away . . .* and he punctuates with a suggestive-face emoji.
Róise does not reply. She tears off the top of a tube of crisps and
begins to eat them with savage urgency, shredding them in her
mouth with the speed and violence of logs in a wood-chipper.

Ten minutes later he sends her a link to a *Grazia* list of classic
romcoms, saying, *Also, saw this, coincidence! Made me think of you!*
Róise finishes the crisps and instantly regrets not having taken
her time and enjoyed them. Crisps were a ritual when she was a
child; her parents were strict about junk food, and she had only
been allowed them once a week as a treat. She liked the thick
crinkle-cut sort, sucking the salt off each one individually until
her tongue was stinging, eating them ridge by ridge to make
them last longer.

Twenty minutes later he says, *Just listened to that band you mentioned – big fan! Gave you a cheeky follow there on Spotify while I was at it, always seeking music recommendations and looking forward to being educated further!* A winking emoji this time. Her stomach churns with nausea. She reaches into her bag and pulls out a second sleeve of crisps.

Half an hour after that: *Guess you ladies must be having a pretty fun night! Hope you get home safe later, I'll drop you a message tomorrow about the small matter of a second date* [the suggestive emoji again] *Toodles! Xx*

Her sick smells foul and vinegary as it slops into the toilet bowl. Afterwards, she brushes her teeth until her spit is marbled with scarlet like a melted smear of raspberry ripple.

When Róise looks at her emails the next morning, she finds that Will has added her on LinkedIn. 'Nothing sexier than a man who could potentially refer you for a job in HR,' says Harley.

Róise is reluctant to text *let's just be friends!* because she does not want to be his friend, and it seems a little too brutal to text, *I have no interest in you on either a sexual or a platonic level, kindly delete my number.* She fudges a reply to his (many) messages. *Hi, had a great night thanks! Trying to fit a lot of things in at the moment, with work and everything else, so I'm sorry but I don't think I'll have any time free to meet up soon. Can't be helped unfortunately, just have a lot on. It was good to meet you!*

He replies several minutes later saying, *No worries at all! How about this: let's set a date for, say, dinner, a week or two from now, and if you find you're still snowed under, we can reschedule. Deal? No pressure*

*at all if you're too busy when the time rolls round, we can always postpone.
Hit me up with a date you think might suit. Xx*

Hey, she responds (deciding to be kind with him), *that's really
nice of you to suggest. But I do sort of wonder if dating is the right thing
for me right now. I feel like my last situation may still be a bit too fresh,
and now may not be the best time for me. Thank you, though!*

Róise, he writes, in a tone she reads as patronizing, *come on,
now. I don't know about you but I think we got on well and it'd be a real
shame to let that go to waste because of things in the past getting in the
way. Wouldn't you agree?*

Honestly? she responds. *Not really. We got on fine but that was it.
I think it's better to just leave it there, tbh.*

Were we on the same date? There was definitely a connection there.
When ten minutes go by and Róise does not reply, Will adds:
*Maybe don't go on dates if you're going to spook so easily? Just some
friendly advice.* Her heart is walloping her chest and she deletes
the conversation, deletes the app, blocks his number on her
phone, before she has the chance to reply with something she
will regret.

She scrolls unseeing through her work emails later that morning,
annoyed and embarrassed, glaring at the grey clouds gathering
beyond the endless windows of her office. She hears the sound of
her name across the room. Someone is talking about their work
Christmas party next week, and how much sparkling wine is
rumoured to have been ordered for it.

'Sounds right up our Róise's street,' Adam has just said, flashing her a smile. Róise has never attended forced office merriment

outside of working hours in her life, but his smile makes her think she may have to make an exception this year. She feels strange when people in work call her *our Róise*; it's something she used to think of as a purely familial prefix. Her sister has a PhD but will never be 'Doctor' or 'Professor' to them, always just *our Ciara*. When any of her co-workers call her *our Róise* she recoils a little, feeling as though she has been adopted into a work family against her will; it is an uncomfortable reminder of how long she has been here, when she at first intended it to be a short-term stopgap.

She forgets this briefly when Adam smiles at her. She is Team Hathaway Recruitment. She lives and breathes for this company. Our Róise? she thinks. I'm all yours.

petrichor

Maggie admires the commitment of the person she sees down near the docks practising their roller-skating at eight o'clock on a Saturday morning. It is dark and cold, occasional sprays of rain freckling Maggie's face. The sky is scarred with clouds and the henchman shoulders of the shipyard cranes are silhouetted on the horizon. The roller-skater weaves across the wet ground in balletic loops as Maggie jogs past, panting desperately.

Maggie and the girls met up with Liam earlier in the week to visit the continental market; they sat around a table in the bar tent under six p.m. darkness, drinking hot chocolate spiked with rum.

'Mum's putting the Christmas decorations up on Friday night,' Liam warned her. 'I'm sure she'll ask you round to help, so you may come up with your excuse now.'

Maggie's Aunt Aoibhlinn has about twelve different nativity scenes that she assembles around the house at Christmastime. They are a mix of plaster, knitted, bronze, and wood-carved figurines, and one made up of plastic *Star Wars* action figures. The set-up is made more confusing by the fact that Aoibhlinn always positions the Magi some distance from the stable until their official arrival on the Epiphany, so the house is strewn with lost-looking biblical characters for about three weeks over Christmas.

'I actually genuinely can't,' Maggie lied. 'I've got to get up early on Saturday.'

'Do you, aye?' Liam snorted, not falling for it. 'Why's that then?'

'I'm going running,' she said without thinking.

'Since when?' queried Harley, looking mildly revolted at the idea.

'I'm just, you know, trying it. For the health.'

'Where are you going?' Róise asked, apparently out of interest rather than suspicion.

'Titanic Quarter.' Maggie felt a pang of sadness, remembering that Lydia had suggested this part of the city while they were purchasing the trainers, because the area was flat and would be quiet in the mornings. She added, 'I'm going early so there'll be fewer witnesses if I pass out after running the length of myself.' Mercifully, no one interrogated her further.

'Are yous decorating the house?' Liam asked.

'Lydia always used to,' mused Róise. Liam gave a nostalgic nod and smiled.

Lydia and Liam had been an annoyingly practical couple. Lydia hung pictures and put together items of furniture as soon as she brought them home. She changed lightbulbs as soon as they blew out, while Maggie, Harley and Róise would go for weeks using table lamps and phone torches before they got round to replacing the bulb in the big light. When they invited people round, Lydia prepared bowls of snacks and dips whereas the other three were content to direct guests to the kitchen and tell them to help themselves. Within a day of returning from trips, Liam and Lydia had always unpacked all their things and stored their suitcases on top of the wardrobe. Liam could not open a slightly rattling drawer or notice a loose hinge at his parents' house without asking for a screwdriver to fix it immediately. Aoibhlinn would shrug and tell him not to bother, and he would frown at the screws and ask, 'How long has this been broken?' and sigh when she told him however many weeks or months. Lydia always contacted Frankie straight away when she noticed drips and rips and rickety fixings that looked like they might become a problem. In the months after she died, curtain rods collapsed and shelves started to wobble and pictures fell down from the crumbling plasterwork, and none of them felt up to the imagined hassle of doing anything about it. Last week, Maggie indulged in hearty self-congratulation after finally texting Frankie about the mould in the bathroom, like a child who had tidied her bedroom without being asked.

She has wondered in passing if Liam might want to help them put up Christmas decorations – and by 'help' she means do it entirely himself while they sit around and drink mulled wine – but he rarely comes to their house anymore. He does not talk very much about Lydia. When he and Maggie are round at Aoibhlinn and Sean's, his parents seem cautious about mentioning her by name. Shortly after Lydia's death, Aoibhlinn had swooped in with an offer to pay for bereavement counselling, and Liam had accused her of trying to throw money at the situation because she wanted him to simply 'cheer up'. Aoibhlinn had protested, and they'd argued. He had later apologized, saying he appreciated the gesture; however, since then (Maggie notes), Aoibhlinn has seemed wary of asking how he is managing his grief, perhaps concerned Liam will hear it as an entreaty to get over himself and stop moping. Words like 'grief' and 'loss' are rarely brought up in conversation now. Sean has instead developed a habit of asking, 'And how's the aul mental health?' as though Liam's mental health is a well-known character at their local pub. Liam gives very convincing answers, but Maggie is never quite persuaded. In her early twenties, Lydia was always impressed by men who had the vocabulary and understanding to be able to talk about their mental health, and by her late twenties she had discovered that many of these men were doing no more to proactively look after this much-talked-about mental health than the average man in the Victorian era. Liam, Maggie suspects, is one of their number. He confessed to her some months ago that he had gone to one counselling session at the start of the year, and that the counsellor was a woman about Maggie's age who responded with earnest platitudes about being kind to himself. He left the session and went out with his friends, bumped into the counsellor in a bar in town, told her he would not be making any future appointments, and had sex with her in the men's toilets. She exited the bathroom when the coast was clear, saying that her friends would wonder where she was, and that she would meet him at the bar. 'Buy me a drink first,' she joked, and he pretended to laugh. Liam found out afterwards that she had later asked his friends where he'd gone, and they told her he had gone home, because they assumed he had, when in fact he was sitting in the locked toilet cubicle crying until closing time.

They had not exchanged contact details, but she had his phone number from the counselling referral, and she sent a text two days later asking how he was and if he wanted to meet up sometime. Liam blocked her number.

'Mags,' he said when he told Maggie, 'I felt so fucking ashamed. It was like I'd cheated.'

'What's her name? You should report her, Jesus Christ,' Maggie said, deliberately missing the point because she didn't know what else to say. She went on, 'Are you going to try someone else?'

'Doubt it. Wasn't really helpful. Even before the toilet debacle.'

'Someone else might be different, though.' Liam looked sceptical. Maggie understands this now that she herself is in therapy. She thought she would get used to Astrid, that she would eventually feel less like every session is a job interview in which she is stumbling over the questions, have an epiphany or two and feel the kind of affinity with Astrid that she might feel telling her darkest secrets to a stranger in the small hours of a house party. But after several months of counselling, Astrid still has the feel of a friend of a friend at a house party with whom small talk has quickly run dry, and around half an hour into their fifty-minute sessions, Maggie feels the urge to pretend she needs to use the toilet or refill her drink, and swiftly excuse herself. Despite this, Maggie is reluctant to look for an alternative, cannot imagine what it would be like to endlessly try out therapists like first dates, wonders how many people have been seeing their therapist for years because breaking up with them feels too awkward, because they are too exhausted to keep trying until they meet the right one.

So Liam never went back to therapy, and he never comes round to put things up in the house anymore. Maggie has always considered herself and Liam to be close friends as well as family, but it is only in the last year that she has realized how much she relied on Lydia to organize their socializing. When he and Lydia were together, Liam came round to their house and went out with them so often that Maggie stopped asking if he wanted to go to the cinema or for coffee together. After they broke up, it took a couple of months for Maggie to acknowledge that she could not simply expect to run into Liam in their kitchen anymore. Now, she made a concerted effort to invite him to things, feeling bad that she'd fallen out of the habit of spending time with him organically, without Lydia; she remembered to text him every couple of weeks with the same guilty impulse as when she realized the council tax was overdue. He agreed to join them at the continental market, and he was coming out for Christmas dinner with them in a couple of weeks. Maggie sneaked a look at him across the table in the bar tent. He had his head tilted back slightly, breathing in the spiced wine and woodsmoke in the air as though he had not been outdoors in a long time. She thought that, if asked, Liam would probably help them carry an overpriced Christmas tree back from the nearest supermarket; but the chances of him coming into the house to decorate it for them were slim.

'I said last year we should buy discounted decorations after

Boxing Day so we'd have them for this year,' said Harley. 'And then I forgot.'

'We should do that this year, though,' Maggie suggested.

'We won't remember,' said Róise.

A cold, claggy sweat sticks Maggie's layers of clothes together as she stumbles and slows to the sort of pace she might adopt when hurrying to catch a train without quite wanting to break into a run. She sees the *Titanic* museum in the distance and decides she will run to it and then stop. A stitch bites into her side as she speeds up and she stops a few yards short, wincing, curlicues of hair stuck to her forehead by rain and perspiration.

'Maggie?'

Just in front of her, Cate has one leg braced on the steps outside the museum to stretch it out, and is looking at her curiously.

'Oh, that's not fair,' Maggie half groans. She has not seen Cate since the day of Lydia's memorial and had hoped that the next time they crossed paths would be on an occasion when Maggie was groomed to perfection and perhaps entertaining a group of admirers with an amusing anecdote. She wonders if she should be concerned that Cate so easily recognized her now, when she is scarlet in the face and wheezing profusely. Cate, by contrast, looks like a shop-window mannequin, dressed as though she is modelling her running clothes rather than sweating into them.

Cate approaches Maggie. 'How you been?' She says it casually, nothing in her tone to indicate that the last time they saw each other they were naked in bed together.

'Yeah, you know. Busy. You well?'

'Can't complain. Do you go running around here, then?'

'I have been, yeah. Running. Well, today.' Maggie wrinkles her nose. 'I've never been running before and I'll be honest, I don't love it.'

'This is only the third time I've been out, in fairness. I didn't stretch properly the first couple of times and really fucked my shins.'

Maggie glances down automatically at Cate's legs and then forces her eyes up, embarrassed, trying to pass the movement off as a nod. 'Good to know, I'll take that on board.' *I'll take that on board?* she mocks herself silently. She is trying to sound aloof and unflappable, not like someone doing market research on *The Apprentice.*

'I was about to go and get a coffee,' says Cate. 'Fancy joining?'

'Yes,' Maggie agrees immediately, then adds with an eye-roll, 'I need something to wake me up,' as though her keenness is for caffeine rather than Cate.

The barista overfills Maggie's drink and a layer of foam shivers dangerously on the top like the head of a pint of stout, threatening to drool down the sides of the cup if disturbed. Cate warms her hands around her own mug and inhales.

Maggie takes a too-big sip of too-hot coffee that burns the roof of her mouth and Cate asks her, 'How are you, how was your friend's memorial thing?' She sounds, to Maggie's ears, as though she is asking as offhand and frivolous a question as *how was your holiday?* or *how was the film?*

'Yeah, good!' she replies. 'I mean, not *good*. But I'm grand. Thank you. For asking.'

'I never asked what happened,' says Cate. 'I don't know if it's a difficult subject. What was she, our age?'

'Yes,' Maggie says formally. 'It's okay, I don't mind you asking. She was in a car accident. She was getting a taxi home from a night out and the driver wasn't licensed. He was a bit messed up himself – he'd been drinking, turned out. The peelers tried to get him to pull over and he sped up. Crashed into some scaffolding round a building on Bedford Street. They both died.'

'I think I read about that,' Cate says, looking almost impressed, as though Lydia is a minor celebrity. 'That was your friend?'

At the time, Maggie remembers that the local media took the incident as an opportunity to remind the public of the dangers of getting into unlicensed cabs, advising patronizingly that people should book their lifts in advance and not allow alcohol to mar their judgement for the sake of a quick ride home. Maggie and Harley wrote angry emails saying that it was in bad taste to suggest that Lydia had cruised to her death simply because she was drunk or couldn't be bothered to book a fonaCAB. They received no replies, and the news articles stayed unchanged.

'That's awful, I'm so sorry,' says Cate. 'Were you out with her? That night?'

Maggie drinks more coffee although her tongue is still stinging. 'No. We were all in a sort of fight at the time. I wasn't speaking to her; neither was Róise. Harley was trying to be on both sides.' Cate rolls her eyes slightly at the mention of Harley. Maggie stops, and says, 'I'm oversharing, it doesn't matter now.'

'You're not oversharing,' says Cate. 'What were you all in a fight about?' Maggie resents and admires the ease with which she asks personal questions. She imagines telling Cate the details of their fight with Lydia in a future moment of shared intimacy; now, she decides, is not the time, when she is lisping from coffee burns and shivering inside an amphibian skin of damp Lycra.

'None of your business,' she says, smiling.

'Tease,' says Cate, but does not press her on it.

As they talk she watches Cate's hands grip tighter around her cup of coffee, clinging on to its slowly ebbing warmth. Sometimes, when they are in bed together, Cate turns over in her sleep and pulls Maggie tight against her as though she, too, can be drained of heat. Most times Maggie lies awake at daybreak, suspended somewhere between the night's euphoria and its crashing aftermath, listening to Cate snoring in the opposite direction. The bedsheet is ice-cold between them. Sometimes Maggie coughs, rolls over, pulls on the duvet, all in the hope that Cate might stir; the result, however, is generally no more than a mild arrhythmia in her breathing. The times she cannot hear Cate's breathing, Maggie wonders for a few detached moments whether she might have died, and wonders how she would feel if that were the case, whether she would be crippled with grief or even, horribly, relieved that the plot – their plot – had at last been advanced. Then Cate sighs or sniffs or shifts in her sleep, and Maggie shuts her eyes and waits for her touch, which does not come.

'What has you out running, then?' Cate asks. 'Training for the marathon?'

'Away on, I can barely run the length of myself. No. Lydia and I always used to make these very ambitious drunk plans to start running together. I had the shoes, but I don't have her anymore. But I thought I'd try it anyway.'

'You going to keep it up?'

'I suppose so,' says Maggie with a shrug. Now that the beads of sweat have retreated from her upper lip and she is no longer panting, running doesn't seem quite so awful.

'Maybe I'll see you out again,' says Cate.

'Have you heard of a mad notion called "making plans with someone"? You know you don't have to just rely on stumbling into me at parties and parkruns.'

'Incredible alliteration. You can tell you did an English degree.' Maggie waits to see if she will follow up. Cate tilts her head to one side. 'Do you want to make plans with me, then?'

'That's what friends do, isn't it?' Maggie says carefully, lightly mocking.

'Is this you friend-zoning me now, is it?'

'Would you like to appeal the verdict?'

Cate drinks the last of her coffee, which must surely be cold by now. 'I don't like to chase people,' she says, her lips curving into a smile.

'Maybe that's why your shins are fucked,' says Maggie.

The next day Maggie is hobbling, tightness tugging at the backs of her legs as though she is a collapsible chair desperate to collapse. She goes to her aunt and uncle's house for Sunday dinner and Liam asks why she is walking like C-3PO.

'I told you,' says Maggie, bolstered this time by the confidence of honesty. 'I went running.'

'Fair play to you, Mags,' says her Uncle Sean. 'Good for keeping the aul mental mechanics oiled.'

Maggie, who has arranged to meet Cate for an early-morning jog on Tuesday, nods silently. She straightens one leg and winces as the muscle pulls taut; she flexes it again, and again, until the pain seems if not neutralized, then normalized at least. The ache twinges later on when she sees the figures in the dining-room nativity scene, all lunging in varied stages of genuflection. She vows to warm down properly next time.

rhapsody in blue

Harley wakes to the sound of a chirping landline next to her bed. She claws the handset out of its cradle and croaks, 'Hello?'

'Good morning, this is your wake-up call,' Ash on reception mocks her serenely.

'What time is it?'

'It's ten a.m., madam.'

'Fuck.' Harley puts down the phone to drown the laughter coming from the other end and sits up slowly to survey the damage. One half-drunk bottle of sparkling wine bobbing in a cooler of melted ice-water. Two glasses. Two towels abandoned on the carpet after use. Two empty miniatures of shower gel in the bathroom. One of the new waitresses from the hotel bar, asleep naked in bed. Harley remembers that they both finished their shifts at three and that one of them, or both of them, had stayed on to have a drink, or more than one drink, and that one of them, or both of them, had the idea of using Harley's employee discount to get a room at the hotel, since it was so late. Harley cannot remember if the waitress offered to buy the wine since Harley paid for the room. Then again, drunk in charge of a debit card, Harley never lets anyone pay for drinks. She probably insisted on getting it herself. In the interests of feeling as though the expense was not a complete waste, Harley takes the undrunk prosecco with her to the bathroom and finishes it while she lathers hotel soap into her armpits, splashes water into her eyes (in an attempt to rehydrate the contact lenses she passed out wearing), and then reapplies makeup with crayoned imprecision.

The waitress has woken when Harley returns; she smiles and teases, 'Thought you'd fucked off.'

'I'm about to,' says Harley, pulling on pants and yesterday's clothes and covering the wine stains with a cheetah-print frock coat. 'Check-out in forty minutes.'

A text from Frankie sent at eight this morning indicates that he will only be available before noon, and queries whether he should call at the house or pick her up elsewhere.

Is there any chance, she replies, *you could swing by town and get me? My place of work has very well-reviewed parking.* She sends him a pin with her location. He responds with a thumbs-up.

Harley sneaks across the foyer towards the hotel restaurant while the reception desk is briefly unmanned, almost sliding on the clean floor tiles. The hotel building is an old red-brick factory on a street corner, and the inside has been laminated and leathered to within an inch of its life. It is one of the establishments owned by Cate's family. The hotel manager is a thirty-year-old man called Ollie, one of Cate's cousins, who has no previous management experience but went travelling a lot in his twenties and thinks this counts as a tourism and hospitality qualification.

He often makes observations that suggest the staff should be emulating the atmosphere and cuisine of whichever luxury yurt park he remembers staying in six years ago. In reality, the rooms are of a very basic standard at a piss-take price. Harley is glad not to be working in the restaurant anymore, remembering the horrified confusion of guests being charged four pounds fifty for a bottle of still water. 'I'm not paying that,' people sometimes said, and Harley shrugged and replied, 'Fair, I wouldn't either,' and took it off the bill.

'You can't keep doing that,' Ollie tried to tell her sternly.

'They weren't happy, I thought you said "customer satisfaction is key"?'

'You've got to *upsell*,' Ollie whined. He loved the word *upsell*, although Harley doubted he knew what it meant.

'What am I meant to do, tell them they're drinking Enya's tears?' She knew she would not be sacked for backtalk. They had a rapid employee turnover thanks to the number of young female staff members Ollie slept with and subsequently ignored.

Harley sidles behind the bar with the intention of making herself a coffee to go. 'Are you in today?' queries one of the duty managers, who wasn't on shift last night while Harley was getting slaughtered.

'No, just passing through. Left my phone charger here yesterday,' Harley lies smoothly. She hits the double espresso button on the coffee machine, and glances around the restaurant as she waits for it to pour. It isn't busy; the breakfast slot for hotel guests has passed, but a few people have come in to avail themselves of the brunch menu. This was another of Ollie's big ideas;

whereas before there was simply breakfast and dinner, they now have a brunch slot between ten and midday, lunch between midday and three, a pre-dinner menu consisting only of small plates between three and six, a Sunday roast dinner menu, and an incongruous Mexican tapas menu available only on Wednesdays.

Harley does a double take at a couple, a man and a woman, tucking into pancakes at their table. She does not recognize the woman, but the man is Róise's ex-boyfriend Brendan. He looks in Harley's direction a moment after she notices him, recognition spreading across his face. He lifts his arm uncertainly in a half-wave, and a chunk of pancake and bacon drops off his fork and onto the floor. Harley smiles tightly, willing the coffee machine to speed up.

Brendan has always been just all-right-looking to Harley. He has good legs and a gently sporty build rather than a straining gym body, although his face does very little for her – he often has the slightly bewildered look of someone who has just been clubbed in the back of the head with a hurley. Harley never found Brendan particularly charismatic or funny, but Róise liked him, and he was kind to her, until he wasn't.

Brendan rises from his seat and approaches Harley at the bar. 'How's the form?' he asks her. He looks uncomfortable, and Harley feels like pointing out that no one made him come over to speak to her. She remembers him being like this when he was going out with Róise, voluntarily initiating a conversation with Harley or Maggie or Lydia and then tensing up like someone being forced to engage in small talk with a drunk at a bus stop. Harley wondered at the time whether he was like that when he was working behind the bar, or whether this was an awkwardness reserved for Róise's friends.

'Grand, thanks,' Harley replies.

'Do you work here, aye?' he asks.

'Yeah, I'm just on my way out.'

Brendan, apparently having run out of questions, stabs his thumb over his shoulder towards the woman at their table. 'That's just Kerri. She's a friend.'

Harley nods. 'Thanks. Didn't ask.'

Brendan clears his throat. 'How's things? Are yous still living in the same place?'

'Same place, aye.' Harley forces the plastic cap too hard onto her coffee cup and the lid splits at the edge. She fumbles for another one.

Brendan looks down at his hands on the bar counter as he asks, 'How's Róise?'

Harley sighs. 'Róise's good.'

'I was maybe going to drop her a message – do you think that'd be . . . I dunno, weird?'

'Not for me to say, mate.'

'Did she have a good birthday?'

'Oh, top-tier,' Harley snaps. 'We went out on the lash and the next morning went to an anniversary Mass for our dead friend.'

'Shit,' Brendan says hollowly. 'Has it been a year since——?'

'You know what, I take it back,' Harley cuts him off, swinging her bag over her shoulder. 'Maybe it's not for me to say, but honestly, there's nothing you can text Róise that's going to make things better. Stay away from her.' She storms towards the

restaurant exit, the strap of her bag getting caught on the door-
knob on the way out.

Harley visits the nearest cash machine and requests a hundred
and fifty pounds. It is declined; so is her attempt at a hundred and
twenty. At a hundred, she strikes success. She will simply, she
reasons, have to be a little miserly with her assets until payday.
No whispered reassurances of 'This round's on me!' and no offering bumps to strangers in toilet cubicles.

She hands thirty to Frankie as she cannonballs into his passenger seat ten minutes later.

'Rough night?' he queries, pocketing the money.

'Late shift,' she says, palming the bag in his cup-holder.

'I bet it was.'

When they are out of the car park he says, 'Do you want
dropped home?'

'Would you be able to stop for five minutes at our house,' she
ventures, 'and then drop me in Stranmillis? I need to pick up
some things. Sorry, I know it's an absolute joke to ask you. But
I'm running really late. I would owe you forever.'

Frankie shrugs. 'All right, then. But I'm warning you now, if
you boke in this car, you're paying for it.'

Harley is not listening; she shifts in her seat, wincing, pulling
at the crease in the rear of her jeans, then furtively checks the
label on the side of her underwear. 'What's wrong?' says Frankie.

Harley sits straight again, and stares ahead, pushing a long
breath out through her nose. 'These aren't my pants.'

★   ★   ★

Harley whips in and out of the house to put on fresh clothes and swap handbags, landing back in the passenger seat with a flurry of 'Thank you, thank you, thank you so much.'

'No worries. Please calm down.'

Nerves begin to swell in Harley's stomach as they drive through south Belfast. Frankie notices. 'Do I need to pull over?'

'No, no. I'm not sick, just anxious. I've not practised.'

'Practised for what?'

'Piano lesson.'

He laughs monosyllabically, thinking she's joking. When Harley doesn't join in, he says, 'Am I driving you to a piano lesson?'

'Yes, and as I said, I'm very grateful.'

'Year Nine carol concert coming up, is it?'

She throws him a haughty side-eye that they both know she doesn't mean. 'Grade five exam, actually.'

'My mistake.'

'I failed it three times when I was at school.'

'I failed Geography at school but can't say I had a second wind for learning about igneous rocks in my thirties.'

'I'm not *in my thirties*,' Harley retorts, then indicates. 'It's a left turn at this postbox here.'

'I know.'

'Well, you did fail Geography, so I couldn't be sure.'

Of the three times Harley failed grade five piano as a teenager, she considers at least two of them to be her sister Marianne's fault. When Harley was fourteen, Marianne ran off to Dublin with her then boyfriend, and between frenzied unanswered phone calls to Marianne's switched-off mobile phone, their mother wailed at Harley to stop practising on the upright piano in their living room because it was exacerbating her migraine. Harley's disastrous exam results came back around a week after Marianne did. 'These things happen,' Mum said, with a pitying glance over the examiner's comments. That Christmas, Harley received an electronic keyboard with a headphone socket. This did not have the feel or sound of an acoustic piano, and she struggled to adapt; she still practised on the living-room piano where possible, until Marianne had friends over while their parents were out and one of them spilled a pint of cider down the keys, sending it wildly out of tune. After her second failed exam attempt, Harley vowed she would have one more crack at it, and then Marianne stole her keyboard to 'lend' to a university housemate who was in an up-and-coming gospel dubstep band. Harley said to the examiner after her third and most diabolical performance: 'Listen, I know I've failed. Can you just tell me now?' The examiner folded away his notes and smiled and said that she would receive the results within a few weeks. When she did, they were full of single-digit numbers and words like *hesitant* and *lacking in movement*. Harley, by then eighteen, told her parents that she had passed, and stopped taking lessons. Her teacher Mrs Erskine, who had spent ten years listening to her stumble through scales and sonatas, seemed to think this a wise choice.

Harley resumed piano lessons in the spring of this year, and tries not to feel ashamed each time she passes the primary-school-age children who attend their lessons before and after her. Harley remembers having a mildly tearful drunk conversation with Lydia a couple of years ago in which she (Harley) lamented her lack of any real hobbies. 'When I finish an afternoon shift it just feels like everyone's going off to *do* something,' she moaned. 'Everyone at work has their silly novel they're working on, or their Friday-night stand-up residency, or their side-hustle selling hand-painted clay badgers online.'

'You're not in a romcom, Harley; you don't need a secret passion for baking artisanal cupcakes.'

'I know, but like, a single hobby beyond the sesh would be nice. Ash at work is constantly fucking *reading*. Remember when I used to read?'

'You were good at the piano.'

'I was famously terrible at the piano.'

'Well, yeah, you weren't *good*. But you wanted to be. Why don't you do that again?'

'It was bad enough being shit at it when I was thirteen, I don't want to be shit at it when I'm thirty.'

'Fine, then. Stick with what you're good at. Drinking, pulling, complaining.'

At Lydia's funeral, one of her teenage cousins played a haunting classical piano piece as Liam, Lydia's father, and the other pallbearers carried her down the aisle. Harley had a wild image of what might have happened had she taken Lydia's suggestion seriously – whether it could have been her playing up there instead.

Harley went straight for neat whiskey at the afters – did you call it an 'afters' at a funeral? she wondered. There hadn't been a wake beforehand. Lydia's mum had told Harley, Róise and Maggie that she did not want an open casket, and that a closed casket would invite gauche speculation from her extended family about the nature of her daughter's injuries, which she had no desire to discuss. Lydia's parents instead organized a post-funeral buffet with a generous bar tab, held in the upstairs room of a pub near their family home.

Harley was on her fourth neat whiskey when she noticed Lydia's cousin standing nearby. She approached the girl and asked her the name of the piece she'd played during the service.

'It was Finzi's *Eclogue*,' she replied.

'It was lovely,' Harley whispered, and she took a swallow of whiskey that she hoped would scatter the dense throng of sobs that had rushed to her throat. 'It should have been me up there,' she added. The cousin seemed to think she meant something else by this, and clearly did not know what to say. Lydia's aunt came suspiciously to her daughter's side. 'I was just saying,' Harley blethered on through violent hiccups, 'how nice the music was. All those lessons – obviously paid off.'

'Clio's actually self-taught,' the mother said, beaming. She looked as though she was about to say more, but Harley mumbled a quick 'Excuse me,' and ran for the door.

Liam was outside alone, squatting on his haunches against the wall and nursing a bottle of beer. 'Harley,' he said pleadingly. 'Please. I'm not here.'

'I won't speak,' she said. 'I just need some air.'

'You can speak. As long as it's about literally anything else.'

Harley crouched next to him. 'Do you have any fegs?'

'No.' He paused. 'Do you have any gear?'

'No.' They sat in silence for a few moments. Harley took another sip of her whiskey. 'Do you think I should start piano lessons again?'

After a stumbling recitation of her scales, Harley begins to pick at her flaking nail varnish, and when she has concluded her third piece she can see that specks of dark blue have scattered across the ivory keys. She wonders when was the last time she properly scrubbed her nails, thinks about the sort of horrors that a forensic team might pluck out from under them with tweezers: crisp dust and grains of coke and waitress DNA.

Mrs Erskine nods after the final chord. 'It's coming on,' she says diplomatically. She takes her glasses off to rest on a chain around her neck and replaces them with a different pair, reading glasses this time. She reaches a sheet of paper down from the top of the piano and frowns at it while Harley waits, trying not to slouch. Mrs Erskine does not put up her decorations until the week before Christmas, but a few festive cards from her pupils are already on the mantelpiece. Harley makes a mental note to buy a card and gift for her when she gets paid. She remembers her mother sending her into her last lesson before Christmas every year with a shiny tin of biscuits that Mrs Erskine always looked delighted to receive, despite it probably being the seventh such offering she had accepted that day.

'So,' Mrs Erskine says, 'for the February exam window we would need to be getting your forms and fees in around now.'

Harley opens her mouth to reply that she has brought the sixty-five-pound exam fee with her, but Mrs Erskine looks up from her list of dates and swaps her glasses around again. 'I'm going to suggest,' she says kindly, 'that we postpone until the May exam season. I'd just be concerned that where you're at now, and with the Christmas break coming up, we might not be ready.'

Harley reads a gentle scold for her lack of practice in her teacher's raised eyebrows, and nods with great enthusiasm to disguise the sprawling ambush of feeling that has leapt to her eyes. 'Yeah, no, absolutely. I know it needs so much work. I know I'm nowhere near ready.' Mrs Erskine gives a benevolent shake of her head, and Harley is suddenly compelled to say, 'I'm so sorry, this month has just been difficult. I had a bereavement last year and it's just been the first anniversary.'

Mrs Erskine is suitably sympathetic. Harley can almost hear Lydia's voice teasing her for her excuses. *Playing the dead friend card, Harley, you spoofer! See you in Hell.*

Maggie is watching TV in the living room when Harley returns to the house that afternoon. Harley throws herself onto the sofa and winces as she feels a bruise throb somewhere on her lower back, an injury that must have been sustained last night, though she can't remember how. 'Is Róise in?' Harley asks.

'You just missed her. She's gone to get food for the turtle.'

Harley shoots a glance at Barnaby in the corner, as though suspicious he might be eavesdropping on them. 'Question,' she says.

'Shoot.' Maggie mutes the television.

'I saw Brendan this morning.'

94

Maggie's expression darkens. 'What was he at?'

'I was leaving work. He was having brunch with some girl.'

'Dickhead,' Maggie mutters, personally insulted by the notion.

'He said she's just a friend. But that's not even important – question is, should I tell Róise I saw him?'

'So he *spoke* to you?'

'Aye, came over and wanted to know how we all were. Asked about Róise and then said he was thinking of messaging her, like he was asking my permission.'

'What did you say?'

'I wasn't going to say anything,' Harley admits, 'and then I told him to keep his fucking distance. But I don't know; maybe she'd want to hear from him. She never talks about him anymore, so I don't know how she feels.'

'She hates him, surely.'

'Well, I don't know. People do get over things.'

'She barely left the house for six months.'

'She's getting out and about *now*, though.'

Maggie grabs her phone and opens their shared Spotify account, thrusting the screen towards Harley's face. 'She's still listening to *Red*. Unless that was you.'

'No. I'm more of a *Reputation* sort of girl. Anyway, what does *that* prove?' Harley groans. '*Why* did he have to come and talk to me? I even brought up Lydia, like a fucking eejit.'

'What?'

'I wasn't thinking, just said it had been her anniversary; and he was like, *Jesus, has it been a year?* I didn't want to keep talking, I just told him to stay away and then walked off.' Harley groans, presses the heels of her hands against her face, and declares, 'Right, I've decided. There's no way I'm telling Róise. She's just had a big birthday, it's a year since Lydia, a year since the break-up, and Mercury is in fucking retrograde. Cocktail for disaster.' Harley does not know if Mercury is really in retrograde, but it seems to add weight to her argument, because Maggie nods sagely as though it all makes sense. Harley sighs. 'I need a drink. Do you want a mimosa?'

Maggie snorts. 'It's two o'clock; bit late for brunch.'

'Well, it's too early for neat vodka, so do you want one or not?'

'Aye, go on.'

'I'll ring Róise, ask if she does too.'

'She'll be back soon, she's just gone—'

'Yeah, but I need her to pick up some orange juice,' Harley says, already holding the phone to her ear. 'And prosecco.'

she drinks tequila

The following Friday night, Róise makes a deal with herself as she draws near the hotel. She will do a shot of tequila to anaesthetize her, she will stay at the party for half an hour, and if it is as awful as she expects, she will leave.

She ignores the sign next to the lift for *HATHAWAY CHRISTMAS PARTY: FLOOR 3*, and heads to the hotel bar. The bartender serves her tequila in the sort of thick-bottomed shot glass that looks like a loupe for inspecting antiques. It is a nice change, she thinks, from the sticky plastic thimbles she's used to in bars and clubs; it makes the tequila feel more like a civilized amuse-bouche, rather than the volta beyond which a night tumbles inexorably into decline.

Róise's heart bounces into her throat when Adam steps up to the bar next to her and says, 'All right, our Róise? What you drinking?'

He taps the edge of his American Express on the bar surface as he says the last part. Róise nods towards it. 'What you buying?' She still doesn't mind the *our Róise*. The way he says it sounds like an in-joke, as though he is not so much saying it as mocking the people who do.

He mirrors her nod, gesturing towards the empty shot glass on the bar. 'Tequila?'

'Ooh, go on then.'

'Pint or half?'

'You're doing it with me, though,' she commands him quietly.

Adam sucks air in through his teeth like a builder surveying damaged infrastructure. 'God, I haven't had tequila in . . .' He pauses to consider. They are, Róise thinks, not too far apart in age, and yet he behaves as though tequila shots belong to a far-off youth with which he has largely lost touch.

'That silence means it's been too long. I'm not taking no for an answer.' She raises an imperious finger to point at him, not knowing quite where this attitude has come from. She is not an especially experienced flirt. Brendan told her when they started seeing each other that she had an aloof sort of mystery about her that he found very alluring; then, she gathered, he found out that it was largely un-enigmatic social anxiety, and it became a lot less sexy.

Adam is pulling a face at the tequila while Róise manages not to gag. 'Look at you,' he teases her, 'hard as nails. It's a young person's game, tequila.'

We're literally the same age, she wants to point out, but doesn't. 'Same again, please,' she says instead to the bartender.

Adam barks a laugh into the air. 'I can't do that again.'

'Not with that attitude, you can't,' she retorts. 'Suck it up, it's my round.'

'Are you trying to get me drunk, Róise?' he says, clutching at invisible pearls.

Every quip that passes between them gives her a rattle of mingled excitement and fear. Things are easy to navigate when they are at work and the lines between them have been drawn by their job descriptions and pay grades. Here, now, she feels that the line has been redrawn, by him, and she is not entirely sure where it is. Róise is concerned that he will keep cracking jokes, and she will continue making jokes back, until she says something and realizes as soon as it is out of her mouth that she has transgressed across a line that she did not know was there.

'I'm getting this,' Adam says, flicking his card at the bar staff.

'Don't be daft, it's my turn.'

'No arguments. I'm your superior.'

'Are you pulling *rank* on me? I thought tonight was going to be like one of those corny scenes in classic novels where the lord of the manor hangs out with the lowly peasants of his estate and it's a thoroughly equalizing moment where they all realize there's not that much that separates them after all.'

Adam is laughing at her the way you might laugh at a toddler mimicking swear words. He pays for the tequila.

'You're just paying me to bully you into doing shots at this point,' she says.

'Money well spent,' he says. 'Cheers.'

When the drinks are down them, Adam looks over his shoulder at a posse from HR getting into the lift to go up to the party. 'Jesus, I hate these things,' he mutters. 'I should go back up. You should run now, no one's seen you yet.'

'There she *is*!' Juliet announces, sashaying across to Róise with Leanne from Accounts in tow. Juliet hugs her, drunk and clearly feeling fond. 'Have you had some prosecco yet, Róise? Come on, I'm getting you prosecco.'

Róise catches Adam's eye as Juliet drags her away, the arrival of their colleagues feeling like a cold hose turning on the comfortable intimacy settling between them, like a teacher accosting you dancing with a lad at the school formal and telling you to leave room for Jesus. She decides, nevertheless, that it is probably for the best.

An hour later, after too many drinks and an intense monologue from Juliet about how the man she is dating is quite the catch but very sexually selfish, Róise stumbles to the bathroom and decides that she should probably quit while she is ahead. She has availed herself of the company-sponsored wine and has had a pleasant flirt with Adam that ought to be enough to sustain her over the Christmas holidays. She doesn't know what he does for the festive period, whether he has parents or in-laws to tour, whether he stays in Belfast or goes away somewhere, and who he does whatever he does with. She knows everything he does between nine and five, Monday to Friday of any given week, but outside of that she does not really know anything about him.

When she emerges from the toilets and makes a sharp turn for the party to recover her coat, she nearly collides with him.

'Róise! You don't smoke, by any chance, do you?' Adam asks her, dropping his voice sheepishly, as if anyone at the party is likely to hear him over the not-particularly-festive rendition of 'Galway Girl' that has started blasting through the speakers.

'Do *you* smoke?' she asks.

'Not normally, but I'd take one now if you had it.'

'I don't smoke. Not really.' He waits. 'They're in my jacket, give me a minute.'

'You're getting a pay rise on Monday,' Adam calls after her.

'I'll hold you to that.' She fires the words over her shoulder without looking at him.

Outside, Adam says, 'So, I know why *I've* got nothing better to do on a Friday night . . .' He exhales smoke from the side of his mouth. '. . . but what's your excuse?'

Róise wonders suddenly whether he thinks her tragic for coming to the office Christmas cringe-fest. 'Free wine, mate,' she says dismissively by way of explanation.

'Good woman yourself.' Adam has not worn a coat outside, but he doesn't seem cold. Róise tries not to look at him in case she stares. There is no hyperbole in his handsomeness, no part of him that has its volume turned up to the highest setting; it is a languid, quiet allure, the kind that goes practically unnoticed until you realize it has crept under your bones.

His phone buzzes in his pocket and he unlocks it while Róise tries to sneak a glance at the screen, partly to ensure there is not a photo of a wife and three adorable children beaming out of it.

Adam locks the phone a moment later with a grunt. 'Remind me in the new year to stop looking at work emails on my phone.'

'You get work emails on your phone?' She frowns incredulously. 'You're such a lick.'

Adam laughs. 'Do you not?'

'Absolutely not.'

'That explains why you never respond to me after five; I thought you were just playing hard to get.'

A small thrill runs through her at the idea that he might be trying to *get* her, although she knows it is silly to think that Adam is doing anything more significant than making small talk with worn platitudes of office banter.

'What's your excuse, then?' she says, almost hoping he won't hear her, or will pretend not to.

'My excuse?'

'Why have you got nothing better to do on a Friday night? Has your missus got other plans?' Róise does not particularly enjoy saying 'your missus'; it sits sour in her mouth, feeling like something from the same sort of archaic wheelhouse as 'the aul ball and chain'. The alternative, however, is a less casual 'your wife or girlfriend', which sounds as though she is presenting him with a form to complete. *Select all that apply.*

Adam gives a short bark of laughter. 'No. I am, as the lord of the manor in your classic novel would say, presently unattached. You?'

She bites the inside of her cheek to stop herself from smiling. 'Same.'

'What happened to that lad you used to be with? When I ran into yous in Lavery's ages ago . . . Barry?'

'Brendan. That's long done.' Adam looks curious, and she decides to indulge him. 'He cheated on me.'

'Grim. Sorry.' He does not ask any follow-up questions. Róise

102

almost feels disappointed. It has been over a year and still the
only people who know about it are Maggie, Harley and Liam.
And Lydia, of course. She wonders if Brendan has told anyone
the full story, or whether he has framed it differently. She thinks
of him meeting women on dating apps and telling them how he,
a humble hero, ended his relationship with Róise because it was
simply kinder, fairer to both of them. She imagines the cheating
details staying firmly in a locked drawer until he gets serious with
someone, and when he eventually tells the story he will redact
certain specifics and add things like *the relationship had been over for
a long time anyway*, as though Róise had been a mouldering flat
that he had moved his possessions out of long before giving official notice to the landlord.

Róise and Adam toss their stubs into the sewer. They can hear
'Shake It Off' blaring from the third-floor conference room, and
he says, 'Jesus. That might be my final straw.'

She had planned to leave and yet she is following him to the
lift, watching him press the button and getting in with him. 'Are
you telling me you *don't* like Taylor Swift?'

'Listen, Róise, you've already enabled my terrible smoking
habits and coerced me into tequila, but I draw the line at Taylor
Swift.'

'Taylor Swift isn't a vice, she's a *doctrine*,' Róise insists as the
lift stops and dings to open. Adam steps out ahead of her and
stops, apparently thrown. She registers slowly that the hallway is quiet and lined with bedroom doors instead of function
rooms.

'Wait, what floor is this?' he says. Later, she will ask herself if

103

he knew it was the wrong floor, if he hit the wrong number on purpose.

'We're supposed to be on three,' she says.

He looks at her; she is standing between him and the doors. 'Get the lift, then,' he tests.

'*You* get the lift,' she replies.

She is backed against the lift button and although she has not pressed it she imagines it glowing orange, a branding iron pressing into her back. His hands on her skin are cold from the outside, and his mouth breathes her full of fever. He is telling her to wait. *Don't move.* He's going to get a room. Later, she will wonder whether he already had a room, whether he had plans for her, or if he would have asked someone else back if she hadn't been there with her notions for shots and her cigarettes that she doesn't, strictly speaking, smoke. Later, she decides, can wait.

wait here, i've gone for help

The four of them – Harley, Róise, Maggie and Liam – try not to
be disappointed in the potatoes. When they made the booking
for dinner several weeks ago, they all gathered around the phone
as Maggie asked about the Christmas menu options, and whether
there was any flexibility with them.

'That's the set menu, I'm afraid,' the member of staff said on
the other end of the line.

'Oh, I know, we're not asking for anything off-menu,' Maggie
hastened to reassure him. 'We were just wondering – so, the
turkey option comes with roasties?'

'Yes . . .'

'And the seared steak comes with mash.'

'Mm-hm.'

'And one of the starters is gnocchi?'

'Yep.'

'We were just wondering if we could have – sort of – potatoes
for the table, along with our main courses. Like three big plates
with gnocchi, roasties and mash, so everyone can have a bit of
each. We can pay extra for it, we don't mind.' The restaurant

manager seemed to decide it was a reasonable enough request and asked Maggie to email through their pre-order with a note about the spuds.

The servings are too small and the roasties aren't crispy enough; the mash, furthermore, tastes bland and unseasoned. 'Is everything all right for you?' their waiter asks.

'Lovely, yes, thank you,' they all nod with an enthusiasm they do not feel.

In previous years when they made their festive dinners at home, Harley would be on mash duty, Lydia did the roasties and Róise always made a wildcard potato option, gnocchi or rösti or dauphinoise. Liam brought the turkey and Brendan did the vegetables. Maggie was always most confident stirring a large cauldron of mulled wine and spices, or at most, artfully arranging a cheeseboard towards the end of the night. Maggie can cook well enough but feels nervous preparing food for other people, convinced she will manage to give everyone salmonella or somehow set herself on fire. Harley makes moderately good dinners from time to time but largely exists on a diet of white wine, hangover pizza and leftovers from the hotel restaurant buffet. Róise has always been the most accomplished with food in the house, but she seemed to lose interest in cooking altogether at the end of last year. One night last Christmas, Róise was violently sick after several glasses of Baileys and allowed Maggie to help her to bed, where Maggie saw (but did not remark upon) an empty sweet tin and a large scattering of jewel-bright wrappers, almost a parody of a rose-petal-strewn boudoir. These days

Róise munches her way keenly through nibbles and bar snacks, but Maggie hasn't seen her touch the oven in months. Now, however, she eats all of her roast dinner, continuing well after the rest of them have begun to complain of feeling full and needing naps. She finishes the last of the roast potatoes despite wrinkling her nose and mumbling, 'They're not as good.' They all know what she means. The restaurant spuds are dry and flavourless. Lydia used to toss the potatoes in goose fat and season them with garlic and rosemary and roast them until they were the colour of sunset.

The waiter comes over just as Harley's hand darts suddenly against her chest and she swallows. He – and for a wild moment, the others sitting around the table – mistakes her gesture for a surge of feeling, concerned she might be about to make a tearful disclosure of sentiment.

'Heartburn, sorry,' she murmurs, breathing out slowly. Harley did not eat all day in preparation for this meal and earlier, her first sip of a margarita on an empty stomach metabolized almost immediately, slapping her in the face with a bitter buzz. Her friends laugh and the waiter joins in with unearned familiarity.

'Can I get anyone any more drinks?' he asks. Harley notices him noticing her as he jots down their orders. He is, she observes, an average hospitality himbo: early twenties, dirty blond, generous with his smiles. If she were less full and tired and more giddy with glee and pre-game prosecco, she thinks she would probably try to pull him.

They pretend to spend time perusing the cocktail menu, affecting the performance of being mad into their botanicals and not just spoofers who look at the most affordable gin on the menu and authoritatively recommend it with a garnish of *that pairs really well with elderflower tonic*, because most things taste fancier with elderflower tonic. While they were waiting to be seated earlier, Maggie pointed to a bottle behind the bar and commented, 'That one's a really nice citrusy infusion,' as if imparting nuanced expertise and not simply guessing from the pictures of lemons on the label.

'Cheers, guys, I'll put that through for you now,' the waiter says with a wink and some animated finger guns. He lifts the unused wine glasses and makes a show of pulling a face as they clank together. Harley imagines he makes try-hard jokes if a mishap occurs during sex; she pictures him doing the same *whoops!* face after elbowing her in the breast or finishing three minutes in.

After returning and passing out their drinks, he lingers. 'It's Harley, isn't it?'

She squints at him. 'Sorry, have we . . . ?'

'Sorry, we met a while ago in the Spaniard. I think you know my friend Cate.'

'Oh, right!' She feigns recognition. 'What was your name, sorry?'

'It's Fergal.'

'Oh yeah, I remember!' She does not remember. It must, she thinks, have been the night she and Maggie and Róise won a pub quiz somewhere in town; the prize was an eighty-pound bar tab and they spent it on several rounds of expensive shots. They had won the quiz thanks to their combined knowledge of Jennifer

Lopez romcoms and the discography of the Bangles. They ended up in the Spaniard around one in the morning and ran into Cate with an entourage of friends. Between Maggie declaring she was going to read everyone's tarot and the three of them being bought a round of drinks by someone they were convinced at the time was Barra Best (in hindsight, it was definitely not Barra Best), Harley does not recall Fergal.

'I reckon you're in there, Harley,' Liam comments once Fergal is out of earshot. Maggie says nothing, and Harley wonders if she is hurt that Fergal did not also recognize her as one of Cate's acquaintances. Róise returns from the bathroom and asks what they're talking about.

'*You* should go for him,' Harley remarks to Róise. 'I will quite happily waive my claim in the interest of you getting your hole.' She feels the comment land more patronizingly than she intended, can sense everyone pretending not to acknowledge it as though it sits in the centre of the table like another lack-lustre dish.

'Don't need your help with that, actually,' Róise dismisses. 'I fucked Adam.'

'Adam from work?!' Harley yelps, delighted.

'Adam your *boss*?!' Maggie gapes in a stage whisper, as if the HR department might be eavesdropping from the next table.

'I don't know who Adam is,' offers Liam, 'but I hope you had a good time.'

'Adam from work. He's my superior but he's not my *boss*. And yes,' Róise confirms serenely, 'I had a very good time.'

Róise has barely begun her inventory of details when Maggie

gasps and passes a low exclamation of, 'Jesus Christ; *DEFCON Five*,' across the table.

'Do you mean DEFCON One?' Róise asks, deciding to be pedantic since her anecdote has been derailed. 'Five is the least severe.'

'Brendan's here,' replies Liam by way of confirmation. Liam and Maggie are facing the restaurant entrance while Harley and Róise glare at them from the opposite direction.

'What's happening?' mouths Harley. 'Who's he with?'

'Some lads,' says Liam, before adding decisively, 'Here, I'm just going to go over there.'

The three women hiss at him, but he banishes their curses with a shrug as he gets up from their table and makes for the bar.

'Are you okay?' whispers Maggie.

'I'm grand,' Róise says. 'I'm just surprised it's taken this long to run into him.'

Maggie glances over their heads at Liam and Brendan, who are shaking hands and greeting each other amicably. 'Is he fucking mad?' she says. Harley becomes very focused on stirring her cocktail. Róise downs her own in silence.

According to Lydia and Brendan, it was a one-time mistake. They had run into each other on a night out when they were both, they maintained, in a very bad place. The bad place in question was Thompson's, a nightclub housed in a city-centre garage and populated by fledgling sesh-heads.

Lydia had been out for work drinks after a corporate away-day and had spent the evening fielding questions from her drunk manager asking where she saw herself in five years, and she wondered if these questions signified an upcoming promotion, or whether he was subtly trying to determine whether she would be availing herself of the company's generous maternity leave. She wasn't sure she was keen on either. She found herself drinking with greater speed and urgency, to the point that when several of the new graduate hires started clamouring to go to Thompson's at midnight, she flung a hand in the air to vote in favour. They all cheered and she felt ill.

Lydia saw Brendan waving to her over the crowd in Thompson's like a drowning man signalling the coastguard. She was having her ear bent off by a twenty-year-old business analyst whose work suit made him look like a tall child about to make his confirmation. She abandoned him instantly, edging through the sweaty throng to get to Brendan. He gestured towards the exit and they went outside together, gulping mouthfuls of cold air as they emerged from the heavy heat of the club.

'Well, what about ya?' said Brendan. 'What has you here?'

'Fucking work,' Lydia replied, her words slippery with inebriation.

'Same.' Brendan told her he'd been on a bar crawl allegedly organized to celebrate a co-worker's divorce, though there'd been little celebration involved; as they'd sunk more pints, the man had gone on long and bitter rants about how women always said they wanted to be with nice fellas and then always treated them like shite, and every time he'd gone to the toilet he'd come back with watering eyes that suggested he had either been snorting something or crying (perhaps both). 'Some of the younger lads wanted to give him the slip and come here, and I wanted to escape, so . . .' Brendan shrugged, cocking his head towards the muffled techno playing inside.

'Choices were made,' said Lydia, for the sake of saying something. She realized, now that she was outside, that she had nothing whatsoever to say to Brendan, drunk or sober, and the high of seeing someone she knew who was not a work colleague began to ebb as quickly as it had come.

Brendan looked just as lost for words, and he said (as if to make small talk), 'Here, have you got any sniff?'

Lydia gasped. 'We should *get* some.'

The best thing they could procure was an E that Lydia bought from a sixth-former in the toilets. She and Brendan split the pill and danced for what felt like five minutes or five hours. Lydia had no idea what time it was when Brendan indicated he was going outside to smoke. She remembered taking a drag of his cigarette and looking at the people queuing for the club and saying, 'You couldn't pay me to be nineteen again.'

'Nah.' Brendan snorted at the idea.

'Do you ever wonder, like, will I feel the same way in ten years? I always wonder will I be nearly forty and think, *Jesus, you couldn't pay me to be in my twenties again*, or will I just be stagnating in the same job, still renting, drinking too much, same relationship, and be wishing I was back at the beginning when it all still fucking felt good?' Brendan was stubbing out his cig against the wall and was not volunteering any response or nods of encouragement, and she kept going: 'Like, you know that Peggy Lee song "Is That All There Is?" ' – and she started warbling.

Afterwards, Lydia could not say whether Brendan had kissed her to stop her talking, or to stop her singing, or whether his kissing her was about her at all. She wrapped herself around him unthinking, as automatic as accepting a line or a shot she did not need or want simply because it had been offered to her. The song stayed stuck in her head for the rest of the night – in the alley while he was inside her, in the taxi home, in bed alone as she fell asleep.

Brendan, who had always taken a minimalist approach to texting (responding to multiple-clause WhatsApp messages with *Ok x* or a simple thumbs-up), wrote Róise a badly punctuated letter explaining what had happened. He attached it to an email as a Word document that she did not see until two days after he had sent it, and only then because she had logged in to her email account to check whether the menstrual cup she had ordered online had been dispatched yet. *This is the hardest thing Ive ever had to write*, he began. He told her that he was feeling low and lost and directionless, which she understood. He said that he had been using a lot of unhealthy coping strategies (drinking, drugs, watching repeats of *Downton Abbey* in the small hours of the morning) as a distraction, which she understood. He then told her he had got completely wrecked on a night out and got off with Lydia, which Róise did not understand. Brendan had always said that of all her friends, Lydia was the hardest to have a conversation with because whenever he talked to her she recycled the same anecdotes and opinions and punchlines, as though she had not remembered ever speaking to him before and did not care for his input. 'You don't even *like* Lydia,' Róise therefore accused him when they later talked about it.

'I *do* like Lydia!' he protested, forgetting which argument he was meant to be having.

'Oh, so you *like* Lydia, then?' she snapped bitterly. He had no response.

He had used those words, *got off with Lydia*, in his letter, and Róise afterwards wondered why. She wondered whether he had tried and rejected a number of different synonyms – bucked, shagged, rode – and decided they all sounded too harsh, too aggressive; whether he thought *had sex with* sounded too clinical, that *slept with* hardly applied to something they had done outdoors several metres away from a club full of teenagers on acid. Perhaps he thought *got off with* might be a nebulous enough term for Róise to assume they'd simply kissed, and that she would either think there'd been no more to it, or that there *had* been more to it but not want to know.

Maggie and Harley came home from a party that Friday night to find Róise and Lydia in the kitchen together. Róise was eating cold leftover Chinese food with a look of hollow savagery in her eyes, and Lydia's face was wet with tears. 'What's happened?' asked Maggie.

'Tell them, then,' Róise said quietly.

Maggie was horrified when Lydia told them. 'Does Liam know?' Lydia shook her head. 'Well, were you ever going to tell him? Jesus fucking Christ, Lydia. What were you *thinking*? I fucking told you, I *told* you this would end badly. And you *know* he's been cheated on before.'

'Oh, yeah, exactly,' Róise said, turning on Maggie. 'How awful for Liam. I obviously can't imagine the sense of betrayal he's going to feel when he finds out.'

'God, I'm so sorry, that was a really stupid thing to—'

'My boyfriend fucked my best mate – but here, at least it's only happened to me once.'

'I didn't mean that, I'm sorry!' Maggie protested.

'I think we should all calm down,' said Harley.

'I am calm,' Róise said through the last mouthful of her food. She swallowed and threw her fork in the sink. 'You do need to tell Liam,' she told Lydia. 'Ideally face to face, although if you'd rather use Brendan's letter template then I'm quite happy to email it over to you.' She looked at Lydia. 'Why in God's name are *you* crying?'

'Róise, I'm so sorry,' Lydia whispered. 'I wasn't myself, I was completely out of it. I was talking absolute shite and there was no – no actual *feeling*, or anything like that. I'm sorry, I know that sounds terrible. You know when you wake up and there's a massive transaction on your bank card because you've decided to buy fucking . . . ten weeks of archery lessons? And you're like, who even was that person?'

'That was *one* time,' Harley interjected. 'We'd just seen *The Hunger Games*, and I took a notion.'

'So, what, it just came out of nowhere?' Maggie demanded of Lydia. 'Or have you and Liam been having problems?'

'It's not been . . . perfect.' Lydia's eyes were fixed on the kitchen floor. 'It's not because of him. I'm just – my head feels like a bag of bees at the minute.'

115

'Why didn't you *say* anything?'

'How the fuck could I, Maggie?' Lydia lifted her head to glare at her. 'He's your brother, or as good as; how are we meant to have a proper conversation about Liam when all you're going to tell me is "I told you so"?'

'What's happening with you and Brendan?' Harley asked Róise. 'Are yous broken up now?'

Róise crossed her arms and refused to meet anyone's eye, staring down towards the washing machine. 'He finished it.'

'*What?*' yelped Maggie.

'He didn't feel things were working. So he's out.' Róise looked at Lydia. 'I suppose you've done me a favour. Thanks, *pal.*'

'Róise, I'm so, so fucking sorry,' Lydia said. 'There was something not right in that E. I would never do something like that. I love you.'

'You sold me down the river for some teenager's gutter pills and a twenty-second ride off the most average prick in Belfast. If that's what your love looks like, I don't fucking want it,' said Róise. She threw the takeaway carton away, the bin lid clanging in the silent kitchen.

In the restaurant, they watch Brendan chat nervously to Liam at the bar. Brendan seems to be determined to maintain eye contact with Liam, as though he fears if he glances around he might meet Róise's gaze and be suddenly turned to stone.

Róise's nausea is tempered only by the fact that she knows there is nothing left in her stomach to vomit up. Forcing the last of the potatoes into her stomach was like cramming pillows into an already-full hot press and knowing that they would probably spring out as soon as the cupboard was opened. Her dinner was in her throat before she had even shut the toilet door.

Brendan's hair is cut shorter than she ever remembers it being and he is wearing a navy jumper that looks almost identical to all his other navy jumpers, although she can still tell it isn't one she's seen before. The friends with him are ones she does not recognize. It is jarring to be reminded that he has not simply ceased to be, but that, unobserved by her, he has continued his life of haircuts and navy jumpers and pints with the lads.

'Are you okay?' Harley murmurs.

'I'm going to shoot on,' Róise decides abruptly, reaching for her bag. She leaves cash on the table for her share of the dinner.

'Róise, wait, we can all just pay and then get a taxi together,' says Maggie.

'It's grand, I fancy a walk. Yous all stay out. Barnaby needs feeding. I'll text when I'm home.'

'Should we go after her?' Maggie asks helplessly as Róise ploughs out of the restaurant.

'Let's give her some space,' Harley says, 'and then head home and check in on her.'

Maggie glances across the room again and reports flatly, 'They're coming over here.'

Brendan and Liam are both carrying a drink in each hand, and put them down on the table in front of the two girls. 'Thanks,' says Harley.

'Thank Brendan, he got the round in,' says Liam. 'Where's Róise?'

'She wasn't feeling well. Thinks it was the potatoes.'

'She's *left*?'

'*Liam*,' Maggie intones quietly, so Brendan can't hear. 'Can you blame her?'

'Here, listen, sorry,' Brendan says, clearly uncomfortable. 'I don't want to interrupt your night. It was good running into yous, but I'd better catch up with the boys.' He seems a strange mixture of relieved and disappointed at Róise's departure. 'Maggie, Harley, hope you're well.' He does not wait for a response, leaving to look for his friends.

'Liam,' Maggie begins.

'Maggie. Don't start with me,' Liam says as he lowers himself into his chair.

'You couldn't have waited two seconds to see how Róise was before you went over and chest-bumped your best pal?'

'Is she okay? Did she actually go home or is she hiding somewhere?'

'She went home, she didn't feel well,' says Harley.

'Christ. Did you put her in a taxi?'

'Why do you suddenly give a fuck?' Maggie snaps.

Liam's temper flares, and he stabs a thumb over his shoulder in the direction Brendan went. 'I dunno if you remember but he also rode my dead girlfriend; I'm not exactly doing hula hoops right now, personally.'

'Sorry. I'm *sorry*.' Maggie sighs. 'It was just a bit weird.'

'Aye, it's fucking weird for me and all.' Liam takes several deep breaths. 'I thought it might feel better to just be the bigger person and go over there. I didn't mean to upset Róise.'

'We know you didn't,' says Harley, wanting to move the conversation on.

'I don't know that I'll be much craic tonight, if I'm honest. I might head off too.'

'Liam, come on, I'm sorry. Stay for a bit, let's talk about it,' says Maggie.

'Maggie, no harm to you, but I'm not in the mood,' Liam replies tiredly, putting on his coat. 'Let's assume you've already told me I need to talk about things and that I need to go to counselling and that I should try running because it's "actually surprisingly therapeutic!" I know I need to and I know I should and I know I will, but not fucking tonight, all right?'

Harley says, '*Running?* God, Maggie. You've *changed*.' She means it as a joke but it is the wrong time. Maggie looks stung by both of them, but does not retaliate.

'To be fair, I don't know how effective all the 5Ks and therapy can be when she's going running twice a week with the girl who's been fucking her about for months,' Liam says in a calm voice. 'But here, what do I know? Enjoy the rest of your night; let me know you get home safe.'

They watch Liam leave, then Harley turns to look at Maggie. 'So. Cate. Let's unpack that a little, shall we?' she says in the cool, placid tones of a therapist.

Maggie has met Cate to go running every Tuesday and Saturday morning for the last three weeks. They jog for half an hour around the Botanic Gardens, breath ghosting out of their mouths in the cold air. Maggie worried at first that she would not be in good enough shape to sustain a conversation while exercising, but this turned out not to be necessary. Their jogs are bookended by small talk but they do not speak while running. Maggie has begun to wonder if she simply imagined the days when their laboured breathing was the result of drunken sexual congress and not light cardio.

If Cate does not want to see her, Maggie reasons, she would be very easy to ghost. They have spoken no oaths of love or loyalty, and have no close mutual friends to engender a custody argument. Cate must feel some affinity with her, to be committed to running together on a biweekly basis.

'Does biweekly mean twice a week or every two weeks?' Cate asked her at the park gates last Tuesday.

'No idea. I always mix up biannual and biennial.' Maggie then looked it up on her phone and found that biweekly could mean either twice a week or fortnightly. 'It works both ways,' she said, 'so to speak.'

'All these fucking bi-s. Ruining it for everyone,' Cate joked, with a self-critical roll of her eyes.

Maggie felt reassured by this quip. She had begun to wonder if Cate was actually straight, Maggie an experiment that had spiralled, Frankenstein's-monster-style, out of control.

'I won't be around for a couple of weeks now,' Cate told her on Tuesday as they picked up takeaway coffees after their run. 'Family stuff, the usual Christmas tour. Obviously you keep going without me if you want.'

'I'll probably take a break too, I'll be busy,' Maggie lied, hoping it would make her sound more in demand and less available. Cate did not ask about her Christmas plans. Maggie added, 'Sure, let me know in the new year if you want to pick it up again.'

'I will! Merry Christmas.' Cate tapped the rim of her cinnamon latte in a toast against Maggie's cup, smiled, and left.

'I didn't know you'd got so into running,' Harley comments, swilling the feathery pulp at the bottom of her cocktail.

'I didn't think I would,' says Maggie. 'I probably wouldn't have, without – you know, the accountability factor.'

'Mm. So you're enjoying it?'

'Running? Yes. I mean, it's absolute agony half the time. But I sort of like it.'

'And are you and Cate . . .' Harley's mouth twitches in amusement. '. . . well matched? Pace-wise?'

'Yeah. Surprisingly. She's in as bad a shape as I am.'

'Catch yourself on. You're much fitter than she is.' Harley, to Maggie's relief, does not press the matter further; she twists around in her seat, looking for someone to bring them another round.

The house is in darkness when Róise arrives home. She kicks off her shoes in the hall and walks into the front room without turning on the light. Barnaby's tank sits aglow in the corner; he is on his rock, resting in the gentle ambience. She does not approach him, wonders if he can see or sense her, wonders if he knows or likes her. Lydia used to chat breezily to Barnaby as she fed him, supplying his imagined responses in a gruff voice that made him sound like an octogenarian who had been propping up a bar on the Falls Road since two in the afternoon. Róise prepares a small plate of kale and slivers of red pepper, placing it awkwardly next to him. She regards Barnaby with general apathy and occasional guilt. Some weeks after Lydia's passing, she had researched online whether it was humane to release pet turtles into the wild, and was disappointed to discover that it was, in fact, not. He ambles towards his food and clamps his jaws slowly around a ruffled leaf edge. Róise turns away.

In her bedroom, she sits down and sips from the days-old pint glass of water on her nightstand. It tastes like dust. Last Sunday morning, still slightly weak after the Friday-night Christmas party, she stretched a claw-hand out of bed to search hopefully for a glass of water that was not there, and instead came into terrifying contact with the spines of the cactus she had almost forgotten she owned. She went to fetch herself water and tipped an uncertain quantity into the pot. She splashes the dregs of her glass around the soil now, watches it for a few moments, as though expecting it will swell with nourishment before her eyes. Nothing happens.

Róise refills the glass in the bathroom. The cold tap has migrated slightly to the left and veers away from her when she tries to turn it off. The damp patch above the shower has grown, and a Dalmatian-spatter of mould has also taken over the grouting. Their landlord sent a maintenance man round to look at it during the week, and he spent twenty minutes switching the asthmatic extractor fan on and off before concluding it needed to be updated. Frankie is considering having the entire bathroom redone. (Harley put in a request for a detachable shower-head.) Róise feels tired at the prospect, as though he has suggested she personally prise off the tiles with her bare hands. She wipes off her makeup, brushes her teeth, ignores the moisturiser in the bathroom cabinet that the three of them each assumed belonged to one of them, until it sat untouched for so long that they realized it must have been Lydia's.

Róise knows she wants to leave this house, has known it for some time; she is not even sure she wants to live with her friends anymore. When they all first moved in together years ago, it felt exciting because it was like being back at uni again. Róise assumed they would evolve naturally from twenty-something buck eejits into secure and self-actualized young women who had skincare regimes and remembered to pay the council tax on time. But she is thirty now, and so is Maggie, and Harley will be soon, and they are still living as though they are students. They have traded lectures for jobs and the cheapest wine in the off-licence for the second cheapest wine in the off-licence, but apart from this, she is not sure how much has changed.

When Róise is in bed, she begins a message to Maggie and Harley. *I'm home safe*, she says, then deletes the last word, then amends to *I'm back at the house. Xx*. She then types out, *I don't want to be here anymore*, realizes how it looks, deletes and redrafts. *This place is falling to fucking bits*. A low, hollow pounding begins in the kitchen. This has happened before; the pipes are old and need replacing. *There's a demon in the boiler again*, she tells them wearily.

★ ★ ★

By eleven, Harley and Maggie have vacated their table and moved to stools at the bar. Harley motions to the waiter for another drink. Fergal's glances are growing on her; the margaritas are working as a strong assist. She is serving the absolute worst bar banter, privately disgusted with herself. She moves on to wine and when Fergal asks, 'Small, medium or large?' she does the ridiculous pantomime of acting as though he's sweet-talked her into a large glass, and he starts playfully calling her *trouble* and she flashes him a wink as though they have a unique and smouldering flirtation instead of being just another steaming hallion leering at her wine mule.

When Maggie's eyes start to lose their focus and she refuses the next round of tequila, Harley says coyly to Fergal, 'You'll do a shot with me, won't you?'

He looks pleased, and then wistful, as he says, 'I can't really, while I'm working . . .'

'Fair. Maybe when you finish, then.' She knocks back the shots before he can come up with a reply, and then excuses herself with a quiet mumble of, 'Bathroom.'

In the loos she stumbles against the cubicle doorframe and drops onto the toilet seat like a sack of spuds, fresh air from an open bathroom window cooling the sweat and tears that mix on her face.

About three hours later they are on his sofa, Fergal squeezing her breast as though he is trying to wring out a sponge. Harley concedes hazily to herself that this may not have been a good idea. She weighs up the clumsy, inexpert sex that is implied by his aggressive groping technique with the sheer awkwardness of having to tell him she isn't into it and fleeing his house to try and get a taxi at two thirty in the morning on a Friday in December. She would, she considers, be faster walking home, although it's late and she's had a lot to drink and does not particularly want to cross a road plastered and get hit by a squadron of freshers joy-riding in a Fiat 500.

Fergal looks thoroughly satisfied with himself when she manages to claw herself away. 'I'm just going to . . . go to the bathroom,' she says, smiling weakly. 'Where is it?'

'Top of the stairs, straight in front of you.'

'Thanks. Do you want anything?'

'From the loo?' he laughs. 'I'm all good, thanks.'

'Yeah, right . . . back in a sec.'

Harley wishes she owned a cleanser that was as effective at removing makeup as Fergal's mouth. There is a pale halo around her lips where all her foundation has been sucked off. She necks some mouthwash from his bathroom cabinet in the hope of numbing her brain for the next ten minutes.

Fergal is all sharp edges and flat surfaces; it is like having sex with a dismantled cardboard box. Harley dissociates briefly while his nose is prodding her in the crotch. He moves upwards, fumbles with her wrists and pins them experimentally above her head. She wants to slap him like an Irish mammy and give him a stern talking-to: *you're not a dom, Fergal, for God's sake stop embarrassing yourself.* Instead, she rolls her eyes, which he seems to mistake for a moment of impassioned possession. She does not want to have to think about what to do with her face so she pushes him until he is at arm's length, then turns over, braced on her hands and knees. He smacks furiously into her from behind, and when she looks up at the wall above his headboard she lets out an audible groan at the Jack Kerouac poster pinned there, a sound that he interprets as a sigh of pleasure. He chokes out an orgasm and Harley counts five seconds before she disengages. 'Bathroom,' she mumbles, grabbing as many of her clothes as she can from the floor as he flops onto his back.

'Did you come?' he asks fuzzily, dragging the sweat off his forehead.

She pretends not to have heard and tries not to laugh. She dresses in his bathroom and tries three different taxi firms, but none of them are picking up within the next hour. The fourth tells her the wait will be twenty to twenty-five minutes and she jumps at it. The operator asks for the address; she hesitates. She knows she is in east Belfast, remembering passing the library in the taxi not long before they reached Fergal's address, so she says, 'Could you just pick me up at Holywood Arches Library?'

'Okay,' the operator says uncertainly, adding, 'I don't think it's open?' as though cautioning Harley against turning up there in the hope of borrowing some Mills & Boon at three in the morning. *Do I really sound that drunk?* Harley complains inwardly.

'Yeah! I'll juzbe ousside thurrrr,' she says. (*Ah. Apparently I do.*)

'All right, that'll be about twenty minutes, then.'

Harley checks the map on her phone to see how far she is from the library and, mercifully, it is less than a five-minute walk. Plenty of time to say her fond goodbyes to Fergal.

'Don't be daft, you can stay over!' he laughs at her when she returns to his room to retrieve her bag and shoes.

'Nooooo, honzly, I'm jus'gon go.'

'I mean, if you sit tight, I'm pretty sure I'll be good for round two in, oh . . .' He looks at an imaginary wristwatch.

Harley feels her stomach writhing and has to bolt for the toilet again. She doesn't know if it is the tequila or the prospect of further intercourse with Fergal that makes her boke; possibly a combination of the two.

Vomiting clears her head somewhat, and she dips back into his bedroom to snatch up her bag and announce brusquely, 'Right, I'm away!' She is at the bottom of the stairs by the time he has his pants on and out the door by the time he has emerged, hissing, 'Come on, you don't have to—'

'I'm just getting a taxi! Work in the morning!' she calls back to him, walking away from the house as fast as she can before breaking into a run.

Harley makes it to the library fifteen minutes after ordering the taxi. She waits a further fifteen minutes, then phones the taxi firm to ask if it's on its way.

The operator – a different one this time – sucks in air through his teeth and says, 'You could be waiting maybe forty-five minutes, love.'

'But the woman before said twenty-five, and I've been waiting half an hour.'

'There's no one picking up near there, town taxis are all booked out.'

'Could I just – can you pick me up from Connswater McDonald's?' she asks glumly. 'Just whenever's . . . soonest.'

Maggie does not answer when Harley phones her. She got the measure of Harley's plans for the rest of the night when they were paying the last drinks bill, and left her to it, telling her to text later or she'd be hammering on the restaurant door tomorrow to tell them that Fergal was not only a terrible waiter but also possibly a murderer. She texted Maggie from Fergal's house and Maggie replied with a thumbs-up that Harley assumed meant she was only half awake.

Harley is not expecting Frankie to answer when she calls. 'Fuck!' she exclaims. 'I thought you wouldn't answer.'

'Why'd you ring, then?'

'I don't know. Why aren't you asleep?' A car roars past her with a Vengaboys album punching out the sunroof.

'Where are you?'

'Holywood Arches Library.'

'What the fuck?'

'Sorry, my taxi was supposed to be here by now, but they're saying it's going to be ages. I was just ringing – just wondering – if I could pick up. Maybe a thirty bag? I've got cash.'

'Do you need a lift?'

'No, course not. I just thought—'

'You're on your own.' It's not a question. She hears him clear his throat, or sigh, or groan on the other end of the line. 'Give me ten minutes. I'll come and get you.'

Harley lingers by the C. S. Lewis sculpture outside the library, the author and his wardrobe life-size and cast in bronze, his hand resting on a small chair behind him. Harley tests the chair before sitting on it; it would not do, she thinks, to conclude the night with the destruction of a local cultural attraction. It is firm enough to support her weight, so she sits slouched over and scrolls mindlessly through her phone. She fancies it looks from a distance as though she is about to be dragged backwards into Narnia.

Frankie pulls up in less than ten minutes. 'Been busy tonight, mate?' she jokes in taxi-driver patter when she is in the front seat, before adding, 'Thank you so much. Seriously.'

'I'm not going to make a habit of this,' he says, checking his blind spot.

'You love it really,' she croaks feebly.

two

what the water gave me

Maggie visits her mother every New Year's Day, in a cemetery populated by weeping madonnas and pensive stone angels. Several graves down from her mother's, there is an angel lying in the foetal position on the large slab of a tomb, and every year her blanket of moss has grown. Maggie wonders if she will live to see the creature consumed completely. She has never told anyone that she once came here alone when the place was empty and lay down next to the angel, the cold from its limbs crawling slowly into her bloodstream. She listened to her own pulse thrumming in her ear and imagined it was the heartbeat of the earth below. A few months ago, she was tempted to disclose this to her therapist, and floated the topic by asking, 'You know Mary Shelley?' to which Astrid replied, 'No.' Maggie felt foolish, and did not continue. Astrid had already listened to Maggie express herself through a multitude of obscure cultural references and internet memes, but at this particular juncture, Maggie felt that perhaps the poetic resonance of a gloomy eighteenth-century teenager who loitered around her mother's tombstone would sound too full of notions to be taken seriously.

Liam has come here with her a few times, lightening the mood by pointing out humorous names on gravestones, reading the dedications aloud and commenting on how they all sound the same. 'Do you never look at them and think they sound like horoscopes? *Gone but not forgotten, forever in our hearts, we'll meet again* – they're the most generic phrases but people obviously read them when they're picking the inscription and think oh my God, that's *so* true . . .' Liam has not come to the cemetery with Maggie since Lydia died; she feels it would be awkward to ask him. She doesn't know if he has visited Lydia's grave; perhaps he makes jokes there, trims the weeds, leaves flowers. Perhaps he lies on the ground and asks her questions, pressing his ear to the earth as if hoping for an answer.

Maggie reads the print on her mother's headstone, though she knows it by heart: *Sinéad Regan, 1968–1989. Beloved mother, daughter, sister and friend.* Maggie has always felt uncomfortable at the order of this list, that 'mother' – a position occupied at that point for only a year – had come before friendships with far greater longevity, and sisterhood that had lasted a lifetime. Maggie remembers nothing about her mum, having only family anecdotes and old photos of Sinéad's strawberry-blonde perm and smiling eyes to go on. She finds it fairly awkward when people come out with trite cliches like, *your mother would have been so proud.* These were all very well when she was a child, but she finds it difficult to reconcile maternal pride with the idea of a twenty-one-year-old now that Maggie herself is thirty. Sometimes she thinks of her mother looking proudly up or down from who knows where at the age she would have been had she lived, although Maggie struggles to age up the photos in her mind and instead ends up imagining the actor Emma Thompson (which can, at times, be just as comforting).

Maggie does not remember being told of her mother's death, doubts she even was formally told, when it happened. Attempting such a conversation with a baby seems just as nonsensical as breaking tragic news to a Yorkshire terrier. Maggie's aunt once disclosed that she had taken to putting on her sister's jumpers and cardigans, in the hope that baby Maggie would feel comforted by familiar arms. Aoibhlinn could smell the echo of perfume around the collar and kept finding Sinéad's stray hairs woven through the yarn. 'When you were older,' she told Maggie, 'I'd pluck hairs off your clothes and I'd have to check myself. I never stopped thinking they were hers.' Maggie wished she could say something to reassure her aunt that it had been worth it, that she had felt the ghost embrace of her mother wrapped around her and that it had somehow helped. She cannot, however, remember this far back; the earliest memory she has is of being three years old and sitting in a hospital waiting room with her aunt and uncle because a swallowed fridge magnet was making its leisurely way through Liam's colon.

A little over a year ago, Maggie texted Liam asking if he still wanted to go and see the ten-year anniversary re-release of *Mamma Mia* in the cinema that evening, and he responded, *maggie I have some really bad news*, and Maggie remembers the feeling of dread that dropped like a cartoon anvil into her stomach, as she thought he was about to tell her of the sudden sad passing of Christine Baranski. She even went so far as to google this before responding to Liam, and while she was doing so he sent another message which read, *where are you, are you alone?* and she said, *what's happened?* and Liam phoned her and said, 'Maggie, where are you, what are you doing?'

'I'm just in the house. What's happened, is something wrong?'

'Is Harley there? Is Róise?'

'They're both out. Liam, what's happened? Tell me.'

'Lydia was in an accident.'

'What? When – what? Is she all—'

'Maggie . . .' Liam's voice was catching, fading, like someone being dragged underwater and out to sea. 'Maggie. Please don't make me say it.'

They never made it to *Mamma Mia*.

This New Year's Day is chilly but bright, and the girls have got the train to the seafront. They walk along the sand as a lacework of foam brushes up against the shore. Harley squints out to sea and asks, 'Can you see England from here?'

'The question should be why the fuck would you want to,' says Róise.

Further along, Harley stops, hands on hips, bent slightly at the waist, wincing. 'PMT?' Maggie assumes.

'It's this fucking coil. The cramps are killing me. Bloody uteruses.' She pauses. 'Uteruses? Uteri? Is it like octopi?'

'It's actually *octopodes*,' Maggie says in a mock-professorial voice.

'Do octopodes have uteruses, though?' Harley muses. She then wonders aloud whether bleeding in the sea will attract sharks.

'Can we just get in, please?' sighs Róise. 'Before we convince ourselves there's a kraken in Helen's Bay.'

They put on wetsuits that, like Maggie's running shoes, were purchased under the influence of gin. They all went in the sea once two years ago and decided it was a deeply primal bonding experience that they wanted to repeat, so they invested in the gear and then spent months unable to coordinate a date that suited all four of them. The one time they did fix a date on a Sunday afternoon, it rained very lightly and Harley suggested, 'Pub?' as an alternative, and no one took much convincing.

The waves flop over each other as though hauling themselves out of bed hungover, and a grey wind brushes past. Maggie zips up her skin and scrapes back her hair and follows Harley and Róise into the water, leaving her bag and coat in a pile with theirs on the sand. She glances back at them nervously, trusting none of the dog-walkers on the beach will thieve them. It reminds her of being in clubs, where she is never fully content to abandon jackets and handbags on the floor while they dance, always anxious they might vanish in the time it takes her to finish the last verse of 'Bohemian Rhapsody'.

When she wades into the water, the cold makes Maggie's throat constrict as though she is already drowning. It becomes slowly more bearable, the rippling silk of the waves weaving around her as she bobs shoulder-deep. Several feet away, Róise still seems to be struggling to adjust, her breath catching in gasps. 'Come here, warm up,' Harley says, drawing the two of them into a floating ring with her. Róise clings to them, shuddering. A few moments later, she says, 'I have to get out, sorry.' She stumbles through the water until it spits her out on the sand, and she wraps herself shaking in a towel.

'Do you think she's thinking about . . .' Maggie wonders.

'Nah. I'm sure she's fine,' Harley dismisses unconvincingly. She takes Maggie's hands as they bob in the water and try to forget.

For New Year's Eve two years ago, Lydia's parents agreed the four of them could stay the night in their house up the north coast, as long as they promised not to break any of her late grandmother's collected football mugs, each one enamelled with GAA players photographed in various stages of sullenness.

'This is the kind of old woman I want to be,' Lydia said, stabbing a finger at the display of cups arranged in a glass-fronted cabinet. 'I want my grandchildren to come round my house to cupboards full of weird memorabilia. I'm going to be one of those aul dolls with a drawer of souvenir spoons and a wheelbarrow that belonged to Madame de Pompadour.'

Maggie remembered Lydia wanting to be an old woman from the age of about eight. Lydia and Harley were both told they needed glasses midway through primary school; Harley hated hers and only reluctantly agreed to wear them after she performed in their school end-of-year assembly and tanked brutally because she couldn't read her sheet music at the piano. Lydia loved having glasses, and chose a pair with small slots on the arms where a chain could be attached. She was disappointed when the optician supplied her with a fluorescent orange shoelace-looking cord to loop around her neck, and in the privacy of her bedroom she instead pulled apart a set of glass rosary beads from her First Communion, glueing them to her spectacles to lend them some glamour. Her parents were furious at this act of vandalism and she was not allowed out to play with Maggie and Harley for two weeks.

When they were in secondary school, Lydia decided she wanted to write an agony aunt column for the school newspaper, and asked Maggie to help her come up with problems so she could write several sample responses as part of her pitch to the head of English. Lydia called the column 'Dear Betty' and wrote her replies as though she were a sage old dame of about a hundred and nine years old.

Dear Period Panic,

I'm so sorry to hear of what sounds like a veritable smorgasbord of menstrual disarray! I endured fourscore years of Auntie Flo and her company was consistently, profoundly tedious. I hope you take some small comfort in knowing you will one day be an old woman with glorious anecdotes about bleeding through an ivory dress on your wedding day. (Fortunately, I'd already had four perfect weddings by that point, and my fifth husband was a man with a sense of humour.) If you're intensely unwell every month and worried about your blood loss, you might consult a doctor to make sure the old plumbing is all shipshape, or to get help if it's not. Medical concerns notwithstanding, I would encourage you not to be embarrassed about the heaviness of your monthly flow, if you can possibly manage it. Some of us are blessed with a tiny fairy fart of spotting each cycle, but most of us, I promise you, are dealing with a Whitechapel crime scene. It's quite, quite natural, and although you will feel many things

at your time of the month (rage, despair, incongruous sexual urges), you
must never feel shame.

Their head of English praised Lydia for her flair and initiative, and said that under no circumstances whatsoever would the column be published in the school newspaper.

As an adult Lydia continued to give advice, usually unsolicited, usually at four on a Saturday morning just as Maggie was beginning to feel she might want to go to bed. After one too many vodkas or bumps of coke, when Lydia would start to authoritatively tell them what they ought to be doing with their lives, Harley used to murmur, 'Betty's arrived,' to Maggie and Róise, and generally excused herself to go to the toilet. Lydia's dawn-time observations were often reductive and mawkish and full of platitudes, declarations that suggested she had either not fully listened to the problem at hand, or had wilfully misunderstood it. There were sometimes kernels of clarity, though; every once in a while, Betty would come out with some advice that made things seem just a fraction less bleak.

'I love her, and all,' Liam once sighed to Maggie, 'but fuck me, she really does think she knows best, doesn't she.'

'That's just Betty talking,' Maggie defended her in amusement. 'She just wants to help.'

Lydia brought expensive champagne for their New Year's Eve toast in her parents' house, and a bottle of Bushmills for after. 'You do know how to treat a girl,' said Harley, eyeing the label.

'Thank my bosses,' said Lydia. 'I looted the leftovers from the Christmas do.'

'How's work?' Maggie asked perfunctorily.

Lydia pulled a face. 'Let's not.' To this day, they still don't quite know exactly what Lydia did for work. Her corporate job always seemed at odds with the person they knew. Maggie would have been less surprised if Lydia had made a living crocheting characters from the *Wombles*, or embarked on a career as a television psychic.

At midnight, they cheered and toasted and cried at the closing scenes of *When Harry Met Sally*. At some point Lydia left the room and came back with her coat on. 'Come on, lads. Bring the whiskey.'

'Are you mental?' Maggie laughed.

'It's stopped raining,' Lydia replied by way of justification.

She wasn't wrong. It was also two degrees and the wind whistled over the water and ruffled the sand. The sea was five minutes from the house; they followed Lydia down the seafront path and onto the beach. She passed round the bottle and they all swallowed slightly too much, their throats burning as if with dragon-fire.

'Jesus fucking *Christ* it's cold,' Maggie shrieked as a gust of wind whipped up her hair.

'You want to get your blood pumping!' Lydia enthused, bouncing around like an annoyingly upbeat personal trainer. Before any of them could respond, she took off at a run along the beach.

'Wouldn't be for me, now,' Harley hollered after her.

'She's got the whiskey,' Róise pointed out.

Maggie found that galloping along the sand after Lydia proved surprisingly cathartic. When they caught up, Lydia was shrugging herself out of her coat and wrenching off her shoes. 'Who's coming in with me?'

'You must be *joking*,' said Maggie; and then, persuaded, she slouched out of her jacket.

'Fuck it,' is all the reasoning Harley seemed to need, and started to strip.

'Fuck you all,' Róise mumbled, but she joined in too.

Lydia was off and running again, barrelling towards the water, Harley following, arms flailing. Maggie's feet slapped the wet sand as she ran and when a wave sliced into her at waist height she let out a heathen scream.

'*FUCK ME, THAT'S COLD!*' Harley bawled.

'*THIS WAS THE WORST IDEA!*' Maggie screeched as another wave smacked and sprayed her.

'*I CAN'T FEEL MY FUCKING LEGS!*' roared Róise.

'*HAP-PY NEW YEAR!*' Lydia flung her arms out and caterwauled at the moon suspended before them, silver and almost full, strung with threads of cloud; and although Maggie had whiskey in her throat and salt in her nose and tears in her eyes, she was laughing.

Out of the water now, Maggie snatches up a towel and sits down next to Róise. 'Train back is going to be a nightmare,' she comments, slapping sand uselessly off her feet. 'I hate sand. I call first shower when we get home.'

'Shower's broken,' Róise reminds her flatly. When they all returned to the house after Christmas, they found that the boiler had given out completely, and Frankie had struggled to find anyone to come and fix it before the new year. 'Fucking landlords,' Róise grumbles.

'Well, like Harley said,' reasons Maggie, 'at least he's tried. Plenty of landlords wouldn't bother.'

'He *says* he's tried, anyway. Harley's only defending him because she's got a notion for him.'

Maggie is halfway through a deep breath of sea air, and promptly chokes on it. '*Frankie?*'

'Aye, she fancies a bit of that.'

'Since when?'

'No idea. I've only clocked it recently.'

'For fuck's sake,' Maggie groans. She looks out at Harley, still bobbing around in the water. 'Is he single?'

'You after him now as well?'

'She *can't* shag our landlord. What happens if she ghosts him and he just leaves us to rot every time something breaks? What happens if he kicks us out?'

'Well, for a start,' Róise says sensibly, 'if Frankie's a middle-aged man who's ready to evict a girl for ghosting him, then he's the real loser here, frankly.'

'Mm. True. And what's the second thing?'

'What?'

'You said, "for a start". I assumed there was more.'

'Oh, yeah: I think we should move out.'

'When you say "we" . . . do you still want to live together? The three of us?'

Róise chews the inside of her mouth. 'Sometimes I don't know. Maybe we need to grow up.'

'We *are* grown-ups!'

'Maggie, we drink gin and tonics out of pint glasses and the delivery driver from the Chip Company knows us by name. We haven't grown up.'

'And you think living alone is the path towards not drinking pints of gin and ordering hangover chicken goujons?'

'Maybe. Maybe not. I don't know.' Róise drags a hand through her hair, sand catching in her curls. 'But we have to get out of that house.'

Maggie sighs, dropping her head towards her knees. 'I love that house.'

'No you don't,' says Róise. She sounds cross, but when Maggie looks at her, she seems sad, almost hopeless. Róise goes on, 'We used to love that house. It isn't ours anymore. It's not been ours since.'

Maggie flinches away from a gust of brisk wind. 'Do you think we'd have stayed there if everything hadn't happened?'

'Everything did happen.'

'But if it—'

'Something would always have happened.'

'I know,' Maggie says glumly.

Róise hugs her knees tight to her chest. 'The house is falling apart. Lydia's gone. We're thirty, Mags, we can't obsess over *the good old days* for the rest of our lives.'

'You know, centuries ago, nostalgia used to be diagnosed as a disease.'

Róise makes a scoffing noise in her throat. 'That's just something ageing millennials say to make them feel better about romanticizing the messy years.'

Maggie laughs. 'So. We're moving out.'

'Yes.'

Maggie says only, 'She's not going to like that,' nodding towards Harley as she emerges lead-limbed from the sea.

Róise shrugs. 'Time marches on.'

Maggie peers out across the water, wondering if there are octopodes out there.

resolution

Harley slides behind the hotel reception desk with what she realizes is a resting misery face when Ash says, 'Rough night?' She has
noticed an uptick in the frequency of people saying this to her,
and half the time (she notes with indignation) she's not even been
out the night before. She doesn't sleep well these days, bruises of
fatigue blooming beneath her eyes. She struggles to fall asleep in
silence, but finds the television too distracting and music not distracting enough. After trialling numerous audiobooks and radio
channels and guided meditations, she is now ninety episodes into
the back catalogue of a video-game podcast hosted by three Australian comedians, which she finds oddly soothing in spite of
(or perhaps because of) not having any interest in video games,
comedy or Australians.

'Boiler's broken in our house. No heating and cold showers,'
she tells Ash by way of explanation for her weary appearance.

'Jesus. Happy new year,' they reply. 'What's your landlord
said?'

'He's been really good about it, to be fair to him,' Harley insists
loyally. 'Someone's meant to be coming to fix it tomorrow.'

'Well, we've got heating,' begins Ash.

'Show-off.'

'. . . so you're welcome to come to a party at ours, if you want. But if you're going to be like *that* . . .'

'What, tonight?'

'Aye, we're doing a sort of not-quite-new-year party. It was meant to be low-key but Ari's now invited half of Belfast, so—'

'So any old slapper can come now, is that it?'

Ash shrugs. 'Offer's there if you want it.' Harley hesitates, and Ash performs an unnecessarily theatrical head-tilt of suspicion. 'You're not doing a *dry* January, are you?'

'I resent your tone.'

'*Are* you?'

'*No.*' While she has made no hard and fast commitments to specific areas of self-improvement, Harley has the vague sense of intention that accompanies every new year, of endeavouring to broadly Do Better. A house party means she will slosh too much wine around the kitchen and talk too loudly to strangers and probably text Frankie to ask for a bag around midnight and then end up getting fingered by someone's cousin in the downstairs lavatory. None of these things, she thinks, are necessarily *bad*; but they're nothing new. Short of a keys-in-the-bowl scenario or a surprise cult sacrifice, Harley feels there is very little new ground to be covered in the house-party genre, and she is very, very tired.

'I don't know . . .' she says to Ash.

'Ah, go on. Everyone will love you.'

★ ★ ★

Harley is staggered to discover that Ash's bathroom has under-floor heating. She cannot believe she knows someone her age who not only lives in a house with under-floor heating, but *owns* a house with under-floor heating. She cannot believe she knows someone her age who owns a *house*.

She lingers in the bathroom, leaning against the towel rail (also heated) and letting the warmth seep into her back. Her skin has not quite shed yesterday's sea chill. The party downstairs is mostly Ari's friends; Harley does not want to cling to Ash and Ari all night like a child following their parents around at a family christening, but her energy for drinking and socializing is already half diminished. She asked Maggie and Róise if they fancied coming along, but they both have work in the morning and seem spent after the excesses of the festive period. The bathroom is calm and clean and Harley almost wishes she could curl up in the free-standing bathtub and fall asleep.

She stares at the toilet cistern and realizes she is longing for the companionship and liveliness of taking drugs in a bathroom with someone. She would swap Ash and Ari's polished new-build with its jasmine reed diffuser and pillowy loo roll for the most mildewed, skid-marked, grimy-floored toilet cubicle in Belfast if she could be wedged in there with someone, chatting and chopping merrily. Harley tries to recall whether she has a single dusting of any substance sitting around at home, thinks wildly about texting Maggie or Róise asking *hey, are either of you up?* like a brazen fuckboy, inviting them again to Ash's house and asking them to bring any leftovers they can find in her nightstand. But the likelihood of leftovers is slim and she doesn't think either of her friends will vault out of bed at the eleventh hour on a Tuesday to answer the call of the sesh.

Harley's thumb hovers over Frankie's number in her phone. He probably won't be available to drop off. Surely someone downstairs has something, surely she can find the will to make fast friends with the right people.

Frankie responds straight away. *Sound, what's the address?*

Frankie texts when he's outside Ash's house. Harley necks her glass of wine in a swallow that feels too large, almost angular as it goes down her throat. She approaches the car and bends down to the passenger window. 'Happy new year,' she says.

'New year, new you, is it?' Frankie replies, gently mocking.

Harley laughs, her breath catching strangely, almost sob-like. 'You coming in?' she says, cocking her head towards the house, as though she has taken it for granted that he's there for the party. Frankie's eyebrow flicks upwards. 'Come on, I owe you a drink. At the very least.'

'That's good of you, but I don't know if you noticed: I'm driving.'

'Just the one, then.' She avoids seasoning her words with any flirtation, aware that if she beckons him even faintly seductively and he declines, she will be forced to move out of her home address not by Róise but by sheer embarrassment.

Frankie considers, looks at her, then turns off the ignition. 'One.'

Reinvigorated by Frankie at her back and the bag in her pocket, Harley practically beams at the other party guests as she moves past them inside. She plucks a beer from the heaving fridge, cracks the lid and hands it to him, pausing to pour herself another wine. 'Sláinte.'

'Go raibh maith agat.'

Harley dings the rim of her glass against his bottle, takes a sip, and says, 'Right. Bathroom.' She nods her head and he follows, as though she is leading him up to examine a plumbing fault.

'Do you want some?' she asks upstairs, tapping a small quantity of powder onto the pristine lid of the toilet.

He shakes his head. 'Driving.'

Harley rolls up her train ticket from Helen's Bay and hits two lines of coke in quick succession. She sighs, lightly pinching the bridge of her nose. 'Much better.'

'Rough day?' he says, apparently amused.

Harley sits on the plush bath mat and leans her back against the tub. 'Are you sending someone to fix the boiler tomorrow?'

Frankie frowns at this line of questioning. 'Yeah, they should be round between eight and twelve.'

'In the morning?'

His mouth twitches slightly. 'Sorry, I know it's not your usual office hours.'

Harley doesn't laugh. These questions, in her mind, suddenly seem very urgent. 'Is it being replaced or are they just patching up the old one? The fella that came round to fix it last time said it was ancient.'

'I don't know, I'll wait and see what he says.'

'What about the bathroom, is that getting redecorated?'

'Did you lure me here to have a business meeting about my property development plans?'

A bright smile flashes onto Harley's face, and she turns it up towards him. 'I fucking love that house.'

'I'm glad.'

'No, listen, I mean it. I fucking love that house. So many memories. You raised a wonderful heap of bricks. You should be so proud.'

Frankie's laughing at her again. 'Someone's getting sentimental,' he says. He sits next to her on the mat, gauging that she has no immediate plans to move. 'Tears and all.'

Harley blinks. He's right. 'Stop it,' she scoffs, but there's a sob in her throat again, higher this time, choking each of her words brutally and individually in turn.

'Jesus, *Harley*,' he says, with confused sympathy. 'You all right? Do you want one of your mates up here?' Harley shakes her head furiously. 'Do you want driven home?'

Harley sniffs, touching the tip of her nose dismissively as though she is simply reacting to a few rogue flecks of cocaine. 'Róise thinks we should move out.'

'Because of . . . the boiler?' Even as he says it, Harley can tell he already knows the answer. 'No. I get it. Thought you might. Given everything.'

'I don't want to go.'

'Maybe you should. Give me some peace.' He says it good-humouredly, which somehow makes her feel worse.

Harley shakes off her feelings, sweeps her hair to one side, briefly massages the back of her neck. 'You'd love that,' she says provocatively, looking him in the eyes and smiling. 'We'll see.'

'You know best.'

When she kisses him it is slow and deep and deliberate, in a way that (she hopes) does not betray she has been thinking at length about what it would be like to fuck him, and in a way that (she hopes) will make him think at length about what it would be like to fuck her.

Someone outside tries the bathroom door and finds it locked. Frankie moves back from her slightly, blinking as if shaken suddenly awake.

'There's another toilet downstairs,' she murmurs, her words slurred with wanting.

'We should move,' he says. He gets to his feet and offers her his hand.

Harley follows him reluctantly from the room. When they are on the stairs, Frankie says, 'I should probably head off, actually. Do you want a lift anywhere?' Harley notes that he has already half turned away, as if anticipating that her answer will be no.

'No, thank you,' she says formally. 'I'm going to stay on.'

'Sound. Thanks for the drink.' He hands her back the beer, barely drunk. 'See you . . . when I see you.'

'Safe home.'

When he has gone, she returns to the bathroom, now empty again. The towel rail still radiates warmth, and yet gooseflesh prickles along her arms and her shoulders are shaking. Harley takes her house keys from her pocket, the one for the front door slightly bent and tarnished. She holds the back-door key between her finger and thumb, dips it into the bag in her other hand, scoops up a small peak of powder to sniff. She swipes the key with her tongue to pick up the residue between its notches, and a metal tang lingers in her mouth like blood.

keep 'er lit

Within minutes of Róise returning to the office after her Christmas leave, Juliet scoots across the floor in her swivel chair, legs paddling against the sallow office carpet. *She knows*, Róise thinks at once. She spent half the holidays imagining awful and increasingly ridiculous scenarios: an ominous summons from HR, a Greek chorus of co-workers turning their gaze on her as she crosses the office, a team meeting in which she is singled out and ordered to wear a scarlet letter on her lanyard. She replayed the night of the Christmas party in her mind, trying to remember whether Juliet had registered her departure, whether she would ambush Róise in the bathrooms at work with the usual 'Happy new year!' and 'How was your holiday?' and then suddenly, 'So . . . what happened with you and Adam?'

The urgency with which Juliet propels herself across to Róise's desk turns out to be a false alarm. By the end of Róise's first day working here she was fully briefed on Juliet's entire romantic past and the urgently narrated dramas of her romantic present. Juliet lives in a village with one and a half pubs, and there is hardly a weekend that goes by where there hasn't been a new and scandalous development in her eleven-person-strong social circle. She takes no interest whatsoever in Róise's personal life. After a full inventory of the Boxing Day feuds that went down in her hometown, Juliet finally clears off back to her own computer. The chair wheels are at too awkward an angle for her to lever herself crablike across the room, so after a couple of failed attempts, she gets up from the chair and walks it to her desk like an embarrassed parent leading away their chastened toddler.

No one else says anything to indicate they know what happened between Róise and Adam at the Christmas party. No one seems keen to mention it at all; apparently a group of them repaired to McHugh's after the hotel, and two of the interns got warnings from the police for indecent footering in a bus shelter. Adam's been in a meeting with the window blinds drawn since first thing this morning, and Róise hasn't seen him yet. She stares blandly at her computer calendar and does no work, watching the door and waiting for him to appear. They have not spoken since leaving the hotel the morning after the party. As they were gathering themselves in the room, he spoke to her in a pleasant and ambiguous manner that seemed to indicate he had enjoyed himself but did not give any clues as to how things would unfold when they returned to working together day to day. Over the holidays, Róise found herself by turns disappointed and relieved that he did not have her phone number. She felt at times that it would have been nice to hear from him, a gently validating text to wish her happy Christmas or to say that he was looking forward to seeing her in the new year. She also, however, imagined him texting one degree too keenly and her having to hand in her notice out of pure awkwardness.

'Róise,' says Adam, when he at last emerges at eleven o'clock. 'Need your help with something.' He nods towards the door of his office, which he shuts behind her when she's in the room. 'Have a seat.' Adam sits in his own desk chair opposite and then says, 'Sorry.'

'Sorry?'

' "Have a seat",' he mocks himself, cringing slightly. 'I sound like I'm interviewing you.'

She gives him a small smile. 'What can I help you with?'

'Oh, nothing at all. I just wanted to check in. See how things are. Make sure it's not weird. Probably proceed to make it weird.' He leans his elbows on the table. 'How are you?' he asks sensitively.

A sharp burst of laughter escapes her. '*Adam.* We just had sex, I didn't witness a murder. I don't need a referral to Occupational Health.'

'Sweet! Okay. I just thought I'd – you know. Check.'

'Don't you worry about me.'

'Grand. Yes. Should we' – he tosses his hand carelessly in her direction – 'I don't know, go for a drink or something?'

Róise has no wish to go on anything remotely resembling a date. However, she does not know how to respectably convey that she would like to clear his desk and lock her legs around him for the next ten minutes, so she says yes. She wants as little time as possible to overthink it, so she suggests they simply meet this evening straight after work. Adam agrees. She returns to her desk with a low, slow feeling of effervescence in her abdomen.

'I didn't plan for that to happen, at the Christmas party,' Adam tells her over a gin and tonic. 'Swear to God.'

'I know,' she says. 'I manage your diary, it definitely wasn't in there.'

Adam laughs. He carries himself with more ease than Róise expected. She was concerned he might have been made awkward and try-hard by what passed between them (and what could potentially pass that way again), but she need not have worried. He flirts in a casual, muted manner that suggests he is quietly confident she wants to be flirted with.

'So, go on. You know all the ins and outs of my daily life. Tell me something juicy about you.'

'I dispute that,' Róise scoffs. 'I know what time you've to be places and who you're meant to be meeting on a daily basis. But I've no idea what your job even entails, let alone anything else about you.'

'Savage. Do you really not know what I do?'

'Do you have the power to give me a pay rise?'

'No.'

'Then I don't care.'

'Well, for what it's worth, I sit on a lot of interview panels, and I'm very good at clocking when someone's dodged a question.' Róise waits, and he says again, 'Tell me something about you.'

This feels, to her, a more invasive request than the night of the

Christmas party when he asked (quite cordially) if he could put a finger up her rectum. She replies, 'My name is Róise McGarvey, I'm thirty years of age, and I work as an admin assistant to a nosy bastard.'

'Solid start. Go on.'

She sighs, and continues. 'I come from Omagh, I live in Belfast with three— with two of my oldest friends. And a turtle.'

Adam stops her. 'Did you almost give away that one of your oldest friends is a turtle?'

'No.'

'You were about to say "three" and then you changed it to two friends and a turtle.'

'The turtle belonged to a third friend who used to live with us.'

'Ah. And, what, you kept the turtle as a damage deposit?'

'No. Our friend stopped living with us because she stopped living.'

'Shit.' He swallows, pauses for a moment. 'When did that happen? If you don't mind me asking.'

'Just over a year ago?'

'God, I'm – that's awful, I'm so sorry.'

'It's fine. It was a while ago. She sort of fucked my boyfriend and broke my heart. And when I was starting to come around to the notion of eventually forgiving her, she died in a car accident. Silly bitch,' Róise jokes weakly. 'We got stuck with a collapsing house and her stupid turtle. It's fine.' She shrugs. Adam looks uncertain about what to ask or say, and Róise adds, 'Tell me something about you, then.'

'Do you . . . I mean, that's quite a lot. Do you want to talk about it?'

'No.'

'Did you go to counselling or anything?'

'Yes,' she lies. 'I'm sorry I even brought it up. Let's talk about something else.'

'I'm starting to think I *should* send you to Occupational Health,' he jokes. 'But, here, if you ever need support or anything, just shout. I can make a referral to the wellbeing service – I'd be discreet about it. Or I'll man the corridor if you want to shut yourself in the stationery cupboard and scream into the mindfulness leaflets for a bit.'

Róise laughs. 'Thanks, *Dad*.' She finishes her drink. 'Same again?'

The conversation, from then on, is steered towards more trivial matters. Adam seems reluctant to talk about his own romantic or sexual past. He talks sometimes about going out in his twenties, but halfway through each anecdote he seems to regret having begun it, makes hasty mention of women he was 'sort of seeing, back in the day' and then tries to change the subject.

She asks why he seems cagey talking about it. 'Did you murder all these women, or are you just trying not to let on you were a slut in your twenties?'

Adam laughs, embarrassed. 'It's just . . . not really who I am anymore.'

'A murderer, or a slut?'

'Both,' he says mock-solemnly.

At one point, he asks what her favourite meal is, and she

160

falters. 'I don't know,' she hedges. 'I'll eat most things. Except anchovies. And raw tomatoes. What about you?'

He sighs yearningly. 'Steak.'

'Why the look of despair?'

'I can't eat it as much anymore. I got gout in my third year of uni.'

'When did you go to uni, the fifteen hundreds?'

'Literally, I had so much beer and beef in my early twenties that I left university with the body of a Tudor nobleman.' Her eyes automatically flick up and down his physique; briefly, but he notices. 'You're thinking, *aye, you still do, pal.*'

Róise says, 'The hotel my friend Harley works in . . . the restaurant does a good steak. If you're still allowed it occasionally, you should go there.'

Adam asks which hotel it is. 'I was going to suggest a hotel near here,' he says, 'if you fancied it.'

'What – tonight?'

'Yes. Last time was a good time.'

'It was a good time.'

'Cut through here,' Adam suggests as they walk through the city centre. People wait shivering for buses and taxis outside the pubs, snatches of music ballooning every so often as someone opens the door to a venue, then shrinking again as it swings shut. Róise follows Adam down a side street, and is drenched all at once in a cold shock of remembering. This is the place, she thinks.

Adam has gone a few paces ahead, but notices her hesitation and doubles back. 'You all right?'

She knows it would be impossible to say exactly where Lydia and Brendan got together in this alley, or whether it was this one at all. Down at the other end, a line is forming outside Thompson's. Adam puts out his hand to her, as if she is afraid of walking by the queuing teenagers. Róise takes hold and draws him against her.

'Róise,' he whispers against her mouth a few moments later, when she has begun to direct his hand under her skirt and between her legs. 'Hotel is five minutes away.'

'I don't want to wait,' she replies.

'Anyone could walk past,' Adam warns, but he's smiling, and his fingertips are brushing the inside of her thigh.

'Make it quick, then.'

'Jesus; easy on the romance, Róise.'

When she comes, she holds him in an almost-headlock, burying her face in his shoulder, lest something revealing should manifest in her expression during a moment of abandon. He laughs softly, tracing his lips along the curve of her ear before easing out of her death-grip. 'Shit,' he mutters as he withdraws his hand. Róise looks down faintly and sees that his middle finger is streaked with blood.

'*Shit*,' she says, deflating. 'Sorry. Fuck, *sorry*. I don't even know when I'm due anymore, it's been all over the place.' This is true; she has not bled in seven weeks, and before that it was three. She got a contraceptive implant when she was twenty-five and her periods have been erratic since, although they've been worse in the last year.

'Ahh, don't worry,' he says pleasantly, wiping himself clean with a tissue from his pocket. 'Happens.'

'We can just – I can get a taxi home instead.'

'Ah – are you cramping, aye?'

'No, I feel grand.'

'Well, I'm still happy to – if you are.' Adam shrugs. 'We can stop in Centra for whatever you use. We'll put a towel down.'

She looks at him with suspicion. 'You sure?'

Adam replies, deadpan, 'I've just fingered you in the street outside Thompson's, but you think railing you on your period might be a bit too indelicate for my refined sensibilities?'

Róise remembers her university boyfriend screwing up his nose at spots of blood on the sheets and saying, 'Babe, you're haemorrhaging,' in a tone of mild disgust. She had accompanied him home to Dublin to visit his parents one weekend, and they were sleeping in his teenage bedroom. Rather than buy neutral linen for the bed he slept in only occasionally, the boyfriend still had an Oasis duvet cover and pillowcase set, so no matter which side of the bed Róise lay on, she was face to face with one of the Gallagher brothers. They did not look impressed by the blood either.

When they wake up in the hotel room the next morning, sex-drunk and drowsy, Adam rolls over, his mouth drifting along her neck, drawing his tongue over the hollow in her throat. Róise remembers too late that she is on her period. In the bathroom afterwards, she bears down and pushes half a hand up there to hoke around for the tampon string, and for several horrifying seconds, panics that she cannot find it. Mortifying scenes flash before her eyes, images of having to present at A&E to have a Tampax Compak surgically extracted from her cervix, before she finally locates the soggy specimen, pulling it out and flushing it down the toilet so there's no chance of Adam seeing it in the bin.

Adam is looking at his phone when she returns to the bedroom. 'Feel free to tell me to fuck off,' he says, 'but do you want me to block out your morning so you can go home and change?'

Róise fastens the clasp of her bra and pretends to look at him askance. 'Are you saying there's something wrong with my outfit?'

Adam laughs. 'I'm just saying. I'll cover for you, if you need me to.'

'If I go home I will want to go directly to bed. I'll just shower here and power through.'

'You feeling rough?' he says, his face creasing with sympathy.

'Not rough. Just tired.' She feels good in Adam's company and enjoyed their night together, but she nonetheless feels as though she has worked an extra shift and needs a long rest to recover.

'Shall we do this again?' he says, sounding interested without sounding too keen.

Róise turns away from him again and pulls on her pants, smiling. 'Sure. Pop it in my calendar.'

filthy animals

'Have you pulled?' Ann asks Maggie in the bathrooms at work. Maggie blanches, until she realizes Ann is looking at the long number written on her forearm, the ink starting to feather on her skin. She explains that it is her login code for the office printer, which she can never seem to remember.

'Does anyone actually do that anymore?' Maggie adds. 'Writing their number down for someone?'

'Probably not. I may have just seen too many romcoms from the 90s.'

Ann is wearing one of her many tailored blazers over a slim turtleneck; it is a style Maggie often wishes she could pull off, but fears that if she wore this combination she would look like a sixty-year-old independent candidate running for election in South Antrim.

'How's the running going?' Maggie asks as they keep pace along the corridor.

'Very well, thanks. Two parkruns on New Year's Day.'

'I couldn't do that. A mile and a half and I'm disintegrating.'

'Started running, have you?'

'Yes, a bit,' Maggie says, embarrassed.

'Do you fancy doing the marathon this year?'

'*This* year? I don't—'

'Just the relay. First leg. Abigail's dropped out; something about a collapsed pelvic floor.' Ann swats at the air as though to clear it of unnecessary minutiae. 'Interested?'

'I . . . yeah, maybe?'

'Think about it. Let me know.' Ann speeds up on their way into the office. Maggie pulls her sleeve down quickly to cover her scrawled printer login.

She has not been running since before Christmas, and hasn't heard from Cate. Against her better judgement, Maggie downloaded a dating app at the weekend, shuffling through a deck of profiles that included four of her ex-girlfriends, two dozen obvious catfishes, and a girl who used to bully her at school who is now seeking someone to join her and her boyfriend in a threesome. Every other bio lists piña coladas and getting caught in the rain as their main interests. Maggie receives several enthusiastic opening greetings of *Hey gorgeous!!* and a shock of heart-eye emojis, usually from twenty-six-year-old women who, when she replies with an inoffensive *hello-well-what's-the-craic*, offer no further response. She speculates cynically that these are baby bicuriouses simply sweeping the apps for a fleeting fix of attention. She chats briefly with a few women who mainly have questions about where to procure the Kate Bush T-shirt she wears in her profile photo. (She is reminded that she has not seen this T-shirt in some time, and makes a note to ask

Harley if she's borrowed it.) She has one short-lived conversation with a burgeoning local influencer who seems to be trying to recruit her to a pyramid scheme. The only sustained exchange has been with someone called Tess, a hairdresser from Cork who drinks pale rosé and owns a cat, and who suggests meeting for a drink on Friday night. Maggie tentatively agrees, although she keeps surreptitiously checking her phone throughout the week, half nervous Cate will message to ask if she's up for running on Saturday morning. By Thursday Maggie has worked herself into a twist of indignation and begun hoping that Cate *will* message, so that she can respond with an airy dismissal (*sorry pal, got a date on Friday so will have to give running a miss!*) and feel temporarily powerful. On Friday she decides that if Cate gets in touch she will simply not respond, and will later post a photo of drinks to her Instagram story as a (not so) subtly intended out-of-office.

Maggie meets Tess at the Sunflower at seven o'clock. Tess has what Maggie's Aunt Aoibhlinn would call 'a face for period dramas', the sort of big dark eyes and wild brown hair that look as though she's been recently roaming a moor in long skirts. A tote bag rests at Tess's feet, the fabric slouching so that Maggie can see it contains a notebook with an iridescent cover and a bottle of whiskey. Tess explains that these are a late birthday present from a friend. Her birthday, she says, is two days after Christmas. 'That's the worst time to have a birthday,' Maggie comments.

'It's the best time to have a birthday,' Tess counters. 'Everyone thinks "poor you, only getting one set of presents", so they overcompensate. People always factor my birthday present into their Christmas shopping. If I'd been born in April, no one would give a thundering fuck. All I'd get from friends is a text promising me a round of drinks next time we were out together, and you'd just know by the time that came round they'd have forgotten about it.'

'I'll take the hint and get a round in then, will I?'

Maggie is quietly relieved that Tess's birthday has been and gone recently. She had an unfortunate spell in her mid-twenties of going on two to four dates with women whose birthdays were in the offing; by the second or third encounter, Maggie had generally decided that she wasn't feeling the romance, whereas her dates were beginning to imply that they would like her to attend their birthday celebrations and be introduced to their friends. Maggie has a blanket veto on meeting the friends of a potential love interest until after they are securely in a relationship; she has identified a personal tendency to become swept up in the intimacy of girl-groups and believe herself briefly in love as a result. When she was twenty-five she dated a woman for six months before realizing that she most enjoyed herself when they were on group nights out and enacting the performance of a relationship to the glee of this woman's closest friends, feeling the most warmth and affirmation when a member of the group seized her hand, sloppy-drunk in the toilets, and said, 'You two are so lovely together – you're so *good* for her!' This has, of course, never been an issue with Cate. The few times they have merged groups on nights out, Maggie has craved the feeling of one of Cate's friends approaching her and saying, 'You two always look so good together,' on the dancefloor. It is a ludicrous thought, she knows. She and Cate have never been on a date, have never met in a pub one to one and done the awkward hug and cheek-kiss, perfunctory admin about who orders the first round, small talk about bus delays and weather and what they've done that day. Maggie has always thought herself fortunate that their meetings are so organic and without ceremony, and yet she wishes Cate wanted even just occasionally to meet her at an agreed time and place with the unspoken expectation of date formalities.

'What are you going to use your notebook for?' Maggie asks when they are settled, pints in hand, at the table.

'I'm a writer,' says Tess. 'So, probably nothing good.'

'Gas. What do you write?'

'Historical fiction, mostly.'

'That's a very broad category.'

'I'm a very broad church.'

Tess speaks eagerly but not self-importantly about her writing. She tells Maggie she's had a story accepted by *The Stinging Fly* and that she dreams of writing a novel set in the 1870s, a long, dark, sprawling Dickensian work distended with detail. She says it would probably never see the light of day because hardly anyone has the attention span for that kind of thing; she includes herself in this, she says, admitting she largely avoids books with cramped font and more than two hundred pages and words like 'epic' and 'richly detailed' in the blurb. They talk about the books they had to read at university, the tragedy of buying all the module texts full price at Blackwell's because their classmates had beaten them to the charity shops, the fact that they have both hung on to their doorstop copies of *The Cambridge Companion to Shakespeare* because they were so expensive and so little used and you never knew if they might come in handy someday.

After two drinks, the expectation that they're going to fuck arrives between them like a silent, voyeuristic third member of their conversation. They are teasing each other as though they are old friends, and Tess's eyes are deep and alluring and locked on Maggie's as if she means to swallow her.

At half past nine when Tess goes to the bar to buy another round, Maggie looks at her phone and wishes she hadn't. *Mags!!! You out??* Xx Cate texted an hour ago. Fifteen minutes ago, she followed this up: *Five Points, mon down!!* Xx This summons reminds Maggie of a time she went out with an English girl who interpreted *mon down!* as a misspelled *man down!* and asked concernedly whether everything was all right. Maggie explained it was a contraction of *come on down*, and the woman said it didn't really work as a contraction if she had to explain it, and Maggie wrote *stop trying to colonize me* as a joke, and did not get a response.

Maggie tenses, waits for Tess to come back to the table, then excuses herself to use the bathroom. She sits on the chilly toilet seat and takes several deep breaths as she runs through her options. The sense of power she expected to wield at Cate getting in touch has not quite kicked in. The feeling is instead not dissimilar to resale tickets popping up for a sold-out festival with her favourite band headlining, with a very small window to make a decision that will empty her bank balance but potentially lead to a life-defining experience.

'You all right?' Tess asks as Maggie returns to the table.

'I feel a bit tipsy actually,' says Maggie, pinching the bridge of her nose. 'I think – I'm really sorry, but I think I should maybe head on after this one.'

'Okay, sound,' Tess says, nodding understandingly.

'I'm not normally a lightweight, honestly. I just feel a bit drunk and I'm meant to be going running in the morning, I don't want to overdo it.'

'Oh, nice! I do the Waterworks parkrun most Saturdays. Yeah, you definitely don't want to be running hungover – I tried once and nearly boked on a swan.'.

Maggie laughs, aching at how nice Tess is being. She almost wishes Tess would say something intensely strange or problematic, to relieve her guilt about leaving.

'We should do this again, though?' Tess continues. 'I promise not to suggest we go running together. That's only a date on *Made in Chelsea*.'

'Yeah, we should do this again!' agrees Maggie, and is surprised to find she means it.

Maggie touches up her makeup on the walk through town and manages to poke herself in the eye with a mascara wand. Her eye is still watering when she gets to the Five Points and she wonders whether this is why she can't see Cate anywhere in the bar area. She texts, *At the Points, where you at?* while she queues for the bar.

Nearly twenty minutes later, Maggie has necked two nervous gin and tonics and is ordering her third. She has run out of cash and the pub does not have a card machine. There is a cashpoint across the road, the barman says. He has already poured her drink and gestures to indicate he will save it for her. Maggie shouts over the trad band to ask him to move it further back from the bar. 'I DON'T WANT TO GET SPIKED!' she explains helplessly. He looks nonplussed, but obliges. When she returns, three men out with an office party try to pressgang her into dancing when the band starts up 'Wagon Wheel', and Maggie wonders if Rohypnol in her gin mightn't have been preferable after all. She flees to the bathrooms, where her phone finally lights up with Cate's name. *Top floor of Lavery's!*

Maggie takes more deep, calming breaths. Cate probably had no signal. She was busy helping a friend who's steaming and throwing up. She was taken briefly hostage by a mafia of urban badgers. There is no point, she tells herself, in wasting time sulking about it; she is already out now.

She relocates, glancing behind her every few seconds, nervous that she will run into Tess and be caught out. She shrinks behind people until she has reached the front of the Lavery's queue and paid to get inside. The top floor is packed, and Maggie shoulders through the crowd on the dancefloor as well as she can. A man a foot taller than her thinks it's funny to rest his plastic pint glass on her head. *Can't find you*, she finally texts Cate. Her message is read, then Cate is typing. *So sorry Mags, just got a taxi back! Shattered. Next time! xx*

In the toilets at Filthy's half an hour later, Maggie admits hollowly to Harley and Róise, 'I think I need to stop seeing her.'

The statement feels devoid of any particular gravitas. It's like shouting a theatrical '. . . and STAY out!' after someone who left weeks ago.

Róise's eyebrow lifts slightly. 'What did she do?'

'Do we need to hunt her down?' asks Harley.

'Don't worry. She's not done anything worse than waste my time.'

'That's a good enough excuse. Bin her.'

'I think I have to.'

'Clean break,' Róise advises curtly. 'None of this "let's stay friends" bullshit.'

She thinks about all the times Cate introduced her as *my friend Maggie* to make sure she knew her place. She makes a scoffing noise in her throat and says, 'We were never really friends.'

Filthy's closes promptly at one o'clock. They join the queue for the Gypsy Lounge upstairs with the rest of the people who aren't ready to accept the night is over and want sanctuary for a further hour or two. The club is crammed full, its low ceiling making the room feel even more tightly packed. The airless atmosphere drenches Maggie in minutes, perspiration prickling in her control pants and a gloss forming on her face. When they are on the dancefloor, Harley clamps her in a clammy hug. 'SERIOUSLY, THOUGH,' she says, detaching from her and holding up a hand in case Maggie plans to interrupt what is clearly about to be a statement of considerable wisdom and importance. 'FUCK THAT HOOR,' she pronounces. 'YOU ARE MAGNIFICENT. *FUCK* THAT HOOR. IS SOMEONE PLAYING THE FUCKING TRUMPET?'

The last query is bellowed into the air as Harley squints around for the source of the music. Some nameless house beat has been thumping since they arrived, but now it is overlaid with a piercing brass solo; there's a musician next to the DJ booth playing over the track. A lacy black bra is looped over the bell of the instrument, hanging by its strap. It is unclear whether this is the addition of the trumpet-player or an ad hoc adornment by a fan in the crowd. Maggie does not know whether it's the gin or the feeling of slow asphyxiation in the stifling club, but her head is light with a sensation of not-quite-thereness. She dances with her friends alongside the shriek of the trumpet, feeling the gentle press of the small hours and elbowing them aside.

broken irish

In the last week of January, with a grand total of three pounds and eighty-nine pence left in her overdraft, Harley sets about going through her small stack of Christmas cards from family members and counting out the money inside them. There isn't as much as she'd like; it is a great injustice, she thinks, that her young cousins making their First Communion were gifted an amount that looked like the proceeds from a large-scale bank heist, while Harley, who has actual bills to pay, gets the same ten-pound Lush gift card from her Aunt Beccy every year. She makes a grand total of twenty pounds in cash and thirty in vouchers, which means she will have to postpone paying her already over-due lesson fees to her piano teacher for one more week, unless Mrs Erskine is willing to accept alternative currencies (namely a voucher for scented candles with season's greetings from Harley's grandmother). She also doesn't have enough money for drugs until payday, although Harley considers that the embarrassment of Frankie's sexual rejection may well be enough to jolt her into teetotalism.

Sometimes she thinks about their last encounter and burns

with mortification, seeing him rigid and horrified at her advances, backing away as one might from a feral dog. Late at night, however, she remembers the subtle murmur of his tongue against hers, slow, unspoken syllables that she was sure meant he wanted her. She thinks of this in the small hours and grinds a vibrator furiously against herself as if sheer force can authenticate the memory. After a few days, she unscrews the cap to replace the battery, and the device comes apart in her hands, a tiny detached spring shooting across the room and burying itself where she cannot find it.

Lydia swore by rechargeable batteries, and Harley finds herself wondering, without really meaning to, whether there might be a functioning toy somewhere in Lydia's old bedroom. Her parents came and cleared a lot of her things around a year ago, claiming some items for sentimental value and bagging up most of her clothes for the charity shop. (Maggie, a dedicated patron of Oxfam, is now prone to drunk existential pondering about how many dead women's jackets she owns.) At the time, Lydia's mother stood in the hall and said to them, 'It doesn't feel right, us going through her things. You girls do what you like with what's left. It's mostly, you know, hairdryers and lamps and things.' She said it as though the room had been left in junk-shop condition, lampshades stacked high and an artillery drawer of ancient hairdryers. When Harley peered inside, however, it looked broadly unchanged: the wardrobes were empty and a mosaic of square patches haunted the walls where photos had once been, but apart from that it was still Lydia's bedroom. It occurred to Harley some time later that in going through her clothes, Lydia's parents had probably happened upon her substantial collection of lingerie, and she wondered if this had been the point at which they'd decided to abandon their review of her possessions. Harley imagined Lydia's father glimpsing her favourite item of latex and at first mistaking it for a swimming cap, then, realization dawning, a scarlet flush creeping up the neck he barely had.

The house is empty and Harley tells herself she will simply have a look in the nightstand drawers, then leave. The bedroom door is always closed, and she has half convinced herself over the last year that Lydia is still in there, simply taking a quiet nap. Harley notices when she steps into the room that someone has put a dehumidifier on the windowsill, and plugged in a floral air freshener near the door; she assumes this is part of Maggie's new crusade against the damp. Harley tries not to pay any heed to the pile of dog-eared books on the floor, novels by glamorous twentieth-century women who drifted bored around Paris drinking wine in the afternoon and hoping to feel things. There are half-empty perfume bottles shrouded in dust on the dressing table, hairpins and lipsticks and odd earrings sorted into Mason jars of different sizes. There is a pot full of buttons in baggies, because Lydia always kept the spare buttons that came stapled to new coats and skirts. Next to the bedside table is a basket full of barely used hairstyling products – hammerhead nozzles and travel-size curling tongs and a crimping device that was obtained for a Mary-Kate and Ashley-themed party and proved almost completely ineffective.

Harley finds a sleek-looking massager in the bottom drawer of the nightstand, along with some silver Kegel balls, a honeysuckle reed diffuser still in its packaging, and about half a gram of coke. Harley is shaking the powder to the bottom of the bag to inspect it when Róise says, 'Harley?' from the bedroom door.

Harley starts and stands up straight, silicon wand still in her other hand. 'Jesus Christ,' she exhales. 'I thought everyone was out.'

Róise comes properly into the room. 'Did you come in here looking for *gear*?'

'No! I came in here looking for sex toys.' Harley pauses. 'Arguably worse.'

'I've been wondering where that went,' Róise says, and Harley follows the line of her gaze to the Cluedo board-game box visible under the wardrobe. Róise looks up and around the room as though admiring the fixtures of a gothic cathedral, and sits on the edge of the bed. 'Explain this, then,' she says, cocking her head towards the vibrator.

'I went to change the batteries in mine and managed to lose a bit from inside it.'

'Buy a new one?'

'I'm broke.'

'You can't switch to analogue until payday?' Harley doesn't answer, and Róise doesn't push it. She lifts a small framed mirror from the dressing table, wipes it clean of dust with her sleeve. 'Put it out, then.'

Harley dumps the contents of the bag onto the surface of the mirror in silence. She has no card or paper money about her person and she feels that to leave the room now is somehow impossible, so she uses a coffee shop loyalty card (one stamp short of a free drink) from Lydia's nightstand to chop the powder into lines, then rolls the card up tightly. Róise inhales hers slowly, in an almost meditative breath that she holds before pushing it out through her mouth.

'I can't come on my own anymore,' Harley says. They are sitting side by side on the edge of the bed, both facing the window, as if divided by a confessional partition.

'Really?'

'Not without the . . . you know. Apparatus.' She resists the urge to wave the vibrator, thinking what a crushing disappointment it will be if she charges it up and it does not work.

'What about during sex?' Róise asks.

'*Please*,' scoffs Harley. 'I haven't had an orgasm during sex since the eighteen hundreds.'

Róise nods thoughtfully. 'I couldn't come for about six months last year.'

'Fair.'

'I tell a lie; I *could* come, but I always cried afterwards, so I didn't want to.' Róise swallows. 'I cried the first time Adam went down on me. He didn't see.'

'You should have said.'

'Fuck off – as if I'd tell him that.'

'You should have said to *me*.'

Róise nods at a shamrock-patterned pint glass on the windowsill. 'Did we steal that on Paddy's Day one year?'

'You put it in your bag when it was still half full and then complained you'd got Guinness on your tampons.'

179

'I fucking hate Saint Patrick's Day.'

'You say that every year,' scolds Harley, 'and every year you go out and every year, without fail, you have a wonderful time.'

'This is pure gaslighting. I cannot remember a single time I've had a good Paddy's Day.'

'Temple Bar, 2015. We made friends with that hen party from Spalding who were all dressed up as members of the Corrs.'

'I think it was B*Witched, actually.'

'See? You remember that.'

'Anything more recent than 2015 to prop up your argument?'

Harley points a finger at her. 'Two years ago. Kremlin. I pulled that girl who looked like a young Diana Rigg.'

'So you mean *you* had a good time, and I was also there.'

'You had a good time! We did a *Grease* medley on the karaoke and you went for a wee behind the Union Street bins.'

'This is not strengthening your case.'

'You lost a shoe in the Uber.'

'I repeat—'

'You definitely had a good time,' insists Harley.

'I'll take your word for it,' Róise grumbles. 'What did we do last year?'

Harley pauses. 'You didn't want to come out last year.' Róise had seen on social media that Brendan had been in New York over Saint Patrick's Day, and she invented a narrative in which he became the folksy darling of an American Irish bar, having some kind of Hallmark meet-cute with a beautiful and driven type-A event planner who was only out because her party-hungry friends had dragged her away from work. Harley remembers that Róise then blocked Brendan on every social media platform, ordered a burner phone online for ten pounds, took two diazepam, and slept for eighteen hours until Paddy's Day was over in both their time zones.

Róise takes another line from the mirror. 'Did I seem mad? Last year.'

'Yes.'

'I hated her.'

'Yes.'

'Lydia.'

'Yes.'

'She made it impossible to fucking grieve.'

'You can still grieve for someone you hate.'

'Easy for you to say – you didn't hate her.'

'I did, in a way. I do, in a way.'

'But you still love her.'

'So do you.'

'Oh, shut up.' Róise watches Harley take a second line, and says, 'We have to move out.'

'Oh, shut up.' Harley pinches the bridge of her nose. 'I know.'

'This house isn't good for us anymore.'

'I know, it's just – difficult. We grew up here. It's sad thinking about strangers sleeping in our beds.'

'Since when have you had a problem with strangers sleeping in your bed?'

'You know what I mean.' Harley sighs. 'I shifted Frankie.'

'*Stop*. Did you actually?'

'He seemed into it, and then he wasn't.'

'Good. He's punching.'

'We can still live together, can't we?'

'If you like.'

'Don't you care?' Harley was the first to come back to the house after Christmas, on Boxing Day when Róise and Maggie were still with their families. The silence was a murky and dense pea-souper, so Harley put on the radio in the bathroom and left her laptop playing music in her bedroom while she watched television downstairs. She fell asleep on the sofa watching *The Vicar of Dibley* and was woken in the morning by Maggie asking why Classic FM and Christy Moore were playing in two separate rooms upstairs.

'Of course, if it means that much to you,' says Róise.

'But what do *you* want?'

'I don't know anymore. Sometimes I think . . .'

Harley swallows. 'Go on, say it.'

'Do you think we're good for each other?'

'We're best friends. Aren't we?'

'The two things aren't mutually exclusive.'

Harley sighs, not knowing how to answer this. 'I don't know what Maggie wants to do.'

'Neither does Maggie, usually.'

'Don't tell her about Frankie, will you?'

'I can't believe you want to redact *that* and not the fact that you went hoking around for our dead best friend's dildo.'

'I'll be putting that in the housemate quarterly newsletter.'

Róise nods at the remaining lines on the mirror. 'Want to

finish this downstairs, and I'll open another wine? Unless you urgently need to retreat with your electronics,' she adds, raising an eyebrow at the vibrator.

Harley laughs. 'No,' she says. 'I've got time.'

home remedy

'. . . and then our landlord picked her up from the C. S. Lewis monument in east Belfast at four in the morning. She said she nearly boked so hard into the wardrobe it would have taken Mr Tumnus's eye out.'

Adam laughs appreciatively. Although Róise uses almost identical terms to those in which Harley first recounted the story, she has the queasy sense of having betrayed her friend by making her out to be some kind of caricatured local curiosity. She stops just short of telling Adam that Harley shifted their aforementioned landlord, and that she went looking for a vibrator in Lydia's bedroom last weekend.

Since Adam suggested that they have dinner as well as drinks this Friday, Róise's immediate concern has been that she must be presenting as an increasingly chaotic drunk during their after-work assignations. Perhaps she is more unpleasant company than she realizes. Or maybe, she considers, Adam is worried that the tequila will sucker-punch her without warning, causing her to suddenly pass out with him inside her. Whatever it is, he seems to be hinting she could do with lining her stomach of an evening.

185

Róise has so far told Adam very little about her friends, but she turned up for dinner this evening with a dossier of Harley anecdotes, presenting them as evidence that she – Róise – is actually fairly tame in comparison.

They are eating at a nice bar (he suggested a French seafood restaurant, she suggested the pub near the students' union that used to advertise three-pound pizzas; they split the difference and chose somewhere that serves oyster starters but also does very cheap, very strong cocktails), but she can't seem to settle. She felt an unexpected ripple of discomfort when she turned down one of the entries off the high street and saw Adam was waiting outside the bar for her; and then again, inside, when he gave his name to the server at the door so she could check the booking. It gave off an odour of preparation on his part that made her embarrassed somehow, as though he had exposed some kind of intimate vulnerability. Until tonight, there has been something about the casual veneer of after-work drinks that made it feel fresh and spontaneous. Róise felt superior to the people around them who were arriving to meet for carefully arranged Hinge dates, cringing at the thought of the administrative back-and-forth that must have been involved. Choosing a venue, proposing a time, messaging *I'm a few mins early, what are you drinking?* and then *Gin and tonic please, I'm two minutes away on the bus!* and then *Sweet, I'm sat in the corner, just past the bar and down to the left!* The thought of exchanging these small, mundane updates with someone feels like baring a part of herself that Róise does not feel is ready to be seen yet.

'How's your food?' Adam asks her. She has been working

diligently on her chicken salad but the more she eats, the more she seems to have. She tries heaping bigger mouthfuls onto her fork but a spinach leaf slick with dressing tries to slide down her throat the wrong way, and she gags silently.

'It's great! I'm filling up so quickly, though. I shouldn't have had the starter.'

'Do you cook much at home?'

'A little bit? Not as much as I used to.' She says it without thinking, and immediately hopes Adam does not ask her to explain. Róise cooked fairly regularly when she was still with Brendan, but after they separated, she replaced evening meals with two over-the-counter sleeping tablets at seven p.m.

'What's your favourite dinner?'

'Why, you going to cook for me?' she jokes. He lifts one shoulder, smiling. Oh shit, she thinks, realizing he actually does want to cook for her. She feels the ghost of the spinach prodding her tonsils and heaves slightly. The idea of going to a man's home with his fridge magnets and his complicated WiFi password and his crotch-hairs in the bathtub makes her feel ill, makes her long for the impersonal neatness of a hotel room.

'Shall we just go back to mine?' he says once they've paid the bill. 'I'm pretty close.'

These are not, she muses silently, the circumstances under which she hoped she would hear him say *I'm close* this evening. 'Yeah, I'm . . . just going to use the loo. Back in a second.'

The food, already unsettled in her stomach, comes up without too much effort. Róise sits on the toilet lid afterwards to compose herself. Adam is as good-looking and charming as ever, and as ever, she wants to go to bed with him; so why should it matter if the bed is in his flat instead of a hotel? But she cannot help it – she feels as uncomfortable as she would had he suggested they head on to a company networking event, or the birthday party of a childhood friend.

'All right?' Adam says, flashing her a quick wink when she meets him at the door of the restaurant. All the blood in her head takes a sharp nosedive to between her thighs. She tells herself they are not walking to his flat; they are going to a shiny, anonymous Airbnb.

He lives on the top floor of a city-centre apartment block. His flat, Róise is pleased to note, is very neat and minimalist. There is no haphazard stack of boring *Lord of the Rings* box sets balanced on the TV stand, no optimistic home-gym equipment, no mortifying musical instruments. The idea of seeing evidence of hobbies feels as distasteful to her as if his home were full of photos of a wife and children, something inherently separate to whatever they are to each other.

'I've only got beers and whiskey,' says Adam, opening a cupboard of glasses, 'and I know you're not a beer fan.'

'Whiskey it is, then,' Róise concedes. She is not much of a whiskey drinker either, but she likes the notion of being someone who sips premium spirits on the rocks instead of throwing them down her at breakneck speed for a shortcut high.

Róise has an anxiety spasm when they sit down on the sofa together and he turns on the TV, fearing she is about to be shown some hideous documentary about the Beatles and/or Charles

Manson, which was Brendan's favourite sub-genre of Netflix. But Adam puts on an ambient fireplace video and turns to rest a hand on her knee. 'Drink all right?'

'Sláinte,' she says, taking a sip.

'What would you be doing of a normal Friday night, if you weren't here?'

'Probably drinking much cheaper booze,' she replies, 'in much better company.'

He laughs. 'Savage. Shouldn't have asked.'

'What about you? How come you've nothing better to be at?'

'I go out with the lads from time to time,' he shrugs. 'But a quare few of them have children now.'

'Not you.'

'I won't lie – half the reason I wanted you to come back here was so you could see I'm not holing up a secret family while I pound you in a hotel room.'

'For one horrible second at the start of that sentence, I thought you were about to say half the reason you wanted me to come back here was so *we* could start a family.'

'You got me. I'm going full *Handmaid's Tale*. You're never leaving.' Adam sips his whiskey. 'Do *you* want kids?' he asks.

Róise can feel her face heating up as though the artificial flames on the television screen are real. 'I don't know.'

'Did your ex want them?'

'I mean, in an abstract way, yes. Just, you know. It's the done thing.' She and Brendan never discussed it in much depth; he made passing impersonal references to children and grandchildren in a way that seemed to assume he would one day be issued

189

with offspring like a jury summons. Róise had imagined what he would be like as a father. He was charming with the children of friends and family members, and she was deeply attracted to the tenderness he displayed towards his six-year-old Labrador, Skip. After she and Brendan broke up, Róise sometimes found herself crying at night about the idea that other lovers and girlfriends would meet and mother his dog. She wonders sometimes if Skip misses her; if he even noticed she was gone.

They have sex on the rug in front of the sofa. Róise wears lingerie she bought online, a complicated lattice of straps that feels as though she has been fastened into a parachute. She was concerned that coming back to his home would mean pyjama cuddles and forehead kisses, but she need not have worried. By the time he finishes, her insides feel bruised. She finds it soothing.

When Róise turned up at the restaurant last night, Adam nodded at her holdall and asked jokingly whether she was planning a weekend stay. She told him no, that she was heading to Omagh to see her family the next morning. Now, as the 273 bus passes through Ballygawley park-and-ride, she is still pondering whether or not he looked disappointed. She dismisses the idea. He was probably trying not to seem too relieved; after spending the whole week in the same office as her and Friday night in the same bed, she is sure he's grateful not to have to make further small talk with her over Saturday lunch.

Ciara meets her off the bus and asks if she's hungry. Róise hasn't eaten since her half-salad last night, unless you count the lime and salt from the after-dinner shots they had at the bar. Ciara suggests the cafe at the bottom of Market Street.

'Any craic?' her sister asks once they've ordered coffee and cake. They speak in low voices because they never know who might be nearby that knows them, or knows their mum. A woman in her seventies once approached Róise delightedly in SuperValu to tell her Róise had once wet herself on the woman's living-room carpet over twenty years earlier, and that she hadn't changed a bit. (Since Róise wasn't openly soiling herself in the bread aisle, she assumed the woman meant purely looks-wise.)

There wasn't much chance to speak privately with Ciara about Adam over Christmas, so Róise gives her a summary in the time it takes for their coffees to arrive. Ciara asks how she feels about it all. 'Be more specific,' says Róise. 'How do I feel about sleeping with someone from work, or how do I feel about sleeping with someone since Brendan?'

'I just mean how do you feel about *him*?' says Ciara. 'Like, as a person.'

Róise thinks it might be cold to disclose that she is trying her best not to see him as a person. 'He's fun,' she says. 'The sex is unreal.'

'Do you think there's something in it? Relationship-wise?'

Róise sips her black coffee. 'Sometimes,' she says, 'when we're together, I pretend I'm cheating on Brendan.' She sees the professional intrigue flare in her sister's eyes; Ciara is a psychotherapist.

'Tell me more about that.'

'No, you tell me. What do you think it means?'

'You can't outsource your self-reflection to me just because I'm a therapist.'

'Fuck sake. What use are you then?' Róise smiles and shakes her head. 'I don't want him back or anything. Brendan. But I'm not ready for another boyfriend.'

'That's allowed. And understandable. What'll you do if it gets awkward at work?'

'Leave, most likely? I'm going to move soon, maybe it's time for a total reset.'

'Really? Where are you moving to?'

'Anywhere else. I mean, not back here. But somewhere else. I need out of that house.'

'Getting a bit much? After Lydia?' Ciara asks.

Róise warms her hands around her coffee cup. 'I still . . . It's been over a year and I can't really believe she's gone. When I'm steaming in the pub with Maggie and Harley I keep accidentally buying rounds for four people instead of three, as if she's just gone to the toilet. I've had to neck the extra drink at the bar before they see. It's costing me a fortune plus my liver.' She shudders. 'Can we talk about something else?'

'We're thinking of moving back to Belfast,' Ciara says smoothly.

'Oh?'

'We're talking about it. Domhnall agrees it makes sense. And if we think there's any chance of moving then really we should do it before Finn gets to nursery age, to give him continuity.'

'Is this really just a ploy to get your child socializing with weeins who don't have culchie accents?'

'Perish the thought,' Ciara laughs. 'But yeah, we're thinking about it. I was a bit worried about Mum being isolated if we just upped and left, but she's got Granny and she's out having the craic with Lesley and Vera every weekend. I swear she's got more of a social life than me.'

Róise nods while Ciara talks more about moving, about things like mortgages and school catchment areas. She feels a low-level disdain for people her age who think it's quirky to claim that they are witless babies in denial about the admin of adulthood, but when Ciara goes off on one about council tax rates or bathroom square footage, Róise feels keenly that her sister's is a world she cannot imagine ever inhabiting.

Róise's granny gets the greatest hits out when Róise tells her she's still single. She kicks off with 'Do you have to be so *picky*?' followed by 'You need to learn to give people a *chance*,' and the timeless classic: 'Who do you think you are, Taylor Swift?' This last one has become an idiom embedded in their family lexicon. Granny is obsessed with Taylor Swift. She has a Twitter account that she uses solely to keep up with Taylor Swift news; sometimes she comes across posts from trolls saying things like *Taylor Swift should be tortured by starving alligators* and she replies earnestly with *I think that's unfair, Kevin. She seems like a lovely girl, and so hardworking.* When Granny asks Róise, 'Who do you think you are, Taylor Swift?' it means she thinks her granddaughter must have notions of being able to take her pick of Hollywood actors and famous musicians.

'You want to get a move on, our Róise; the only ones left are going to be middle-aged divorcés looking for a second chance at youth, or struggling musicians who never grew up in the first place.' Granny gives her a pointed eyebrow-raise as the bell clangs at the back of the church and the organ starts wheezing.

Granny sprained her ankle after Christmas and should still be taking it easy, but it's Molly McElhinney's memorial service and she wanted to attend in person instead of watching online. (Róise, Ciara and their mum bought Granny a smart TV for her birthday last year. It has dozens of channels and on-demand platforms and the only things she ever streams on it are *Midsomer Murders* and Mass.) Granny has started doing soft mutters and harrumphs during the homily, which makes Róise think she has perhaps got used to heckling the celebrant from her armchair at home. She gives Róise a pound to put in the collection basket, and another to light a candle at the end. When Róise was young she had a very unrealistic notion of how long the votives in church lasted once she lit them, watching a little bowl of liquefied wax form on the surface and imagining it burning determinedly for days. While she and Adam were in the restaurant last night one of the waiters came round putting tea lights in amber-coloured holders on each of the tables. The candle was freshly lit when it was set down between them, but several drinks later, she watched the flame give way to spiralling smoke-ribbons.

She blows out the taper after lighting her candle. 'What did you wish for?' Granny whispers impishly, coming up behind her. It's an old joke; the flames ruffle from the breath of their laughter.

hunt the hare and turn her down

One week before Valentine's Day, Maggie's therapist breaks up with her. Astrid sends an email beginning 'Hi all!' like a chirpy maid of honour circulating plans for an upcoming hen weekend. She then says that due to personal circumstances, she will be stepping away from her practice for the foreseeable future. Despite this explanation, Maggie cannot help wondering if this 'Hi all!' has been sent to her, solely and personally, because Maggie's troubles have become too tedious to tolerate, even at a rate of forty pounds an hour. Astrid writes that she will be available for concluding sessions until the end of the month and that she is more than happy to recommend alternative sources of counselling. Maggie has never thought ahead to a time when she would not be seeing Astrid on Mondays, although she always had a vague notion that she would one day walk away with a certificate (real or implied) to confirm that she had Finished Therapy. Restarting with someone new seems like an exhausting prospect. Perhaps Astrid could send her notes to any future therapist of Maggie's, so she doesn't have to rehash the various deaths and disruptions that have led to her having regular panic attacks and shared custody of a turtle.

Maggie has returned, alone, to running. The half-hour silence from one end of the park to the other is now filled with twelve repeat plays of 'The Rocky Road to Dublin'. She keeps pace with its rhythm, picking up speed in the latter verses, almost able to imagine that she is bouncing around at a céilí.

Maggie did her first solo run accompanied by an audiobook memoir by a social media personality who claimed she used to start the day with a double shot of vodka and three lines of cocaine until she discovered long-distance running. The opening chapters were a bleak inventory of the woman's alcoholic blackouts, the descriptions so harrowing they made Maggie feel nauseous and wrong-footed, as though she herself might stumble mid-jog and be stranded paralytic on the ground until a passerby called an ambulance. Maggie retired the audiobook three chapters in and switched to podcasts, but found her thoughts were too scattered to engage with anything vaguely informative. She tried a few episodes from the broad genre of 'two pals shooting the breeze as if at the pub', but it only made her want to be at the pub shooting similar breeze with her own pals, which she found was not a productive mindset for seven a.m. on a Tuesday.

After her Saturday run, instead of a quick blitz in the shower, Maggie decides to take a bath. Frankie sent someone round last week to treat the mould, and the chemical smell has finally left the bathroom. On the wall, however, there is still a shadowy frogspawn of damp patches that suggests the problem has not been fully banished. Maggie sits with her back to it, drinks the cooling dregs of her coffee, and picks up the book she hasn't touched in two weeks. She and Tess have been engaged in pleasant discourse over text about all the books Tess has read, and all the books Maggie owns and means to read, one day.

I've got very basic tastes, Tess says. *I love a One Woman's Journey memoir.*

They talk about Cheryl Strayed and Elizabeth Gilbert and Maggie improvises opinions based on the films with Reese Witherspoon and Julia Roberts. They talk about self-indulgent party-girl memoirs by women their age and admit they don't know if they're cringing at the authors or at themselves. Tess tells her that she always stops reading a few chapters before the end of these books.

Why? asks Maggie.

Tess responds with a voice note. 'There's always this smug sense of clarity and *healing* at the end. It's unrelatable and it's fucking annoying. I don't want to hear that someone's cured their depression through learning square-dancing and now only drinks one night a week. I want to read a memoir that someone wrote between seshes – no, *during* seshes – something that ends with uncertainty. That's life.'

Maggie looks with ambivalence at the book she planned to continue reading in the bath, a recent memoir by a woman being touted as 'the millennial Nora Ephron'. She has around eighty pages left and wonders whether she should sack it off now, to be on the safe side.

★ ★ ★

'Let me guess: "It's not you, it's me",' Maggie jokes during her last session with Astrid.

Astrid laughs. 'It *is* me,' she insists. 'I'm being deported!' Maggie blanches. 'It's fine,' Astrid insists with a cavalier flick of her colourfully manicured hand. 'How have you been?'

Maggie mentally scraps everything she planned to talk about during the hour. She parrots a few platitudes from the audiobook she abandoned, pretending to have found therapeutic solace in running again. She claims to be reconciled with the notion of moving house, with the unspoken acknowledgement that things could be worse (*well, at least I'm not being deported!*). She tells Astrid about her date with Tess, outlining all the positives without disclosing that she bailed on said date to chase after Cate. She spins things so positively that she almost convinces herself; perhaps this is it, the graduation certificate for finishing therapy. Perhaps, she thinks, Astrid is leaving her life at exactly the right time, like a sort of Australian Mary Poppins. Afterwards, Maggie thinks she may (in a desperate attempt at sincerity) have actually blurted the phrase 'Australian Mary Poppins' at the end of the session when she was saying goodbye, but the last hour already seems a blur, and she cannot be sure. In the street, litter waltzes around her on a chill wind. Maggie realizes too late that she never did ask Astrid where she gets her nails done.

party politics

Róise is running out of reasons not to go out for dinner in south Belfast. Adam has suggested a number of possible venues since they started spending Friday nights together, but all of them have been closer to her home than his, and she has no wish to be faced with the *shall we just go back to yours?* that will surely follow. The only person she has ever entertained romantically at home is Brendan, and she feels nauseated at the idea of Adam creeping to their mouldy bathroom in his pants, coming down-stairs in the morning and introducing himself to Harley or Maggie, using the neglected kitchen utensils to make breakfast for her.

She has turned down one south Belfast restaurant claiming the staff are rude, another citing food poisoning that she never had, and several other bougie bars with a vague dismissal of *they've got wile notions.* She proposes alternatives in the city centre, claiming *I've always wanted to try their steak,* and then when they arrive and consult the menu she sees something she would actu-ally prefer to the steak, and she wonders if ordering something else would undermine her subterfuge, and then she remembers that it hardly matters since whatever she eats will likely end up in the toilet bowl.

The sickness was never something she planned to make a habit of. She nursed envy for the people who lost their appetite when they were grieving and heartbroken. When Brendan left her and Lydia died, Róise could do nothing but eat – enormous take-away pizzas orbited by sides of fried chicken and garlic bread, Tayto sharing packets the size of military sandbags, paper sacks of sweets from the supermarket pick-and-mix. She ate until she was full, and kept going until she was sick, and if she wasn't sick she thrust a hand into her gullet until it came up in an acid slop. She binges less often than a year ago, but the sickness has become a habit, an automatic digestif after a large meal. Róise imagines it will reach a natural end one day, in the way that she had one bad night drinking vodka martinis when she was twenty-five and her body concluded that she could simply never have them again. She remembers when her sister Ciara had a proper eating disorder at university, and the sheer amount of admin involved: food diaries and calorie counts and exercise targets and weigh-ins. Ciara shrank until her shoulders looked as though they were hung on a wire coat hanger; her breasts deflated against her toast-rack ribcage. Róise, however, has seen no measurable change in her body at all.

'Have you lost weight?' Adam asks carefully in bed. She is staying at his flat again. He offered to cook for her, but she volunteered a place in town that she pretended to be keen on. She hoovered up a mountain of meat and potatoes and was neatly sick in the restaurant toilet.

'No?' says Róise. She wonders if he says this semi-rhetorically, thinking she will take it as a compliment.

'Sorry, I don't mean to be – you know, personal.'

'It's grand. I've not lost weight; certainly not after that dinner, anyway.' The red wine and chunks of meat in her vomit looked visceral, as though she had been feasting on a blood sacrifice – a starved fox set loose in a sheep-pen.

'Sweet. I just wanted to check you weren't – you know. Work-related stress, or anything.'

'Jesus, I thought you were going to say you were checking I wasn't pregnant.'

'Considering we're riding and work in the same office, that could also fall under the heading of "work-related stress".'

'No, I'm not stressed. Or pregnant. You can tell HR.'

Adam smiles at her. She likes the creases beneath his eyes when he smiles, like folds in a lifted theatre curtain. He props himself on one elbow and asks what she's doing tomorrow – there is a film at the QFT he's interested in seeing. Róise finds herself respecting him for disclosing the proposed activity before she confirms her availability. When she was still seeing Brendan, he would ask, 'Are you free tomorrow?' and she would ask why, and he would insist, 'Are you free?' and it would turn out he wanted her to come to a pub she hated, with friends or family members she hated just as much. When she hesitated he would launch a defence of why his mother meant well and his mildly bigoted childhood friend Finbar was really a sound lad who was misunderstood, and she would have to pretend the chosen venue was the main issue, that the drinks were too expensive or that she was barred after she and her friends had tried to smuggle a dachshund past the door staff. After ten minutes of sulking, Brendan would look at one of his group chats and tell her, good news! They were actually going to a different pub now, and she would have little choice but to get steaming drunk and pretend to be interested in the match on television while Brendan and his friends reminisced about their school-day capers.

'I'm not actually free tomorrow,' she says truthfully. 'We're having a party for my housemate's thirtieth.' Róise regularly tells stories about her two best friends when she is with Adam, but was a little nauseated last week when he referred to Maggie by name in conversation as though he knew her. She now makes an effort to anonymize them, somewhat shaken by the idea of Adam talking about them with the easy familiarity of household names.

'Ah, nice. Is that at yours?'

'Yes.' Róise already regrets saying the word *party*. She should have told him they were having a girls' night, or going for dinner. In her mind, 'party' has invoked an image of a Gatsby-style carnival with a fireworks display and a guestlist of hundreds. She wonders if he wants to be asked, wonders if casually inviting him to drop by will downplay or intensify whatever is happening between them. She considers that inviting him now would at least eliminate the chance of her texting him slightly buzzed at midnight tomorrow, suddenly thirsty for his hand on her lower back. There are many reasons she does not want him to come to her house, but one that crosses her mind now is that she left his flat early one Saturday with the excuse that she was expecting the delivery of a bookshelf she had bought online and needed to sign for. This was already a risky fabrication considering Adam knew she was planning to move house (why would she be ordering bulky furniture at such a time?) and Róise is concerned that he may note the absence of a bookshelf in her bedroom upon visiting and wonder why she lied to him.

'Do you need a hand with anything?' he asks. 'I can drive you to the supermarket if you want to do a big wine shop.' He seems sincere. Róise does not get the impression he is hinting he wants to be invited. She concedes quietly to herself that being transported to and from the supermarket would be much more practical than heaving overpriced crisps and cava back down the road from the off-licence, but the idea of meandering around Tesco on a Saturday with Adam seems like another intimacy to which she is not prepared to commit.

'No, that's nice of you to say, but we're all sorted.' The impulse to offer a concession in return for his kindness overwhelms her better judgement. 'If you want to drop in for a bit tomorrow night, feel free. You won't know anyone there, but if you fancy swinging by, you can. If you want.'

'Yeah, all right. Sounds good.' His response does not suggest he thinks this a landmark of any great moment. He changes the subject. 'I meant to say to you earlier – there's a job that's come up in the Dublin Road office. One of the team managers is leaving.'

'You thinking of going for it?'

'Not me. I was thinking you might.'

Róise bursts out laughing. '*Team manager?* Away on. I can barely manage my own laundry schedule.'

Adam shrugs. 'I did your job, back in the day, and I didn't think I'd be good for anything more senior either. But honestly, most of it's just emails.'

'Am I that bad at my job that you want rid of me?'

He looks uncomfortable. 'You don't think it's going to start getting strange, working together while we're . . . doing this?' For *this* he flicks a hand vaguely towards their naked bodies.

'We can stop, if you feel compromised.'

'To be quite honest, I'd rather lose you as my admin and keep you as . . . *this*.'

Róise is doubtful. Over the years, the idea of moving jobs has begun to feel like needing the loo in the middle of the night when she cannot be bothered to get out of bed. She knows something will need to be done about it eventually, but her get-up-and-go has got up and gone.

'Sure, send me the advert, and I'll think about it,' she lies.

would you be well

'Your sister did a dry January, you know,' Harley's mother tells her on the phone. 'Would you ever think of doing the same?'

'I loved it, Harley – you'd feel amazing,' a saintly Marianne calls out in the background.

Harley drains the glass of prosecco she poured for herself at eleven a.m., considers reminding them of the time her sister spiked the lemonade with vodka at Harley's twelfth birthday party, then decides against it. 'Mm. I'll think about it,' she says.

'How's Maggie? How's *Liam*?' asks Mum, putting coy emphasis on Liam's name. She has had Harley betrothed to Liam in her mind since they were about ten and felt it a great personal slight when he instead began dating Lydia. Harley feels incapable of finding Liam attractive because she grew up with him and was witness to the teenage fashion atrocity that they all refer to as 'the Vanilla Ice years', but Mum still insists on asking *how's Liam?* with a wise matriarchal smile.

Harley chooses not to indulge her. 'Maggie's grand. She's got really into running recently.'

'Has she? Fair play to her. Marianne's got that Strava on her phone now, haven't you?' Mum's voice moves away from the phone to talk to Marianne. Harley picks at a hangnail as she waits for them to finish talking parkruns and personal bests.

'Would *you* ever think of getting into it?' Mum's voice is in her ear again. 'You should see Marianne, the weight's dropping off her. Isn't it, love?'

'I've got to get on, Mum,' Harley says, before her mother can be distracted again. 'I'll not keep you.'

'Well, here – I'm passing you over to your dad to say bye. Enjoy your weekend,' Mum signs off. Marianne does not offer a goodbye on the other end of the line.

'Is that you away on?' Harley's dad says into the phone.

'Yeah, I've got plans with the girls.'

'Lovely stuff. Well, I hope that money gets you a few nice whiskeys. Have one for me and all.'

'I will. Thanks for the card.'

'No bother, pet. Happy birthday.'

'Thanks, Dad.'

Harley hangs up the phone. She picks up the birthday card from her parents and pockets the cash they have put inside it. The front of the card says, 'You're 30 Today!' – simple, factual, neither congratulating nor commiserating. Harley finds it apt. She is the last in the group to turn thirty and was expecting the day itself would either find her grieving the end of an era or rejoicing in the start of a new one. The reality is different. It is either numbness or calm; she cannot tell the difference between them anymore.

★　★　★

Maggie puts on a noughties playlist while they're sitting in front of the mirrored wardrobes in Róise's room, and it is almost as though they are back in university halls again, getting ready for a night out. Their electric-blue eyeshadow has been retired after many years of faithful service, and no one is drinking West Coast Cooler out of a Sports Direct mug because there aren't enough glasses to go around, but the hiss of heat as Maggie clamps curling tongs around the ends of her hair, the tangle of phone chargers snaking out of one exhausted adapter, the autotuned chorus of Ke$ha coming from Harley's speaker – all of it has the feel of a Tuesday night ten years ago. Maggie can practically feel the hairs on her arm stinging from a Limelight wristband stuck on at an awkward angle, her gag reflex triggered by the ghost of chocolate tequila shots past.

The first lot of people arrive early, most of them friends with small children who want to be back home for baths and bedtime stories. 'Sorry, *what?*' says Saoirse McConnell (Queen's University class of 2009). 'Mate, I've pumped enough milk for rush hour at Starbucks, I'm wearing a very heavy-duty breastplate, and I've brought my wedding gin – I'm not leaving this side of midnight.'

'Mine can't sleep without me,' say three other mothers in almost sinister unison. They erupt laughing, one of them trills, 'Jinx!' and they start into an animated focus group about night feeds and teething while Maggie and Róise show Saoirse to the ice and mixers in the kitchen.

'Why don't we invite her out more often?' Maggie whispers fondly when Saoirse has left the room.

'She's got a baby now?' Róise shrugs. 'She missed my birthday because she didn't want to be hanging for Bumps and Flumps or whatever the fuck it was.'

'Is Liam coming?' they hear Saoirse blare from the living room.

Maggie grimaces. 'No, *that's* why.' There was an intensely awkward period at university during which Saoirse used to joke about becoming Maggie's sister-in-law because she had a thing for Liam and felt they had an unspoken mutual affinity. (When Maggie told Liam about this years later, he said, 'Oh, *her*? Barely ever spoke to her – I always thought she was called Amy?') By coincidence, Saoirse seemed to lose interest in coming out with them once Liam began seeing Lydia. 'Can't put my finger on it, but I sometimes get the feeling Lydia is . . . like, *jealous* of me?' she once said drunk to Maggie. When Lydia died, Saoirse shared a photo on Instagram of the two of them in a club together, captioned with three broken-heart emojis. 'She's absolutely sold Lydia up the river for that picture,' Harley remarked. Lydia was squinting, her hand captured claw-like mid-gesticulation, while Saoirse beamed prettily up at the camera with not a whisker out of place.

'Is Liam coming, aye?' Róise asks Maggie.

'Aye, I think he's coming after the match.' Maggie opens the fridge to refill the wine glass she half drained when the toddler-talk commenced at the door. She has realized that spending her working life processing adoption court reports does not make her particularly good at child-centred chat in her free time. A friend once spoke reverently about the blissful maternal synergy of co-sleeping, and Maggie's only offering was to warn her that the risk of sudden infant death would be heightened if she took the baby to bed with her after she'd consumed alcohol. The friend (who had in their uni days been barred from more than one Belfast drinking establishment for trying to steal table lamps in her tote bag) reacted as though Maggie had personally accused her of trying to send the child to sleep by dipping its dummy in absinthe.

Harley comes into the kitchen. 'It's someone else's turn,' she mutters, nodding towards the living room. 'Who invited them?'

'You did,' Maggie points out.

'Yes, well, they used to be fun. Where's that gone? I've had to absent myself because judging by their faces, jokes about my own abortion are neither relevant nor funny.'

Maggie lasts longer than Harley in the living room, where she is asked by three different women (all of whom she has not seen in at least five years) whether she wants children, in the absurd sort of way people on reality TV dating shows ask, 'What's your type?' as if the answer is a succinct and easy one. *Brunette, tall, nice eyes. Two kids, a boy and a girl, ideally before I'm thirty-five.* Maggie often feels her answer is 'No,' and has said as much, and is then treated to a pop-psychology diagnosis about how a dead parent has probably dented her maternal instincts. On other occasions, friends and family members have shaken their heads and speculated that the cases she sees in work – children whose birth parents struggle with addiction and conflict and mental illness – might have left her disproportionately biased, speaking to her as though she is someone who has developed a wildly irrational fear of zombies by watching too many films about the apocalypse. Sometimes when people ask if she wants children, she says, 'Sure, maybe, someday,' thinking this is vague enough to avoid being psychoanalysed, and instead she is interrogated in detail about how she would engineer the whole thing: would she adopt, use a donor, would she carry the baby herself or would her partner, is she worried she might not bond with a child if they shared no DNA?

'Sorry, I'd better get the door,' Maggie eventually excuses herself.

Liam turns up with friends around nine o'clock, Cliftonville F.C. scarves thrown one by one on the coat rack. 'Mags, I can't remember who you've met: Ryan, Ben, Knoxy, Tommy, Dara . . .' He points at each of them in the now bustling hallway like a schoolteacher doing a headcount.

Dara, the last in line, jerks a thumb over his shoulder and says, 'This is my girlfriend Caitlín.'

Maggie is surprised that her wine glass does not shatter theatrically in her clenched hand, as Cate follows Dara through the front door.

'Cate?' This is not Maggie's confused exclamation, but Róise's. She glances sideways at Maggie.

'Ahh, do yous know each other?' Dara says, oblivious and apparently pleased.

'Mutual friends!' Maggie steps in to cover, trying to modulate the shrillness in her voice. 'We met at Vanessa Clarke's hen party.' Cate stands in total silence, looking very much like someone who has tried to edge out a soundless syllable of flatulence and has instead soiled the seat of her pants.

'Ahh, right, nice! I was working away the day of the wedding, gutted I missed it,' says Dara.

'Anything for the fridge?' Róise interjects, steering Dara down the hallway.

'So how have you *been*?' Cate says with overcooked cheeriness. When her boyfriend seems out of earshot, she adds, 'I'm . . . sorry, I didn't know we were coming to your house until we literally just got here. Dara just said we were going to a party.'

Maggie does not know which of her many questions could be satisfactorily answered in this particular moment of quiet chaos, so she says only, 'Caitlín?'

Cate looks relieved to be asked a question she knows how to respond to. 'People always struggled with *cawch-leen* when I went to uni in England. I thought of shortening it to Cait and then when I told people it was Cait with a C they spelled it Cate, and I quite liked it.'

'Why does Dara call you Caitlín?'

'Loads of people do. My parents still do.'

'Your parents have known you forever.' Maggie understands as she says it. *So has he.*

'Sorry, this is daft – I'll go, I'll say I'm not well.'

'No – stay.' Maggie cocks her head, as if she is a benevolent bouncer admitting Cate to a club without paying.

'You sure?'

'Of course.' The feeling is now one of having bumped into a favourite schoolteacher and their partner browsing the shelves in

211

Asda, the unearned outrage and bleak inevitability of discovering that, of *course*, the object of Maggie's infatuation has a personal life that does not include her.

Maggie comes face to face with Harley on her way to the bathroom. '*Cate*,' Harley hisses. 'Róise's told me. What the fuck?'

'Have you got any . . . ?' Maggie resists doing an unsubtle mime to indicate she means drugs, but Harley understands.

Harley blanches at the shift in topic. '*Oh*. No.' She thought about texting Frankie earlier this week, but her pride would not allow it. She tried a couple of people who'd sold her gear in the past, but one of them was on holiday and the other responded, *I don't do that anymore, sorry.* Harley read a subtextual 'grow up' in the latter message.

'Can you get some?' asked Maggie.

'I – have you asked anyone else?'

'Like who?'

'Never mind. Yeah. I'll try. Are you *sure*?'

'Don't patronize me.'

Harley plants a kiss on her forehead. 'Sorry. I'm on it.'

In the bathroom, Maggie unlocks her phone, opens her chat with Tess, and pauses. They have been texting a little in the weeks since their first meeting, but have not yet arranged another one. Between feeling rejected by Cate and being dumped by her therapist, Maggie has not felt much in the mood to go on a date and pretend to be well adjusted.

Hey! Are you out? Fancy coming to a party? x Maggie types and presses send before she has time to change her mind.

Less than two minutes later, Tess responds. *Hello! Aw I'd have*

loved that but am down in Cork this weekend. Hope you have a good time!
Fancy pints next Sat? xx

Maggie holds her hands under the hot tap to stop them shivering, and does not notice until they start to redden that the water is stinging her skin.

Harley spends an unacceptable amount of time adding and deleting a *Hey!* from the beginning of her message to Frankie, convinced that it looks deeply uncool but that the text reads as too abrupt without it. She experiments with other supposedly cavalier prefixes and considers that if she sends a message that opens with *Ahoy!* then Frankie might at least respond to check she isn't having a nervous breakdown. *Hello,* she sends at last, *are you around tonight, am looking to pick up. We're just at home; no worries if not.* She hopes that the reference to *we* will imply that the request is a collective one and not a solo effort to lure him out to her.

'Harley,' Róise beckons her in an undertone from the kitchen door.

'Sorry, yeah, I'm coming.'

'Do you think Frankie would drop off for me if I messaged him?' Róise murmurs. 'And would you mind?' Róise's eyes have the half-drawn blinds look that suggests she is already gently drunk.

'Did you not used to have a number for that Omagh lad with the mullet and the really good mandy?'

'He's not been about for ages. Went to work in Reykjavik.'

'Doing what?'

213

'Lead viola in the Iceland Symphony Orchestra.'

'Fuck me. Fair play.'

'Aye, he's doing all right for himself, like.'

Harley's phone vibrates in her hand. *no bother. what you after?*

'What you after?' she asks Róise.

Róise looks blank. 'Are *you* picking up?'

'Maggie wants to.'

'Why does *Maggie* want to?' says Róise, and then answers her own question with a sage nod: 'Cate's here.'

'Why do *you*?'

'Adam's coming.'

Harley sucks air through her teeth in the style of a pessimistic builder. 'Say no more.'

For the next twenty minutes until Frankie gets here, Harley has decided to presume, vainly and vehemently, that he wants to fuck her. She decides that he walked away from her when she kissed him because he feared the sheer strength of his feelings for her, because he thought it would be too complicated to fall for one of his tenants. There is little doubt in her mind that he will instead greet her with uneasy formality, place three small bags of powder quickly on the nearest available surface rather than risk touching her hand, and leave her with unspoken confirmation that they will never flirt over mould again. For the next twenty minutes, however, he is mad for her. He is flooring the pedal at amber lights like a pensioner running late for Mass. She is sketching personality around her eyes with a charcoal pencil and swapping her comfortable supermarket pants for the good guest pants (and then cutting the label off the good guest pants because they were also purchased in a supermarket but he doesn't need to know that).

She starts to wonder whether Frankie might take a look at the mound of everyone's coats half obscuring her bed and assess that it looks like too much hassle to have sex on. She remembers her mother once tutting because Harley had left the gate open at the front of the house. 'Well, that's just an invitation for burglars, isn't it?' she remarked, and Harley wondered what self-respecting criminal would be put off by so flimsy a hurdle as their garden gate, which is waist-height and rust-baked and slouching off its hinges. Still, she'd rather not risk it; she piles the coats up on the unused armchair in the corner of her room.

Here, he texts, a quarter of an hour later. He has parked in the street just in front of their house, still in the driver's seat but with the engine switched off. The doors click to unlock as she approaches, and she gets in the passenger side. He looks as he always does: shadow lining his jaw, coat collar flipped up against the cold.

'Hello,' she says, trying to ignore how far up her rear the good pants have ridden.

'Good party?' he says. The faint slap of an upbeat Taylor Swift song is coming from the front window, and someone in the living room has switched on the ancient rotating disco ball that she'd no idea still worked.

'Gas.'

'Special occasion, is it?'

'No. It's my birthday.'

'Is it, aye?' Frankie looks mildly impressed, as though birth-days are something only earned by a skilled few. 'How old?'

'Dirty thirty.'

'Well. Happy birthday.' He reaches into his coat and she fleet-ingly considers pretending to have left the cash in the house, inviting him inside while she goes to get it, but she can too easily imagine him saying, 'No worries, I'll wait here,' and her having to enact an embarrassing charade of going inside to fetch the money that is already in her back pocket.

'You coming in for one, aye?' Harley cocks her head towards the house, asking the question as though it is clearly rhetorical, as though he stops round their house for parties all the time.

He shrugs. 'If you say so.'

She shrugs in response. 'Well, if you don't *want* to . . .' She cracks the car door. So does he.

In the hallway, she tells Frankie, 'Everyone's dropping their coats in my room. Up the stairs, just to your right.'

In the kitchen, Harley gathers Róise and Maggie in a small, coven-style huddle. She palms each of them a small bag of powder. 'Go easy, okay?' she says to Maggie in particular.

'Why does everyone think I can't handle drugs?' Maggie hisses, annoyed.

'Because the only time we've seen you on them was my birth-day,' says Róise, 'and you ended up on a bathroom floor stroking the loo roll like it was made of swansdown.'

'Yes, well, the only time I've seen you drink absinthe you pre-tended to be Dutch to pull that medieval historian, and I don't remember anyone judging you for that.'

'Come on. Yous judged me a little bit.'

Harley shakes her head. 'Not my style.' She looks behind her to check no one is listening, then tells them, 'If anyone wants their coat, one of you needs to come and do a secret knock on my door.'

'What's the secret knock?' asks Róise.

'I don't fucking know. Do the opening bars of "Blue Monday".'

'Why are we knocking?' Maggie asks, suspicious.

Harley brings her palms together as if in prayer. 'The lord of the manor has come courting.'

'I don't know what that means. Are you getting your period?'

'Godspeed,' Róise overrules knowingly, dismissing Harley with a flap of her hand.

Harley sprints up the stairs, slowing to a strolling pace on the landing, opening her bedroom door casually. Frankie is glancing at his phone screen. Harley thrusts a bottle of beer towards him.

'Thank you,' he says.

'Do you want some?' she asks, tapping powder from the bag onto a small plate from the kitchen.

'Were you being good?'

'Sorry?'

'Hadn't heard from you in a while. Wondered if you were doing a detox,' says Frankie, nodding at the coke.

'No,' she says. She looks at him with an eyebrow raised. 'Thought I'd scared you off.' Harley has no paper money left on her person, so she rolls up a discarded train ticket and takes a hit.

Frankie is examining her intently when she lifts up her head. 'What's your angle?' he asks, shaking his head and frowning.

'There's no angle.'

'Seriously. What's broken? Are yous hiding a secret corpse in the walls?'

'We have no secrets.'

'Then what's your angle? Why am I here?'

'You ran out on me,' Harley comments. 'Last time.'

'You were drunk. And wired. And . . . feeling things.'

'Doesn't sound like me.'

'Didn't want to take advantage.' Frankie shrugs, and he looks at her as he does so. He wants validation, she thinks; he wants to hear that she didn't just go for him because she was drunk and feeling things. He wants to know that she wants him.

Harley offers him the rolled-up train ticket. He takes it, shifts closer, leans over her lap towards the plate. 'Driving?' she jokes.

'Taxi,' he says, and snorts the line. He does not move back from her afterwards.

'Or not,' she says. Frankie raises an eyebrow, smiling. Harley tips her head and adds, 'That's my angle.'

'Since when?'

'Always.'

'Lies.' His nose brushes against hers.

'Fine. Secret corpse in the walls.'

'Fine. Whose?'

'Yours. If you're lucky.'

This is shit wine,' Róise hisses at Maggie, refilling a glass at the fridge, drunk and nap-eyed.

'Why are you drinking it? There's more cava—'

'It's not mine.'

'Whose is it?'

Róise rolls her eyes. 'Cate's.'

'Why's she got you refilling her wine?'

'I offered. So she doesn't come in here.'

'*Why?*'

'*You're here.*'

'*You're pissed,*' Maggie says in a stage whisper.

'*I knowwww.*' Róise shuts the fridge too forcefully. '*Shh.*' It is unclear to her whether she is addressing Maggie or the fridge.

'Where's Adam?'

'On his way, *apparently*. I think he's trying to seem cool by turning up late.' Róise winces. 'I think he wants me to think he's *cool*.'

Róise's thoughts feel woolly, and she reopens the fridge, pours more wine into Cate's glass and passes Maggie a slim tin of something pre-mixed. Maggie immediately returns it to the shelf and says, 'Come on – you deliver that, and let's go upstairs.'

'Thought you'd never ask,' Róise says, giving Maggie a messy double-lidded wink that she instantly regrets.

In the living room, Cate is wedged into the sofa next to Dara, his arm resting around her shoulders. After sloshing chardonnay in Cate's lap (which she politely ignores), Róise stumbles upstairs to Maggie's bedroom. 'I'm steaming. I'm sorry,' she says as she shuts the door.

Maggie is sitting on her bed, and has put out a conservative quantity of coke on the surface of her phone screen. 'Don't be sorry. How's Cate? Still cosied up with her boyfriend?'

'No, I think they're talking to different people?' Róise lies.

'Or he was out for a smoke? Didn't see them together.' Either she is more convincing than she thinks, or Maggie simply wants to believe her.

Róise dumps out more powder and slices up two generous lines. 'Have you got a note?' Maggie doesn't have one, so they inhale through a rolled-up receipt from the Chip Company. Róise takes a deep breath.

'Are you all right?' asks Maggie, trying to pretend that the sharp hit of drugs to her nasal canal has not affected her in the slightest.

'Of course. Why?'

'Because I've not seen you this plastered since—'

'Oh, don't go there,' Róise groans. 'I'm not funeral-drunk, I promise.'

'Is this because of Adam?' Maggie's eyes are watering slightly, so it looks as though the question makes her emotional.

'Was that line too big?' asks Róise.

'Don't start with me.'

Róise's phone vibrates next to her. 'He's here,' she says. She necks the end of her glass of wine. 'You could always borrow him for an hour and pretend he's your boyfriend. See how Cate likes it.'

'Why is she *still* here?' groans Maggie.

'Do you want rid of her?'

'No,' Maggie sighs. 'Go on, go get the door.'

At the front door, Adam greets Róise with a smile and hands her a bottle of wine. He is wearing black jeans and a dark maroon jumper that looks as though it would be soft if she laid her cheek against it.

'Crémant?' she says, reading the wine label. '*You* can stay.'

'Thank fuck for that. Taxi driver nearly mowed into one of those beer bikes in town so I think I may need to sit down.' He looks suddenly stricken. 'Sorry – I shouldn't have brought up – you know . . .' His eyes dart around as though he expects a spectral Lydia to come howling through the walls.

'Don't be daft. What are you drinking, do you want anything put in the fridge?' She reaches for the plastic bags in his hand.

'Yeah, if there's room – I've got some beers. That's for you,' he says, handing her one of the bags.

Róise takes it and looks inside. A waxy-leaved succulent peers up at her. 'This is for me?'

'Yeah, I remember you saying you had a cactus so I thought I'd get you something that's also pretty low-maintenance.' He winces slightly. 'Sorry, I know you're moving out and it's another thing to take with you.'

'Stop apologizing. That's really kind, thank you.' She feels as though she is giving perfunctory thanks for one of the office whip-round birthday presents she's always been determined to avoid. 'I'll . . . I'll put this upstairs so it doesn't get damaged. Do you want to sort a drink out in the kitchen?' She passes the beers awkwardly back to him. 'I'll only be a minute.'

'Sure. Here, Róise . . .' He summons her eye contact, and she is suddenly worried he might be about to kiss her. Adam asks, 'What should I say if people ask how I know you?'

'Oh, no,' she replies, deadpan. 'Did you not get the case notes with your undercover profile?' Adam laughs. 'Just tell them the

221

truth,' Róise adds. 'You're a friend from work.' She leaves before she can see him looking disappointed.

Róise does another line of coke in her bedroom and puts Adam's plant next to her cactus on the windowsill. The plant is a stiff rosette with the purplish tint of a drinker's nose. Earlier today, she became concerned that he was going to turn up with flowers, but this is somehow more unnerving.

Róise leaves her room just as Frankie is sliding quietly out of Harley's. 'Róise, hi,' he says coolly, as though they are colleagues emerging from neighbouring offices.

'Is Harley in there?'

'Yeah, yeah . . . she's just fallen asleep.'

'Are you . . . heading off?'

'Oh, were you wanting some more . . . ?' He fumbles with his inside pocket.

'Does she know you're leaving?' Róise asks, already knowing the answer.

'I don't think she'd want me to overstay my welcome.'

'Have you asked Harley?'

'Have you *met* Harley?'

Róise clenches her jaw. 'Can I have two fifty bags, please?' Frankie hands them over, looking uncertain. He waits.

'Thanks!' Róise says brightly, offering no payment. 'Now fuck off.'

Adam is next to the turtle tank downstairs, chatting to Liam about the football score. 'The famous turtle!' he says to Róise as she approaches, looking down at Barnaby.

'The famous Adam!' Liam says enthusiastically, pointing from Adam to Róise. Liam agreed to come to their house for a party on the condition that he could be extremely drunk by the time he arrived. He has only been here twice since Lydia died, and Róise tried to convince him to adopt Barnaby on both occasions, without any success.

'*Famous*,' Róise snorts, not looking Adam in the eye.

'Lovely meeting you, mate,' Liam says, pulling Adam in for a hearty clap on the back. 'Excuse me, I need another drink.'

'He seems nice,' Adam says. 'So he's Maggie's brother?'

'Cousin, technically, but his parents raised her when her mum died, so basically, yeah,' she says, each syllable staccato.

'Are you all right?'

'Yeah! Of course! Why?'

'You seem . . .' He narrows his eyes slightly as they look into hers. 'Are you on something?'

'Yeah, do you want any?'

'Coke?'

'Aye.'

Adam looks embarrassed. 'I do, but I shouldn't. Had a bit of a bad relationship with it when I was in my twenties.'

'I don't do it *that* often,' she says, instantly defensive. 'Just fancied it tonight. Settle the nerves.'

'Ah yes, cocaine, famously the most calming of drugs,' he laughs.

'Don't do that,' she snaps.

Adam looks thrown. 'What?'

'You always get on like you're fucking *judging* me.'

223

'What are you *talking* about?' Adam looks around as though he senses he has been lured into a trap, invited into the second act of an argument in which he is the undisputed villain.

Róise's thoughts are all at once ablaze like the twelfth of July, and she does not stop to consider how it has happened. She storms out of the living room and up the stairs, hoping he will follow her, since this will mean he has only himself to blame for whatever she is about to say to him. Adam comes after her, follows her into her bedroom. She throws another quantity of coke on the bedside table, not really wanting it, a performance of self-medication to show him that Something Is Wrong.

'Róise,' he says, sitting down on the bed next to her. 'Come on, talk to me.'

'I don't want to talk to you.'

'Did you invite me here just to have a go at me? Just tell me what's wrong. Why do you think I'm judging you?'

'Because you are. You always are.'

'For what, doing a bit of coke at a house party? You should have seen me back in the day, Róise, I'm in no position to be judging anyone.'

'ADAM!' she shouts at him. 'We're the same fucking age!' He has no answer to this, and waits for a follow-up statement. 'You and your fucking "*back in the day*" – you never shut up about how you *used* to have a drug problem and shag around and work a shit job and drink tequila and live in minging flats. Your *back in the day* is just my fucking *day*, mate.'

Róise can see a number of very valid defences line up behind

Adam's eyes. She knows somewhere in her heart that she is being unfair. But she is angry, and he is here.

'Do you want to talk,' he asks, 'or would you rather I left?'

'Neither,' she says, irritated.

They sit in silence for a few moments before he speaks. 'I can stay,' Adam offers, 'and you can shout at me for a bit if you want to. Only because I don't think it's really me you're angry with.'

Róise wants to go to the window and tear both of her sturdy little plants from their roots, not caring about the cactus spines shredding the skin of her hands. Instead, she reaches out slowly to touch Adam's arm. His jumper is soft, as she thought it would be. He allows her to bury her face in it, and she is not sure whether she wants to be soothed or suffocated.

At midnight, Cate opens the door of Harley's room with a lacklustre knock. Harley is lying prone on her bed, scrolling unseeing through her phone. Cate looks around for her coat. Her eyes settle on the black-and-white print Blu-tacked to the wall. 'Who's that?' she asks.

'Maud Gonne. Coats are over there.'

'Who is she?'

'Archbishop of Canterbury. Taxi on its way?'

'You don't like me very much, do you?'

Harley sits up. 'She was an Irish revolutionary. Suffragette. Yeats's muse.'

'Right. Like your tattoo.'

'No. This is Joyce,' says Harley, looking at her inked forearm. It says *I'd love to have the whole place swimming in roses* in decade-old cursive; the ink has started to fray and feather like a wrist stamp the morning after a night out. The line is from the last chapter of Joyce's *Ulysses*, which she has, to this day, never read. 'How do you know that?'

'How do I know you don't like me? Because you act like you don't like me.'

'No, I mean, how do you know that about my tattoo? I mean, you're wrong, but still. Same ballpark.'

'You told me once.'

'When?'

'When I asked.' Cate sits down on the end of Harley's bed. 'Have you got any——?'

'I fucking *knew* you were going to ask that.' The bag of coke is in Harley's hand before she can think better of it. Frankie has gone, and she hungers for company like an abandoned mongrel.

'I was going to ask if you had any other tattoos,' Cate says sardonically. They glare at each other, neither wanting to break first. Cate relents. 'But if you're offering . . .'

Harley chops up two lines. When Cate has taken hers, Harley asks, 'Is your *boyfriend* not missing you?' She puts an unintended stress on the word, like schoolgirl teasing, as though she is pointing at a picture of an ugly French boy in a textbook. *There's your boyfriend.*

'He's too steaming. He's at the workshopping-sitcom-ideas level of steaming.'

'Good match, was it?' she asks, meaning the football. Cate does not reply, and Harley wonders whether she has hilariously misunderstood the question, taken it to be a query about her compatibility with Dara, as though people went around speaking of *good matches* like characters in a Jane Austen novel.

'Why *don't* you like me?' Cate demands.

Harley looks affronted. 'You come into my house, on the day of my daughter's wedding—'

'That's not even the line.'

'What's that even from?'

'You've never seen *The Godfather*?' Cate scoffs.

'*That's* why I don't like you,' says Harley.

'Because I appreciate good cinema?'

'Because you act like you're better than everyone else. You're not lamenting the fact that I've never seen *The Godfather*. You *love* that I've never seen it because it makes you feel superior.'

'As if *you* didn't love that I don't know who Maud Gonne is.' Harley is silent, thinking. 'You're trying to work out whether there was a wrong double negative in that sentence.' Harley's mouth twitches. Cate, quite generously, changes the subject. 'What are you doing up here on your own, anyway?'

Harley pushes out a long breath. 'I had sex with our landlord.'

'When?'

'About an hour ago? He left.'

'So wait, sorry – are you hiding up here because you're ashamed you slept with your landlord, or because you're ashamed you slept with *a* landlord, or because you're ashamed you slept with *a*-slash-*your* landlord and he left immediately afterwards?'

'Who said I was hiding? Or ashamed?'

'Aren't we all?' Cate says ruefully, eyeing the half-full bottle of prosecco on Harley's bedside table. Harley is about to offer her some, but Cate reaches across of her own accord and takes it by the neck. She drinks too quickly, hiccups, shudders.

'What are *you* ashamed of?' Harley demands.

Cate thinks for a moment, then says, 'I didn't mean to, you know.'

'Didn't mean to . . . ?'

'Maggie.'

'Does your boyfriend know?'

'No.'

'So you two don't have some kind of *arrangement*. He's not downstairs getting rimmed by my cousin Barry.'

'I've known Dara since we were children. We got together at school. We went to the same uni. Moved in together straight after.' Cate's voice is matter-of-fact, as though she is reciting a history lesson: *divorced, beheaded, died; divorced, beheaded, survived.*

'Does he know you like women?'

'No.'

'*Do* you like women, or were you just—'

'I wasn't. Don't say it.'

Cate looks so downcast, Harley almost – *almost* – feels sorry for her. 'Here,' she says, trying to lighten the mood. 'Nothing wrong with experimenting. I tried fisting once, didn't like it, never went there again.'

'I never really got to try things.'

Harley waves her hand dismissively. 'Everyone thinks that. You could be the Marquis de Sade and you'd probably still have existential FOMO.' She wonders at how quickly this line trips off her tongue, thinks it might have been something Lydia once said to her when Harley was concerned about being a virgin at twenty-two. Cate does not look reassured. Harley tips out more cocaine, not remembering whether their last hit was five or forty-five minutes ago.

When they have each taken another line, Cate swipes her finger across the plate and rubs the dust into her gums. A minute later, Harley can taste it on Cate's lips, on her tongue; her mouth and mind seem to slowly lose all feeling.

Maggie has to cling to the fridge door as she opens it, heart knocking against her ribcage like a neighbour with a noise complaint.

The music has been turned down low in the living room to accommodate a game of Never Have I Ever, which, when everyone is in their thirties, becomes less of a light-hearted drinking game and more of an informal support group. In the kitchen, Maggie shivers from the draught; two friends are standing vaping at the open back door, desperate to keep in with the smoking crowd outside. A plume of vapour drifts across Maggie's path, strawberry-scented and sickly, and her throat constricts.

Harley is suddenly in the kitchen, empty wine glass dangling from her hand. She stares at Maggie. 'Mags,' she says, 'can I . . .' She hesitates, and then says, 'Can I just get past you to the fridge?'

'Yes.' Maggie does not shift.

'Could you just . . .' Harley asks, hand on the fridge door.

No, Maggie thinks. She cannot move. It's happening again.

★ ★ ★

Róise and Harley each take Maggie under one arm and guide her slowly out of the kitchen and towards the stairs – slowly, because she needs a lot of encouragement to put one foot in front of the other. Her breathing is laboured and she looks sick with dread. 'Should we *call* someone?' says Róise.

'She's having a panic attack.'

'Are you sure?'

'Yes. She had a few bad ones last year, they were just like this.'

'*When?*'

'I don't have exact dates, Róise – it was probably when you were in your *Yellow Wallpaper* era,' Harley replies bitterly.

Róise snaps back, 'Well, if you knew that, why the fuck would you give her coke?' Róise tries not to think about the size of the lines she cut up for Maggie earlier.

'She *asked* me! I'm not her fucking mother!'

Cate starts to come down the stairs just as Maggie, still hoisted between Harley and Róise, sinks to her knees around the middle step. 'What's happened, what's wrong with her?' Cate asks, looking at Harley with mild horror.

'Too much fun,' is Harley's curt reply. 'Can you move, please, so we can get up here.'

'Let me help—'

'I think you've done enough,' says Róise, and Harley almost bursts out laughing at how melodramatic it sounds in this moment. Cate lowers her eyes, chastened; or perhaps she is on the verge of laughing too.

'Maggie?' says Liam, coming out of the living room. 'Is she all right?'

'We're just putting her to bed,' Harley says over her shoulder.

'Here, let me lift her. Maggie, come here, you're all right,' says Liam, starting up the stairs.

'We've got her, it's fine!' says Róise.

'Don't be stupid, just let me—'

Adam is on the upstairs landing now, having heard the commotion and emerged from the bathroom. He ventures down the stairs behind Cate. 'Can I do anything? I know first aid – do you want me to—'

'Can you all just fuck off?' barks Harley.

Maggie's heart is pounding in her ears, as though her mind is trapped in the boot of a car and hammering to be let out. She feels as though the floor is warping and caving under her knees. And then, before anyone realizes what is happening, the staircase opens up beneath them.

three

sure you know yourself

No one is mortally wounded. There are a few minor splinters, but most of the wood has rotted to a feathery texture that is soft rather than spiky to the touch. Maggie is scratched and in shock, but otherwise fine. Róise sustains some bruising, and Harley sprains her wrist. 'Will I be able to play the piano?' she later asks the doctor.

'Very funny,' the doctor says.

'No, I'm being serious,' says Harley. 'I've got an exam in May.' She is told it is a mild sprain that should heal within a few weeks.

Everyone flees the party after the stairs collapse, clearly worried that the rest of the house will shortly follow. Cate leaves with her boyfriend, head bent, not making eye contact with anyone. Adam checks none of them are concussed, and asks Róise if she or anyone else needs to stay at his flat for the night, although he seems awkward and slightly too formal. Róise thanks him and declines, and Adam leaves too. The three of them – Harley, Maggie, Róise – go with Liam to his flat, almost empty-handed, unable to access any of their bedrooms or most of their possessions at their own house. Harley passes out on his sofa around three a.m., and wakes up at nine to a throbbing wrist and a surprisingly coherent text that Róise sent to their group chat with Frankie in the small hours of the morning, telling him that the stairs have caved in and passive-aggressively suggesting that he might want to send someone round to have a look at his earliest convenience. Frankie responds with a single thumbs-up.

'Right,' says Róise, visibly hungover and yet still quite businesslike. 'What the fuck now?'

They make arrangements for where they will go while their hallway looks like a small bomb has exploded in it. Liam insists that Róise stay at his flat as long as necessary, since her nearest family is a ninety-minute drive up the M1. Maggie will go to her aunt and uncle's. Harley has no choice but to go home to her parents.

Neither Maggie nor Róise make reference to anything else that happened at the party. Harley wonders if they feel as she does, a strange relief that the headline catastrophe has eclipsed everything else; relief that, for now, they can only speak of practical things and do not yet have to sort through the smaller devastations of the night before.

Harley's mother shows her to her old bedroom. Mum has redecorated it in neutral tones, papering over the black walls that Harley wanted when she was fifteen. The bed frame is the same, a single bed that creaks when she breathes, and her bookshelves are still there, although the titles have all been arranged by the colour of their spine, which was certainly not Harley's doing. When she asks, Mum says that Marianne was photograph-ing them for Instagram. She shows Harley her sister's social media, a grid with autumnal filters filled with beige fashion and expensive coffees and books that Harley recognizes as her own.

Harley asks if she can sleep in the spare room — Liz's old room — since it's larger. Mum hesitates, because the spare room has become Marianne's unofficial bedroom during her periodic break-ups; the drawers are full of her clothes and one side of the room is taken up with her exercise equipment. Marianne's old teenage bedroom is also packed with clothes and knick-knacks and stuffed toys and magazines, possessions more than a decade old that she hasn't got round to clearing out yet.

Harley settles for her own old room, sinking onto the bed and looking up at the bookshelves. Her vision is warped by out-of-date glasses. When she left Liam's this afternoon, her eyes were gasping with dryness under contact lenses that were in their thir-tieth hour of use. The first thing she did when she arrived at her parents' house was ask her dad if he had any of her old glasses. He had always taken them when her prescription was updated, saying he knew how and where they could be recycled. Since this was something he had never actually got around to doing, he presented her with a shoebox full of various pairs of spectacles from the last twenty years, right back to the wiry little frames she'd worn in pri-mary school. The pair she wears now is at least ten years old and the rainbow stripes of the bookcase all blur into each other.

Maggie sends them a message from her aunt and uncle's on Sunday evening, telling them she's just been back to the house.

MAGGIE, Harley responds immediately.

We don't know it's safe, you eejit, says Róise. *Why would you go back??*

We forgot about Barnaby, Maggie replies.

Frankie updates them midweek over text. The hallway and stairs, he says, are going to be 'a big job', and he does not expect the house will be habitable for weeks. 'You don't say,' Harley whispers at her phone screen. He tells them that the builders are clearing the debris, and that he will work out a way of letting them upstairs so they can pack some things. A ridiculous image pops into Harley's head, of Frankie showing her a string of knotted bedsheets by which he escaped out of the window when she had fallen asleep the night of the party.

Instead, a ladder rests against the landing when Harley and Róise let themselves into the house several days later. Harley has procured new contact lenses, and is grateful not to be climbing it half blind. She and Róise take it in turns to go upstairs, throwing their essentials into suitcases at high speed. Róise comes down while Harley is in the kitchen, packing a shopping bag with leftover spirits. The kitchen is a cemetery of empty bottles, beer cans squashed and lying on their sides like felled soldiers.

'Planning another party?' Róise comments, nodding at Harley's clanking bag.

'I'm living with my mother. Needs must.'

'Here.' Róise seems to suddenly remember something, and fumbles with her purse. She pulls out two plastic baggies of coke and hands them to Harley. 'I don't want this, you have it.'

'That's more than I bought on Saturday,' Harley says, frowning.

Róise grimaces. 'These were on the house.'

Harley has been putting off seeing Maggie, because that will mean telling her about Cate. Harley considers not telling her – it was a single, silly, far-from-sober kiss, and Maggie and Cate aren't even together, and everything Cate has done is surely far worse. She thinks perhaps it would even be unkind for Harley to add this to Maggie's hurt, and she then thinks selfishly about how bad she would look should Cate tell Maggie herself. She cannot help thinking of Lydia with gloomy sympathy.

Harley arranges to meet Maggie in a bar near the hotel when she has finished her Friday evening shift. Maggie goes in for a hug when she arrives. 'This is so strange,' she says. 'You really get out of the habit of hugging someone when you live with them.'

They order drinks. 'How've you been?' Harley asks. 'How's home?'

'It's grand, aye. I've watched about a thousand episodes of *Murder, She Wrote*. And my Uncle Sean is obsessed with Barnaby.'

'Did you go to pick up the tank?'

'Yes. And a load of my clothes. You've been back?'

'Aye, couldn't do another day in someone else's minging work uniform.' Harley stirs the ice in her drink. 'How's the head?'

Maggie looks sheepish. 'Fine. I don't think drugs agree with me.'

'Any more panic attacks?'

'No. Aoibh and Sean's house feels . . . safe.' Maggie drinks thoughtfully. 'Can't last forever, I suppose. But it's nice for now.'

'Have you heard from Cate?'

'What do you think?'

Harley takes a deep, shaking breath. 'I need to tell you something.'

Maggie laughs. 'I already know.'

'Sorry, *what*?'

'I know you slept with Frankie. Róise told me that night.' Maggie looks at Harley's stricken expression. 'Oh God, are you really embarrassed about it? *Harley*. I'm no judge of male beauty but he's not the most hideous conquest in the world.'

'Maggie.' Harley presses her hands to her eyes. 'It's not that.'

'Come on, then – spit it out.'

Say it. 'Cate kissed me.' The slight untruth tastes bitter in her mouth. She drowns it with vodka.

Maggie is briefly silenced. 'What?' she whispers.

'She came to get her coat. She was fucking rude.' Harley swallows. 'I gave her a line. It happened really quickly.'

'Sorry.' Maggie stops her, shaking her head. 'Circling back for a second, how do you get from Cate being rude to you offering her a line?'

'I was off my fucking box, Maggie, I'm so sorry. Mad drunk, half a bag down, Frankie had pissed off like a thief in the fucking night . . .'

Maggie looks at her, all at once terrifyingly calm. 'You sound like Lydia.'

'Lydia made a mistake,' Harley says quietly. 'So did I.'

'Did you fuck? You and Cate.'

'No! Maggie, I swear to you—'

'You know, I want to be absolutely raging,' says Maggie, 'but the sad thing is that it actually doesn't really surprise me.'

'Well, yeah, sure you know what Cate's like—'

'I don't mean Cate, I mean you.'

Harley looks into Maggie's eyes, now cold, and feels a scalding rush of temper. 'What a classy thing to say.'

'As *if* you're lecturing me on how to be classy.'

'As if *you're* making this much fuss about one stupid kiss. What are we, in fucking school?'

'If it wasn't a big thing then why were you so scared to tell me?' Maggie snaps.

Harley talks over her: 'Jesus Christ, Maggie, it's not as if she's your girlfriend.'

'I'm not angry because she's my *girlfriend*, I'm angry because she's a *cunt*, Harley. She's been a fucking cunt to me, and you're my best friend.' The frosty veneer is splintering, and Maggie looks as though she might be about to cry. She necks the end of her drink and stands up.

'Maggie,' Harley says, softly pleading as Maggie puts on her coat. She does not know what else to say, so adds only, 'We didn't fuck. I promise.'

'I don't believe you.'

'Why don't you believe me?'

'Because I know you,' Maggie says, and she leaves.

Another party; someone else's, this time. It is later that night and Harley has found friends. Two girls who used to work at the hotel, Tina and Jen, though she cannot remember which is which. They run into each other in town. 'You're still at it?' Tina or Jen marvels when Harley says she's stayed working at the same hotel. The two women were both masters students when they worked behind the bar with Harley, and left as soon as they'd graduated. She remembers missing them, at the time. They were terrible bartenders but wonderful gossips.

They invite her to someone's birthday at a house on the Newtownards Road, and the three of them squeeze into a taxi together. Harley sits in the front seat and tries to check her phone, entering the wrong passcode several times and dropping it down the side of her seat. Her fingers are numb from drinking, although she slurs to the taxi driver that she has a sprained wrist and waves her bandaged hand in his direction. She stayed in the same bar after Maggie left and ordered a bottle of white wine, and then moved on to whiskey, and then stopped in another pub telling herself it was one for the road, and then she met Jen and Tina. She pretended to have been out with friends just prior to seeing them. She sifts through her memories and tries to remember if she ever did coke with either of them during post-work socials, and if so, which one – Jen or Tina? – and whether they were good company. Harley has the bags Róise gave her in a zipped pocket of her purse; she has done two or three or maybe more lines already, but it wasn't as much fun alone, and she ended up forcing the long-suffering waitress behind the bar to listen to a slightly manic tirade about *Game of Thrones*.

The two women have not brought their own alcohol to the party, so Harley decides to assume the contents of the fridge are fair game, and she makes herself a gin and tonic. Someone taps her on the shoulder and she turns around, drafting a defence in case someone is about to challenge her for theft. A boy stretches out his arms as though cheerfully offering himself up for crucifixion. 'Harley O'Farrell! As I live and breathe!'

'We've met,' Harley gauges, pointing at him with mild suspicion.

'Come on, I know you're bad with names, but . . .' He looks at her with encouragement. The pause is too long. 'It's Fergal,' he says at last, bravado ebbing visibly.

'*Fergal* . . .' Harley says, slowly processing. 'Shit! Fergal. Hello.'

'We have *got* to stop meeting like this,' he says, tipping his head to one side, quite the coquette. She remembers now that he was full of these lines that he probably thought made him sound like Cary Grant but that made next to no sense in context. In fairness to him, she concedes, she probably came out with worse, thinking she sounded like Katharine Hepburn and not a bladdered gorgon.

'What you doing here, who do you know?' she asks.

He throws his head back laughing. 'This is my house. Although I can understand why you wouldn't necessarily remember the kitchen.'

Harley cannot recall the bedroom or the bathroom either, but she does not say so. She looks around the room, full of people she does not recognize. Gina and the other one (what were their names, she wonders) have disappeared. It is almost comforting to see a familiar face in Fergal, despite having needed prompting about quite why it was familiar to her.

'Is it someone's birthday?' she asks, squinting at the streamers hung from the kitchen door.

243

'That would be mine.'

'Fuck off! Happy birthday, mate.'

'Thanks, pal!'

Perhaps, she thinks, they could be friends. Even just for tonight. Harley snaps her fingers and points gunslinger-style at him, something she has never done before and hopes never to do again. 'I have a birthday present for you.'

Fergal looks confused at being led to the bathroom, but perks up when she produces cocaine. 'Aw, mint!' he says, Christmas-morning glee spreading across his face. 'We could have done this in my room, though, you know.'

'I like bathrooms,' Harley says, sprinkling out a quantity on the toilet lid, which is very clean. 'Do you live with friends?'

'No, just me. I lived with my brother, but he moved to Edinburgh.'

'Your bathroom is very clean,' she comments, doing two lines in quick succession.

'I'm a clean person. Did you think I must live with someone else to have a clean bathroom?' he laughs. He dithers over which nostril to use, and then snorts a line carefully.

'I did wonder. I don't know why.'

Fergal sits back on the bath mat. 'You know, when I said we could have done this in my room . . .' Harley waits for the suggestive comment. '. . . I didn't mean . . . like *that*. Sorry, I wasn't trying to be creepy.'

'I didn't think you were.'

'You did, and I get it. You made a pretty fast exit last time,' he says, looking sheepish.

Harley sighs, and then smiles at him. 'You're not creepy. Maybe just a bit cringe sometimes.'

Fergal rolls his head back and groans. 'Jesus, that's *worse*.'

A laugh erupts from her, surprisingly unforced. They talk for a while longer. He asks if she's all right. 'You look tired,' he says.

'I am tired.'

'Well, if you need to head on, I'll understand. You don't have to sprint out while I'm in my pants.'

Harley smiles again. 'You should go downstairs. It's your party.'

'Is that code for you needing a shit?'

'Here,' she says, handing him the remaining bag. There is less in it than she thought, but he still looks pleased. 'Don't spend it all in one shop. Find some friends.'

'You don't want this?'

'I've had enough,' says Harley.

The night is cold. Harley wanders down the road alone and tries one taxi firm after another. She should have ordered one before leaving, but she could not stand to be around people a minute longer, even nice ones, like Jen and Tina probably were, and like Fergal somehow turned out to be.

A car pulls up beside her, a printed sign saying TAXI taped crookedly on the inside of the back passenger window. 'Need a taxi, love?'

'I've got one, thanks,' Harley says. The car drives off; she thinks of Lydia and wonders whether she should have noted his licence-plate number. Too late now.

She looks at the last resort in her phone contacts and she taps the screen. It rings three times before he answers. 'I'm really sorry to ring so late,' she says, 'but can you come and bring me home?'

When she has hung up the phone, Harley goes again to the C. S. Lewis statue, her old friend, and sits on the chair outside the wardrobe, waiting. She draws her coat close around her, and her breath mists in spirals. The stars are out.

The car arrives. Harley gets into the passenger seat, her hair tangled and falling into her eyes. 'Been busy tonight, mate?' she jokes.

'Last job and then I'm clocking off,' Dad says with a jocular smile. 'Good night?'

Harley reaches for an answer, and then sobs begin to tear violently out of her. She drops her head so her hair forms a curtain and her father cannot see her face. She feels him put a hand on her shoulders, rub her back as though she is a baby needing winded.

'We'd better get on, before your mum starts to worry,' she hears him say eventually, and he puts the car in gear and pulls away from the kerb. She cannot stop crying. The car slows down a few moments later, and a voice crackles just outside the driver's side window. 'What's yours?'

'Two teas, please. Wee splash of cold water in both.'

When the order is handed to him, Dad puts her tea in the cupholder, and drives on.

'Thanks, Dad,' Harley says, sniffling. The tea warms her hands until she is home.

back in the day

A month after leaving the house, a month in Liam's box room, and Róise is keen to have a proper talk about where the three of them are going to live, which is made difficult by the fact that two of the three of them are now not speaking to each other.

Róise has tried to spend as little time as possible in Liam's flat, other than going there to sleep. She feels guilty taking up space there during the evenings and over the weekend. Liam's box room is crammed with a pull-out sofa bed and piles of things that don't have a place anywhere else in the flat: a snowdrift of spare bedding and towels, two mismatched side tables, a crate of Bordeaux (he does not drink red wine), a cat litter tray (he has never owned a cat), and several battered grey ring-binders that contain his lecture notes from university. 'Sorry the room's not in better shape,' he apologizes every two to three days. She tells him not to be daft. 'I'll be out of your hair as soon as I can,' she says every two to three days. He tells her not to be daft. They coexist very peacefully, but Róise feels as though she is going to sleep each night in her sister's childhood Wendy house, in which Ciara used to pack away clutter to give the illusion that she had tidied her bedroom.

At the end of the month, Róise goes to stay with her sister in Omagh. She has tried for the last two weeks to make weekend plans with Maggie and Harley, but Harley is not responding to texts and Maggie makes excuses, clearly convinced that Róise is trying to lure her and Harley together for a reconciliation. Róise understands; Harley tried a few times to engineer a meeting between Róise and Lydia after they fell out, which Róise did not appreciate.

Róise has scrolled through her contacts, wondering half-heartedly whether she should catch up with other friends from school or university, but most of them were at Harley's birthday party and Róise is not sure she has anything left to say to them until the next large gathering a year or more from now.

Last weekend, she spent Saturday and Sunday in town, sleep-walking in and out of every film showing at the Dublin Road cinema. Adam asked if she saw anything she'd recommend, but all of them are blurred together, Ruth Bader Ginsburg wrestling with Florence Pugh in her memory.

Adam has checked in on her regularly since the party, but they have not spent any time together outside of work. They chatted in the office kitchen and corridors, and it gave Róise a thrill at first, as though they were roleplaying that they were still only colleagues and that nothing was wrong, and she flirted a little with him until he began to look concerned and asked if she was getting enough sleep, apparently reading her coyness as exhaustion.

Róise takes a walk into Omagh town centre on Saturday afternoon, wandering in and out of the shops. She had a vague notion of getting a magazine and going for a coffee, but the Carlisle bookshop at the top of the high street has been shut since last year, and the other newsagents in town only seem to have publications with headlines like 'Alligator MAULED my sister, and then we FELL IN LOVE!' so she decides to pass. She browses the charity shops and buys a second-hand Maeve Binchy and a brown suede-look blazer. She takes a photo of herself wearing the jacket and types out a message: *£7 in Oxfam, it's giving Meg Ryan*, and then looks at the most recent texts that Maggie and Harley have ignored, and closes WhatsApp. She has opened and closed the app several times this afternoon already, wanting to take photos of ludicrous book covers and a crystal yoni egg that someone has innocently put on display among the bric-a-brac, and send them to Adam. She has resisted, afraid of falling into an endless exchange of rolling news. Their text conversations to date have had a clear beginning, middle and end, and have usually centred on where and when they plan to meet up, with an occasional postscript agreeing that they'd had a nice time.

'How's it going with your man, anyway? Should I tell Ma to start shopping for hats?' Ciara asks that evening, spooning some marmalade-looking concoction into Finn's mouth at the kitchen table.

'Oh, shut up.'

'Language,' she says, wiping the baby's chin.

'I've only been seeing him a few weeks.'

'Best ride you've ever had, you said.'

'How are you allowed to say *that* in front of *him*,' demands Róise, pointing at Finn, 'but "shut up" is a step too far?'

'Do you want to keep seeing him? Domhnall's got a friend

in Belfast who you met at the christening keeps asking if you're "back in the game yet".'

'Seriously, Ciara? "Will you meet my mate?"' she says in a mock schoolgirl tone. 'Which friend?' she then asks curiously.

'Alex Maguire.'

Róise pulls a face. 'Didn't he get drunk at the christening and tell everyone he'd eaten his sister's placenta?'

'Yes. He's great craic. Good-looking boy. Works for a charity.'

'I'll pass, thanks.'

Ciara jabs the plastic spoon in Róise's direction. 'Alex Maguire doesn't really want to date you. I made that up so you'd think about whether you want to go out with other people or whether you like this Adam lad. Which you clearly do.'

'This does not seem like a legitimate therapy technique.'

'Don't care, I'm not your therapist.'

'I'm not turning down Alex Maguire because I'm really into Adam, I'm turning down Alex Maguire because he eats placenta.'

'You can't turn down Alex Maguire, because he's not asked you out.'

Róise sighs. 'You're starting to sound like Granny. "Who do you think you are, Taylor Swift?"'

'Well, she's right. Give over listening to the piano version of "Forever and Always" and catch yourself on.'

'Do people pay you for this shite?'

'*Language*, please.'

In the office on Monday, it is Juliet's birthday. Róise vaguely remembers an email sent round with someone's bank details, inviting donations for a gift. She does not remember signing a card, although perhaps it was only offered to those who sent a contribution towards prosecco and perfumed bath oil. Juliet is delighted to be the centre of attention. 'Did you make these?' she asks Róise, pointing to the wheel of cupcakes assembled on the table, cream-frosted and freckled with edible rose petals.

'No,' says Róise, surprised at being asked. Sandra, who clearly spent some money on the cupcakes in Marks & Spencer, looks put out at the suggestion.

'I just remember you making those gorgeous traybakes for the Christmas feed a couple of years ago. You've *got* to bring them in again sometime,' says Juliet. 'Here, get yourself a plate.'

Róise accepts a paper plate and does a short lap of the buffet. She has eaten erratically since being at Liam's, reluctant to spend too much time in the kitchen in case she's in the way, not wanting to take up his space with her groceries. She has spent far too much money on sandwiches and limp salads from the office canteen, she chain-drinks cans of Diet Coke, and she snacks on the biscuits that people leave in communal territory on top of the filing cabinet. She packs her paper plate now with miniature traybakes, a sausage roll, crisps of two different flavours. She eats it all and goes in for second, then third helpings, then eats a sickly-sweet cupcake when she knows she is already full. The rose petals wilt in her bile half an hour later.

Adam calls her into his office in the afternoon. 'Are you all right?' he says quietly, closing the door.

'Yes? Why?'

'Juliet said she heard you being sick. You look a bit pale.'

251

'I'm not wearing makeup.' This is true. She ran out of foundation around a week ago, and it generally takes her at least a fortnight to get around to replacing her makeup when it runs out. She can usually scrounge products from Maggie or Harley in the interim, but this is now, of course, not an option.

'Were you sick?'

Róise did not realize there was anyone in the toilets at the time, and her blush betrays her. 'I think the sausage rolls disagreed with me.'

'Are you sure?' Adam's brow creases as he looks at her. 'Róise, there's not . . . should I be worried about anything?'

'God, *no*. I'm not *pregnant*,' she whispers, appalled. 'I ate too much, and I was sick. Nothing to worry about.'

Adam catches her eye. 'Did you *make* yourself sick?'

Róise almost gags again, managing to protest: 'Are you mental?'

'Sorry, it's none of my business. You're just . . . you eat loads when we're out for dinner, but you've lost weight the last few weeks, and I did the whole bulimic thing, back in the—' He stops, and Róise wonders if he is embarrassed for disclosing personal information, or for starting to say 'back in the day' after the argument they had. 'You don't have to talk to me. But you can, if you want. And I will of course be very offended since I made those rocky roads and it's not a very encouraging comment on my baking skills,' he adds for levity.

Róise wishes he would revert to being the recruitment manager with whom she occasionally flirts, and at the same time wishes he would gather her up in his arms and allow her to cry for the next three to five business days.

'I'm fine,' she says. 'There's no need to worry. Your rocky roads were lethal.'

That evening, Róise settles into her sofa bed with her phone and laptop and a bottle of white wine from the nearest off-licence. The shop displays its wines in a light-piped cabinet that pretends to be a fridge but has no actual cooling function, and the liquid is thick and tepid in her glass. She schedules appointments for the coming fortnight. Maggie and Harley, to discuss their plans for the next quarter. Frankie, to give their official notice on the house and negotiate the retrieval of their possessions and damage deposit. Adam, for an informal chat about her job prospects. Adam again, for a formal chat about their relationship (professional or otherwise) moving forward. The last appointment, due to scheduling availability, will end up being the first. Tomorrow, six o'clock at Lavery's.

'I found a bag of your T-shirts,' says Róise, taking a drag of a disposable plastic vape on the roof terrace. She sampled someone's vape at Harley's birthday party, a strawberry-flavoured mouthful that felt like having a sweet snack, and she bought one of her own last week to distract her from being hungry in the evenings. 'I think you must have brought them round to do laundry at mine. Back when the dryer was working.'

'Is it broken?' asks Brendan. He has both of his hands laid out palms down on the table like someone about to perform a magic trick, or someone recently arrested. His pint is one-third down after two sips.

'Everything's broken,' says Róise. She tells him about the stairs collapsing.

'I always said they felt dodgy. You'd put your foot down and it was like sinking into a bog.'

'Did you fuck! You never said that.'

'I definitely said it at least once.'

'Well. Once is enough, I suppose.'

Róise unblocked Brendan's phone number and sent him a message last night before she had the chance to overthink it. She resisted the temptation to begin, *Hoping this finds you well,* although she did not quite know how else to start, since they have not spoken in over a year. *Hello, hope you're well,* she said. *Fancy catching up? No worries if not. Take care.* He responded almost at once, as though he had been waiting by the phone for her to get in touch. *Hi, sounds great. When you free? x*

She asks how he's been. He's doing well, he says. Same job at the bar she never goes to anymore. New housemates, two lads from work. Training for a marathon. He asks how she's been, and Róise does not know how she can effectively summarize the exhaustion of the last year, much less in response to his pedestrian life updates. She tells him she is also in the same job. Looking for a new place with Maggie and Harley. Going to the gym, she lies. 'I wondered,' he remarks. 'You've lost weight.' He says this like a compliment. He lifts his pint with his whole arm, and Róise tries not to look at the crook of his elbow, the soft flesh against which she once imagined resting her head. 'Go on then,' he says, making a swift underbite to suck up his moustache of stout foam. 'Who is he?'

'Who?'

'You're seeing someone?'

'Why do you think that?'

'You hate the gym.'

Róise's eyes narrow slightly. 'I hate you, and yet here I am.'

Brendan's face drops like a child being refused sweets. 'You *hate* me?'

'Can you really blame me?'

'It's just . . . *hate* is a strong word, Róise. It's been a long time. Life is short.' He puffs his cheeks out in a slow exhale, apparently flummoxed. 'I *am* genuinely sorry for what happened. But I don't want to fall out with anyone. I thought maybe time would pass and we'd be, you know. Friends.'

'Friends.' Róise wishes she had the composure to laugh in his face. She takes a drink of her wine and steadies herself. 'I don't know where to put all this fucking fury. Lydia's dead, and you want to be *friends*, and I've got all this pure rage that's got nowhere to fucking go.'

'Róise,' Brendan says, looking hopeless. 'I don't know how many more times I can say I'm sorry.'

'I don't want to hear that you're sorry. I want to know why you did it.'

'Listen, I know it's not what you want to hear, but it honestly wasn't about you.'

He said this at the time, in his letter and in person. Being demoted to the status of supporting character without agency or impact feels somehow worse than being provided with an inventory of specific ways in which she was inadequate. She looks at Brendan, into his hurt, *are you mad at me* eyes, and knows that it is pointless to persevere. She finishes her wine and rises from her seat. 'Thanks for meeting me. I'm going to head off.'

'Already? Róise, come on, I'm really sorry. It's good to see you – I want to catch up properly.'

She whips her coat up over her shoulders in a movement that is satisfyingly fluid. 'I'm homeless, my best friends aren't speaking, I haven't eaten in nine hours, and I may have to change jobs because I'm getting the ride off one of my co-workers. That's about all my craic, Brendan. Enjoy your night, get home safe, I wish you all the best in your future endeavours.'

Róise can smell Liam's tea from the front door when she lets herself in. She joins him in the kitchen. He is making a cheese toastie with thick crusty bread, mozzarella drooling down the sides like candle wax. 'All right, stranger?' he says.

'I saw Brendan,' she replies.

Liam does not flinch. 'Any craic?'

'He's the same.' Róise shrugs.

'Ah. Sorry.' Liam prods his steel turner towards the sizzling pan. 'Do you want this? I've got bread that needs used up while it's still fresh – I can make another one.'

Róise opens her mouth to decline, and her stomach gives a yawn of betrayal. Liam raises his eyebrows, his face saying *ahh, go on, go on, go on*, Mrs Doyle-style. 'Go on, then,' sighs Róise. 'I'll try it.'

what are we after

Astrid told Maggie, back at the beginning of their counselling sessions, that she would only breach confidentiality if she was concerned that Maggie posed a threat of serious harm to others or to herself. At the hair salon, Tess seems to feel a similar duty of care when Maggie sits down in the black box-chair in front of the mirror, and states that she has been thinking about getting a fringe.

Maggie's original instinct was to lock herself in the bathroom and dye her hair a bold new colour, fire-engine red or chocolate-wrapper purple, until she remembered Harley once tried a home dye that called itself 'Peach Breeze' and gave her hair the colour and texture of Animal from *The Muppet Show*. Maggie has spent this week browsing different colours and cuts into the small hours of the morning, texting Liam, *do you think I'd suit being brunette?* or *honest opinion: should I shave my head?* after scrolling through twelve pages of image results for Kristen Stewart. Liam replied, *you suit your hair the way it is. If you showed up with any of these styles then I'd think you were going into witness protection. Can you please get off Pinterest and reply to Róise's messages xx*

'Now,' says Tess, coming to stand behind her, smiling at Maggie in the mirror, 'what are we after today?'

'I want a change,' says Maggie. The woman in the next seat along from her has gorgeous silver-blonde hair swept to one side, the other side of her head shaved down to duckling fuzz, and Maggie gets cold feet about asking for anything dramatic. 'I was thinking maybe a fringe?'

Tess bends down to peer at Maggie's reflection at eye level, close enough that Maggie can hear the chewing gum clacking between her teeth. She says, 'Okay; and what's brought this on?' like a doctor asking *and when did these symptoms start?*

'Do you not think I'd suit one?'

Tess either isn't listening or pretends to have heard a different question. 'I reckon a couple inches off the end – maybe collarbone length? – and some really subtle pink highlights, if you fancy.'

Maggie is not quite ready to admit that this suggestion sounds extremely attractive; she imagined sweeping into the salon and dictating the terms of a dramatic new style herself, and instead now feels she is being babied. She presses, 'Would I really look *that* bad with bangs?'

'Darling,' Tess says kindly, 'I'm trying to help you.'

'It's just a fringe!'

'It's never *just a fringe*.'

Maggie concedes defeat, and allows Tess to swathe her in a black gown and lead her to a basin. Tess has a fresh manicure, nails filed almost to spikes, and Maggie wonders if they will catch and scratch and tangle in her hair, but Tess's fingers are gentle as they massage the shampoo and warm water together.

Maggie and Tess have not yet arranged a second date. Tess either has not noticed Maggie holding back, or she has noticed but is choosing to be patient. Maggie cannot help but wonder whether this apparent mellowness is an indicator of indifference, but she has too many other concerns clamouring for attention in her head to consider this at length. Earlier this week, Maggie sent Tess a message saying *I need a haircut urgently*, and Tess replied with, *who hurt you*, and Maggie chose not to outline the details of the Cate conflict, but instead told Tess about their collapsing house. Tess was appropriately sympathetic, and booked her in for a Friday afternoon appointment.

'Any plans for the weekend?' Tess asks from behind Maggie.

'Not sure yet.' Róise sent a passive-aggressive calendar invite to both Maggie and Harley during the week, with a brief agenda of items to discuss, the main ones being clearing out the house and trying to find a new one. Maggie does not know whether Harley and Róise have been in contact. She herself has not spoken to Harley since they argued, and Harley has not tried to reach out to her.

Cate has not been in touch either. The predictability of her silence is almost comforting. The loss of her has not come as much of a blow to Maggie, since the last year has been a loop of losing and finding and then losing her again. The feeling is like sitting in a chilly bath that has cooled from piping hot over time, gradually enough that she barely feels the drop in temperature.

Maggie starts at the quick blast of cold water from Tess's hose as she does a final rinse before swaddling her head in a warm towel. When Maggie is back in front of the mirror, Tess brushes

259

her hair carefully, stopping short each time the bristles meet a knot. She gestures with the handle of her comb and explains where she plans to make cuts. 'We'll get rid of the dead ends and add some colour afterwards. Sound good?' Maggie nods.

Tess brings her a coffee while the colour is setting in Maggie's hair. 'You up to anything tonight? One of my friends is doing a DJ set at Union Street, if you fancy coming along.'

'Are you going to give my hair a beautiful finish only to watch it slowly congeal in a lesbian sweat cloud?'

'Who said I was giving your hair a beautiful finish?'

'I *knew* it – there's Veet in these foils, isn't there?'

'Nah, I just went with pure acid. You're going to smell like a crucified cat in about seven minutes.'

Maggie smiles. 'Union Street sounds good.'

After she's been rinsed and blow-dried and had a look at the back of her head in the mirror, Maggie gets out her purse at the counter and Tess gives her a subtle *don't worry about it* shake of her head. 'I do nails, too, so just come back sometime. I put the good ones on Instagram, if you're interested in my shameless self-promotion.' She taps her phone screen a couple of times and shows it to Maggie.

Maggie scrolls down the colourful grid and stops on a set of nails painted neatly with lemons and limes. 'You did these?'

'Yeah, do you like them?'

'Do you remember – sorry, you've probably done loads of them – but do you by any chance remember who you did these for?'

Tess peers at the screen. 'Aye, she used to come in every couple of weeks. Australian girl. Haven't seen her in a while.'

'She got deported,' says Maggie. Tess looks curious, and Maggie adds, 'Mediocre therapist. *Great* nails.'

The first time she came to Union Street with Harley and Róise – before she dented her perineum on a steel pole – Maggie waxed with drunken nostalgia about the fact that the building had been a shoe factory in the nineteenth century, as though she herself had once worked there.

'MAGGIE!' Tess flags her down from the bar. Maggie realizes she was looking automatically for Harley and Róise's heads in the crowd, forgetting who she is meant to be here with.

'WHAT ARE YOU AFTER?' Tess asks. 'MY ROUND!'

Maggie orders a vodka tonic. Tess also gets two shots of tequila, and the salt mingles with the taste of sweat already beading around Maggie's lips. Heartburn fumes in her chest as she swallows the shot, and she forces the lime wedge into her mouth. She spends the next few minutes trying to dislodge the strands of lime pulp that are now trapped between her teeth.

The club is lit with the pink and blue of sunset clouds. Friends and couples lift their interlocked hands over the crowd when they have to pass around people, as though they are making an arch at a céilí. The dancefloor is packed, bodies gasping and sweating and pulsing in time with the drum beat. Maggie is strung between wanting to go immediately to bed and wanting to get so drunk she wakes up tomorrow afternoon missing a minimum of one vital organ. She gulps down her drink like an athlete hydrating after a sprint.

Tess says a quick hello to her friend at the DJ booth. Maggie's attention drifts, expecting not to be acknowledged, or to be introduced as a friend. 'THIS IS MAGGIE!' Tess says simply, touching Maggie on the arm.

'LOVE YOUR HAIR!' Tess's friend comments.

'SHE DID IT!' Maggie replies, pointing to Tess.

'LOOKS CLASS!'

'MAGGIE!' She turns around to see who is summoning her. Cate is standing two feet away, her black hair in a ponytail and her cheekbones bladed in the blue light. She is wearing her snakeskin Doc Martens with denim shorts and a white T-shirt with Kate Bush on the chest.

'THAT'S MY TOP,' Maggie says, pointing.

Cate looks confused, not expecting this to be the thing she was first challenged on. She glances down at her chest. 'IS IT?'

'YOU KNOW IT IS.'

'WHO YOU HERE WITH?' Cate asks, glancing around for Harley or Róise.

'THIS IS TESS.'

Tess smiles at Cate, leans in to Maggie to ask, 'ALL OKAY?'

'SHALL WE GO OUTSIDE?' Cate says to Maggie, as though a private conversation between them has already been agreed.

Maggie pauses. 'SORRY,' she says to Tess. 'JUST GIVE ME A MINUTE?' Tess nods.

Maggie takes a swallow of the cool air outside as though she has come up from underwater. Cate crosses the street to stand on the corner opposite and folds her arms across her chest. Maggie does not know if she is cold or if she is trying to cover up the T-shirt.

Maggie waits. Cate says nothing. 'So?'

'Sorry. I should have told you.'

'Which part? That you stole my T-shirt, that you pulled my best friend, or that you had a boyfriend the whole time we were getting with each other?'

'I didn't *steal* it. It was that night ages ago when I spilled a negroni all over me and you said I could borrow a top.'

'Never occurred to you to give it back?'

'I forgot! Jesus Christ.'

Maggie sighs. 'Would you ever have told me if I hadn't found out? Like, how did you imagine things were going to go?'

'Do you mean Dara?'

'Of course I mean Dara. I didn't want to come out here to talk about a fucking T-shirt.'

Cate looks inconvenienced rather than remorseful. 'I didn't plan any of it. I didn't mean to do either of you over.'

'Have you cheated on him before?'

'Not before you, no.'

'Were there other people, or was it just me? And now Harley, obviously,' Maggie adds bitterly.

'There were a couple of people. Women.' Maggie takes 'a couple of people' in the way that her granny might say she'll have 'a couple of biscuits', which could mean any number south of ten.

Nevertheless, she softens very slightly, against her better judgement. 'Are you worried you're gay? Is that what this whole thing is about?'

Cate looks away, seeming almost huffy. 'I don't know what I

am. I've had a boyfriend since I was in school, I never really got the chance to find out.'

'Are the rest of us just meant to wait around until you do, aye?'

'I never asked you to wait. We never said what we were.'

'You never asked me to wait, but you asked me if I was single, you asked me back to yours, you asked me *Maggie, you out?? wanna come join??* every time you were steaming. You asked me if I wanted to start running together. *You* asked *me* to come out here to talk and now you're acting like you've been summoned to the principal's office. Take some fucking responsibility, Cate.'

Cate bites the inside of her cheek and says, 'I'm sorry I kissed Harley. I don't even like her.'

'More fool you.' Maggie crosses her arms, mirroring Cate. She wants to ask whether Cate is single now, since that information has not yet been volunteered, but she worries Cate will read this question as a proposition. She swallows her pride and asks it anyway. 'So what's your craic now, then? Have you told Dara? Are yous still together?'

Cate rolls her lips together as though rubbing lipstick into them, and says, 'We're still together.' She does not say whether she has told him, and Maggie decides she would rather not know.

They stand in silence for a few moments. 'It's cold,' Cate says eventually.

'Should have worn a jacket.'

'I did. It's inside.'

'In that case, you may go and put it on for the rest of the night, because I want my T-shirt back.'

'I'll give it back to you when—'

'You'll give it back to me now.'

Cate, to Maggie's surprise, does not argue with her. She removes the T-shirt in the club bathrooms and returns to Maggie with her jacket zipped up over her bra. 'Happy?'

Maggie breathes out slowly. 'Dead on.'

They part ways. She sees Cate leave with her friends a few minutes later. Maggie goes outside and takes out her phone, blocks and deletes Cate's number before she can overthink it. Her phone vibrates as several messages come through, and for one truly wild moment, Maggie thinks Cate has used a friend's phone, or found her on social media, gone some kind of round-about way to find her and ask for her forgiveness. It isn't her, of course. The messages are from Harley.

I'm so sorry

I've been an absolute weapon

A classic fool

I hope you're all right

I love you

Maggie hears the music swell behind her as the door of the club opens. 'Hey,' says Tess. 'Everything okay?'

Maggie locks her phone. Tears prickle her eyes, and she pinches the bridge of her nose as if she might stop them like a nosebleed. 'I'm really sorry.'

'It's okay. What do you need?'

Maggie wraps her arms around herself. Cate was right, it is cold. 'I should go find my friends,' she says.

afters

saplings

They planned to bring flowers, but next to the fresh blooms were the days-old discounted bunches, their petals already puckered and brown-edged like ageing skin.

'Maybe we should get her something else,' muses Maggie. 'Flowers'll just be dead in three days.'

'What else are we meant to bring?' Harley says flippantly. 'Bottle of champagne and a scented candle? Great big shiny helium balloon that says "Happy Thirtieth"?'

'I think Maggie meant something else in the horticultural genre,' Róise points out. 'Although by all means continue to be a cunt about it, Charlotte.' A woman browsing potted orchids with her two young children shoots them a glare.

'Language, *Rosie*,' says Harley, sniggering. Róise made the mistake of telling them that the panel who interviewed her last week referred to her as Rosie in all their correspondence, including the letter she received offering her the job. ('I don't know whether I'll take it,' she told her friends over drinks one evening. 'Fair,' said Maggie. 'But how does Rosie feel about it?')

They linger over roses blushing in containers, although the

labels suggest these would need semi-regular maintenance, feeding and mulching and pruning, which they are reluctant to commit to. They examine tiny trees in teacup-sized planters, and wonder if they will stay small or whether there is an absurd chance they might spring up fairytale beanstalk-style and dominate the surrounding area. Maggie spots a display of cacti and wanders over. Most of them are spiky pillars clustered together in a way that looks unnervingly like a reptilian hand is trying to push its way out of the earth.

'Róise,' says Maggie, 'you've got one of these, haven't you?' The cacti are almost completely white, almost completely spherical, adorned with small pink flowers as though on their way to a wedding.

'Mine's never flowered,' says Róise. She checks the label to see if these are a different species. *Mammillaria Hahniana ('Old Lady Cactus')*. 'Fuck sake. What have I been doing wrong?'

'It might not be getting enough light. Especially over the winter,' a man (whom they assume works in the shop) offers from nearby.

'Will it flower if it's outside, then?'

'Very likely.'

'We should get one of those,' Harley decides.

'They're very social plants. They grow better if they aren't lonely,' the man advises them.

'What about this one?' Maggie reaches for a pot with four wispy white crowns nestled in it. 'How much is this, do you know?' she asks the man.

'Oh, I don't work here,' he says. Harley pulls a face when his back is turned.

They pay, then carry the plant pot outside and around the corner to where the car is parked. 'Sorted?' Adam asks when they get in, confused by the absence of flowers.

'We panicked and got a cactus,' says Róise.

Adam nods. 'I got your whiskey. It's in the boot.'

'Thank you.'

'Anything for you, Rosie.'

'Good thing we're going to a cemetery,' Róise murmurs, 'because I am going to kill all three of you.'

Adam gave Róise a set of four cut-glass whiskey tumblers as a housewarming present. At the cemetery, she rips the cardboard packaging and gives one to Maggie, one to Harley, one to Lydia. Harley decants the whiskey. She thinks about pouring Lydia a more conservative measure, since it will not be drunk by her, but rethinks at the last minute and sloshes amber liquid liberally into the glass. 'Happy birthday,' she says.

'What'll we toast to?' says Róise. She holds the whiskey close to her lips. She has grown to like it more since drinking it with Adam; it makes her think of fireplaces and warmth and comfort.

There is a short pause. 'Well,' says Harley, 'I passed.'

Harley sat her piano exam last month, having practised on the piano at her parents' house even though, a decade on, it was still out of tune. She grew used to ignoring the flat notes and focused instead on the placement of her fingers on the keys, and

Mrs Erskine nodded approvingly when she went to her lessons. It was not, perhaps, the triumph she might have imagined – a sudden shift from stumbler to genius, her examiner delighted and her teacher in happy tears – but she did well enough to pass. She could not tell her parents, since she had lied to them that she'd passed when she was eighteen. The first person she told was Maggie. ('As if you need a certificate to tell you you're good at fingering,' Maggie scoffed on the phone, and then she came and met Harley with a bottle of fizz and a smile that told her she should be proud.)

Maggie raises her glass. 'To outstanding musical accomplishments, and to Rosie's new job.'

'Bitch,' Róise says, but fondly. She has yet to accept the job offer. It is a role that asked for excellent communication skills, teamwork skills, people skills, attributes she was seemingly able to spoof in her CV and in the interview. She read the bullet points of the job description and thought of what Adam had said: *mostly emails.* She has elected to sleep on it and decide tomorrow.

'And to Maggie's legs,' Harley adds to the toast. Maggie did her first parkrun this morning, and is training for a 10K in October. The shoes she bought drunk are already wearing down. Harley has christened it 'the Runaissance'. Maggie still feels as though she is being strangled by her breath and tripped by her own feet, but there is a comforting absurdity in finishing each run after being convinced every step of the way that she is about to die as she lived: listening to the soundtrack from the *Mamma Mia* sequel and being slowly asphyxiated by a sports bra.

Maggie sips her drink and looks suddenly crestfallen. 'Should have brought Barnaby.'

(The turtle has remained in the care of Maggie's aunt and uncle. Sean says he is welcome to stay. 'The place'll seem quieter when you leave, Mags. Be nice to keep the wee lad around.'

'I'm not that loud, and he's not exactly chatty,' Maggie said, but she did not argue the point. Barnaby seems quite content there. Sean is talking about getting him a friend.)

'We said that last time,' says Harley. 'We always forget.'

'We could bring him next time.'

'We won't remember,' says Róise.

They return to the house for the last time to drop off the keys. They spent a few weeks trawling online listings and viewing houses before finding a three-bed near the university. Their new landlord has stripped and redecorated the whole place between tenants; the walls are sterile and the furniture is sparse, but it is clean and practical and the rent isn't too bad. The three of them have yet to properly move in, and in each room of the new place, piles of their boxes are stacked haphazardly like scattered ruins.

They thought they would get the most difficult part out of the way and pack up Lydia's room first, but even when her bedding and books were in boxes, she was still everywhere in the house. Róise claimed the moisturiser in the bathroom cabinet, since it was expensive and seemed a shame to waste, whereas Harley decided that hanging on to Lydia's vibrator was, on balance, too perverse a notion even for her. They rolled up Lydia's patterned mugs and mismatched wine tumblers from the kitchen cupboard, and packed them in with all the different pint glasses they had smuggled out of pubs in inside pockets over the years, long glasses and stout tankards and goblets with Germanic-sounding brand names written on them. They took her prints down from the walls and wadded up her throws from the sofa and threw away the bottle of disgusting Battenberg-flavoured liqueur she had left in the freezer.

There were tears – there were so many more tears. There was the gentle, smiling dew around Maggie's eyes when she found the unworn trainers Lydia had bought for herself while they were several gins deep and promising to go running together. There were savage tears, sobs that sprawled in Róise's throat as she emptied the kitchen units, all of them full of things she hadn't used in a long time: roasting dishes covered in dust, a spice rack full of expired jars, unopened packets mouldering at the back of the cupboard. She had been angry for so long, at this house and at everything else, and yet the thought of never cooking and eating here again filled her with a sadness that felt almost unbearable.

There were the quiet tears that Harley shed when she returned to the house to pack up her bedroom and Frankie was there inspecting the building work, and they made polite small talk about nothing, and it was clear – now that the seal around their neatly packaged flirtation had been shredded by messy sexual intercourse of only middling quality – that they were two people who did not know each other very well and did not care enough for each other to try to change this. Harley has always found the end of an informal intrigue, the death of imagined chemistry, to be something that (unlike a relationship breakdown) has no socially normalized code of mourning as yet, and so she nursed her disappointment alone. She passed Frankie again on her way out of the house and tried her very best to be content with not being looked at.

Over the last few weeks the three of them have sat, alone and together, in the bedrooms and bars and broken toilet stalls they grew up in, and they have cried. It is not only that something is ending, it is also the knowledge that things will continue to end, that in the future there will be other, greater moves away and apart, and that they will never be the same four girls and a turtle living together again.

'This isn't the end,' Maggie insists, when they are sitting on the wall outside the house. Adam drove them from the cemetery and left them off so they could return their keys. They have done a quick skim of the rooms to check nothing has been left in drawers or cupboards, but it seems risky to linger in case more of the house decides to spontaneously collapse around them, or – God forbid – one of them starts crying again.

Outside, Harley pours them each another splash of whiskey. 'Last orders, lads.'

'Sláinte,' Róise murmurs.

Their keys go jangling into an envelope, and they drop it through the letterbox. 'Home?' Maggie says, without much conviction. The new house isn't home yet.

'Pub?' says Róise, with a barely-there question mark.

'Pub,' agrees Harley. 'Keep 'er lit.'

The early-evening sun dips low in the sky, the whiskey warming in their hands. They knock back the rest, gather themselves up, and set off towards another night.

Acknowledgements

Thanks in abundance to my agent, Jenny Hewson, for taking a risk on me when this novel was still a hot unfinished mess (as opposed to the hot finished mess it is now), and for all your time, insight and encouragement. To my editor, Orla King, for engaging so thoughtfully with my writing, for knowing and loving these characters and for helping me to fully bring them to life. To everyone at Picador who has worked on and shown so much enthusiasm for this novel; thank you so much.

I owe a monumental debt to New Writing North, whose Northern Writers' Awards scheme changed my life; thank you so much for your support. Thanks a million to Naomi Booth, the most incredible mentor I could have wished for; your insight and enthusiasm improved both my craft and my confidence in ways I can't even begin to describe or repay.

Thank you to the Arts Council England and the Society of Authors for grants that gave me the opportunity to spend more time with my writing, to learn and try out new things. To the

Arvon Foundation, whose evening classes were exactly the kick I needed: thank you to my tutors for reading my work, for taking me seriously, for telling me to stop overthinking. (I'm working on it!)

To the wonderful women of my writing group: Anabel, Hatty, Janine, Natalie, Stephanie, Victoria. You are all formidable both as writers and as people; I can't believe how lucky I was to end up on a writing course with a group so kind, funny, supportive and talented. Thank you all for cheering me on to the end.

GRMA to all the Belfast hallions, for always showing me a good time! Particular and heartfelt thanks to Aimée Walsh − where do I even begin? Thank you for the love and encouragement, the advice, the laughs, the hours of voice notes. You're a legend.

To my best pals in Newcastle, for the mess, the tears, the love and the laughs. To my Warwick Street wife, Chiara Pellegrini; forever in Ernest.

To Jack: I will have to read and write many more books to find words that adequately describe how wonderful it is to love you and be loved by you. Thank you for everything.

Thank you as always to my family: my sister Fionnuala, and my parents Breige and Paul. Thank you for supporting my choices and never telling me that moving to a new city to do a full-time job and a part-time PhD and write fiction in my 'spare time' was an objectively unhinged thing to do (even though it probably was). Thank you for making me laugh and feel loved, and for always welcoming me home.